Readers love
Domestic Do-over
by KATE MCMURRAY

By Kate McMurray

Blind Items
The Boy Next Door
Devin December
Four Corners
Kindling Fire with Snow
Out in the Field
The Stars that Tremble • The Silence of the Stars
A Walk in the Dark
What There Is
When the Planets Align

DREAMSPUN DESIRES
The Greek Tycoon's Green Card Groom

ELITE ATHLETES
Here Comes the Flood
Stick the Landing
Race for Redemption

THE RAINBOW LEAGUE
The Windup
Thrown a Curve
The Long Slide Home

THE RESTORATION CHANNEL
Domestic Do-over
Residential Rehab

WMU
There Has to Be a Reason
What's the Use of Wondering

Published by DREAMSPINNER PRESS
www.dreamspinnerpress.com

RESIDENTIAL REHAB

Kate McMurray

Published by
DREAMSPINNER PRESS

5032 Capital Circle SW, Suite 2, PMB# 279,
Tallahassee, FL 32305-7886 USA
www.dreamspinnerpress.com

This is a work of fiction. Names, characters, places, and incidents either
are the product of author imagination or are used fictitiously, and any
resemblance to actual persons, living or dead, business establishments,
events, or locales is entirely coincidental.

Residential Rehab
© 2021 Kate McMurray

Cover Art
© 2021 L.C. Chase
http://www.lcchase.com
Cover content is for illustrative purposes only and any person depicted
on the cover is a model.

Mass Market Paperback ISBN: 978-1-64108-277-8
Trade Paperback ISBN: 978-1-64108-276-1
Digital ISBN: 978-1-64108-275-4
Mass Market published May 2022
v. 1.0

Printed in the United States of America
∞
This paper meets the requirements of
ANSI/NISO Z39.48-1992 (Permanence of Paper).

Chapter One

NOLAN MIGHT have jumped the gun.

He stood on the set of *Wake Up with Stacey Lewis*, staring at a blandly decorated nook that he was supposed to spruce up. The nook was basically a corner made of two fake walls, inside of which were a bare twin bed and a beige love seat. One of the fake walls had a window with a curtain rod hanging above it. Behind the other one were a few bins of products that bore his name. After some small talk with Stacey Lewis herself, his task would be to decorate the nook using his own branded curtains and bedding and a few random accessories. And he only had about twenty minutes to do it.

Two years ago he could have done this in his sleep, especially since some producer had already chosen home accessories in colors that complemented each other and weeded out the few wacky pieces in Nolan's collection. For a few years there, he'd dropped by Stacey's show a couple times a month to give her audience home-decorating tips. He was Nolan Hamlin, after all. Interior designer to the stars.

And yet....

This was his first television appearance in over a year. He and Stacey were old friends, which was why he'd chosen to end his not-exactly-planned hiatus with her. But now that he was here, he didn't feel confident he could do this.

But it was too late. Stacey walked over and gave him a hug. When she stepped back, she said, "We're on in less than two minutes. You ready?"

No. "As I'll ever be."

Behind the camera, the director said, "Thirty seconds."

The director signaled that the live studio audience should applaud; then he signaled the show was back live. Stacey said, "Good morning again, everyone. It is my great pleasure to welcome back a dear friend to the show—interior designer to the stars, Nolan Hamlin!" She paused for the audience to hoot and holler for a moment. "It's been a long time, Nolan."

"It has, yes." He knew how to do this, so he smiled and gave a little wave to the audience.

Stacey never looked away from the camera. She grinned and said, "To make Nolan feel at home, I've given him a little challenge. Look at this dull little room." She gestured toward the nook. "We're going to brush off Nolan's rusty design skills and give him fifteen minutes to spruce this up using home goods from the Nolan Hamlin Collection, available at fine retailers across the country. Once he's made this room *fabulous*, we'll chat with him about what he's up to these days. Sound good?"

The audience cheered.

"You up for the challenge, Nolan?"

"I am." But that was a lie. It was like he'd forgotten everything he knew about textiles and accessorizing.

"All right. We're putting fifteen minutes on the clock...." She gestured toward a massive digital clock offstage. "And your time starts... now!"

As he'd been instructed, Nolan ducked behind one of the fake walls and started rifling through the bins of sheets and afghans. He heard Stacey say, "We'll check in with Nolan later. But when we come back.... Jessica Benton is here!"

The audience cheered for the actress; then the director yelled, "Cut. We're clear!"

But Nolan still only had fifteen minutes, so he started ripping the plastic off the bedding he wanted to use. Then he spotted a rug rolled up and propped against the fake wall, and that was just what belonged on the floor. The colors would pull the room together, if he used the dark brown throw on the sofa and the white-and-teal bedding.

Maybe he did still know how to do this.

He signaled to a stage hand to help him move the rug, then asked the guy to hold up the bed while he slid the rug under it. He could feel the camera pan by him as the show came back from the commercial break, but he ignored it.

He kept an eye on the giant clock and managed to make the fake room look reasonable. He went for beiges and browns to go with the sofa, but with little pops of teal. He picked curtains, a throw, and pillows for texture, he put a lamp with a teal base on the side table, and he added a jade-colored bookend on a shelf with some books because he liked how the jade went with the bedding, a big puffy down duvet with a cover that was clean and white with a single teal stripe through the middle.

He stood back and admired his work when he had about a minute to go. Best room he'd ever done? Hardly, but he'd had limited materials to work with. It almost didn't matter; the important thing was that Nolan was engaging with the public again. And his appearance here was kind of an advertisement for his products anyway. Plus, he had to promote his new TV show. So, yeah, this little fake room was basic, but in his experience, a lot of people were allergic to color, so his most recent collection was pretty neutral.

Truth be told, his whole life had been colorless for the past year.

Across the stage, Stacey said, "And when we come back, we'll check in with Nolan Hamlin!"

A moment later she jogged across the stage and looked at the nook.

Feeling suddenly self-conscious, Nolan said, "If I'd had more time, I would have steamed the bedding. I don't love that there are still creases in it."

"It looks great for fifteen minutes."

"Thanks." He blew out a breath.

When they came back from commercial, Stacey said, "And we're back with Nolan Hamlin. If you're just joining us, I asked Nolan to design this little room for us in fifteen minutes. And it looks fabulous, doesn't it?" She paused for the audience to applaud. "Tell us about the choices you made here."

Again, Nolan wasn't new to this—he knew the object of this segment was to explain to non-designers how they could best use his products to decorate a room. On autopilot, he explained about textures and colors. When he finished, Stacey turned to her audience and said, "Do you think this is something you guys can do at home?" When there was a general murmur of assent, she added, "Fantastic. All of you have a gift card to spend at Nolan's online store so you can put some of these beautiful things in your own home!" She paused for applause and then said, "Let's chat, Nolan." She grabbed his hand and led him over to the other side of the set.

Two sofas sat at a forty-five-degree angle. He sat on one end of a sofa, while Stacey sat at the closest end of the other—basically they faced each other.

He took a deep breath, knowing even before Stacey opened her mouth that she'd want to talk about Ricky, something Nolan most assuredly did not want to do. But Stacey would feel the need to explain to her audience why Nolan Hamlin, who used to appear on her show once a month, had pretty much disappeared from public life for a whole year.

"We're so glad to have you back, my friend," she said. "For those of you who don't know, Nolan took some time off because he lost his husband a year ago. How are you doing now?" She turned and looked at him expectantly.

He couldn't speak for a moment. It had been a year, and he'd prepared himself for this question, but still, it felt like someone had reached into his chest and punched his heart. "I'm… okay." That felt sort of true. He was trying very hard not to let his emotions show, but still, his voice cracked when he added, "It's been tough."

Stacey reached over and squeezed his knee. "I know, honey. But I'm so glad you've decided to get back to what you really love to do. I know that's what Ricky would have wanted."

Nolan turned to face the audience, because he realized that a slideshow of photos of himself and Ricky was happening on the screen between the two sofas. He couldn't look or he'd lose it.

Ricardo Vega had been a breakout "teen" actor, starring in a popular soap when he'd been in his midtwenties. He'd spent his thirties struggling for legitimacy, mostly getting cast as the hunky love interest in Hallmark Christmas movies and bit parts on TV… and then he'd gotten that diagnosis. Pancreatic cancer. He'd died three months later.

Nolan still missed him in a way that was physically painful at times, but right now, while on television, he had to keep it together.

Stacey picked up a stack of cards from the side table. She glanced at the one on top and said, "Why don't we talk about your new show?"

Nolan let out the breath he'd been holding. "Well, we haven't started filming yet, but I can tell you a little about it. It's called *Residential Rehab*. I've been developing it with the Restoration Channel. Basically, we're helping fix up family homes that seem unfixable. So, like, we'll work with families who inherited houses that were in rough shape. Or maybe they've lived in the same house for decades and never made any upgrades, or they bought a fixer-upper and got in over their heads. So I, and a cohost who is still TBD, will be helping these families complete their renovations and decorate in a modern way that makes the best use of the space."

"It sounds amazing. Any ideas about your cohost yet?"

"Restoration Channel and I are looking for an up-and-coming designer to help me out." And this was something Nolan was resigned to but still chafed against. He could do the show by himself, but Garrett

Harwood, the Restoration Channel's head of programming, wanted to give Nolan someone to bounce ideas off of. He'd been out of the game for a while, it was true. Even before Ricky got sick, Nolan had been focused on TV appearances and his home goods line; he hadn't actually designed a room, let alone a whole house, in a few years. Harwood's argument was that bringing in a young designer, someone who was hungry and creative, would help Nolan keep his ideas fresh.

"I honestly can't wait," said Stacey. "I love your designs so much. I mean, that's incredible. Any idea when the show will air?"

"If all goes to plan, we'll find our young designer in the next couple of weeks, then we'll start filming by late spring and the show will premiere in the fall."

"Sounds amazing. You're all going to watch, right?"

The audience cheered.

So Nolan smiled and tried to think about the show and not Ricky.

"Before we let you go," said Stacey, "I do have a surprise for you."

On cue, one of the stagehands emerged from the back holding a cake with four lit candles.

"A little birdie told me it's your fortieth birthday," said Stacey. "Audience, please help me wish Nolan the happiest of birthdays!"

Nolan hardly knew what to do with himself as the audience sang "Happy Birthday." He laughed, blew out the candles, and thanked Stacey. His birthday had actually been the day before, but he appreciated the thought. He gazed at the cake, unable to keep from remembering that Ricky hadn't lived to see his fortieth birthday.

Nolan's anxiety about this milestone had been intense. Forty didn't look the way he'd expected. Oh, *he* looked all right; he had a good skin-care regimen and people kept telling him the gray hair starting to pop up at his temples was sexy and distinguished. But he'd had this whole life plan. He and Ricky were supposed to still be living in their beautiful house in the Hollywood Hills, perhaps now welcoming their first child. This terrible emptiness in Nolan's chest was not what he was supposed to be feeling while looking at a birthday cake.

He was saved from becoming maudlin when the show wrapped up for the day. Once they'd signed off, a stagehand appeared with a knife and cut the cake into thin slices.

"I know how difficult this must have been," said Stacey. "But I'm glad you're back in the world again. I worried about you."

"I know. It's been a year, that's for sure. But I'm all moved into the new place here in New York now. So let's not be strangers, okay?"

She grinned. "Welcome back to the real world, then. I was so glad to leave LA behind me."

"Yeah. Me too." Probably for different reasons.

Stacey gave Nolan a hug. "Happy birthday, my friend. I hope this year treats you well."

Chapter Two

GRAYSON CHECKED his phone for the umpteenth time as he walked along Fourteenth Street. The Restoration Channel offices were on Ninth Avenue, near Chelsea Market, and Grayson knew his way around the neighborhood pretty well, but apparently his nerves about his impending job interview were manifesting as certainty that he'd never find the building.

But he did, and he got to the reception desk; then he was led to a conference room. Then he almost passed out.

Grayson had met Garrett Harwood a few weeks before. Sitting beside him was a woman Grayson didn't know. But sitting beside her was Nolan Hamlin. *The* Nolan Hamlin.

Lordy, he was hot.

But now was not the time. Grayson was here for a job. If he got it, this would be his big break, something that could propel him to having a career like… well, a career like Nolan Hamlin's. Grayson wanted the whole thing: the interesting design jobs, celebrity clients, his own line of home goods.

"Please have a seat, Grayson," said Harwood. "Guys, this is Grayson Woods. He's a New York–based designer. I met him through Marla Greene. Grayson, this is Helena Bloom, the producer for our new show, *Residential Rehab*. And this is Nolan Hamlin, who will be cohosting the show."

"Yes," said Grayson, still feeling starstruck. Then he remembered he was trying to impress these people. "It's a pleasure to meet you all."

"Marla Greene?" said Nolan. "How do you know Marla Greene?"

Grayson took a deep breath. Marla Greene was a home-improvement media mogul. She had her own Restoration Channel show, as well as several magazines and a series of books about interior design. "I met her at a wedding," Grayson said. Then he realized how stupid that sounded. Nolan's discerning gaze was really throwing him for a loop. "Actually, I designed the wedding. This friend of mine from high school, he married a high-profile lawyer. You know, the guy who argued that LGBT discrimination case in front of the Supreme Court last year? They asked me to do the decorations for the wedding because they thought there would be some press attention. So I did everything. It was at this old mansion in Connecticut. I picked out the chairs and the flowers and all the decorations. I helped both grooms pick out their suits too, actually. And then *Marla Greene Weddings* came up to take photos and feature the wedding in one issue. So Marla was there, and she loved my designs so much, she did a feature on me for her main magazine too."

"Yes," said Harwood. "I love your stuff too, I have to say. Really clever design work. You're an outside-the-box thinker, which I think we'll need here. This show will require some creative problem-solving."

"Thank you."

Grayson glanced at Nolan, who looked impressed. He wrote something down on the pad of paper in front of him.

It was hard not to stare. Grayson knew Nolan had taken a much-publicized year off after his husband had died, and he looked like he'd aged some in that year. He was still gorgeous, of course; remnants of an LA tan, warm, light brown hair, a square jaw, a delicate nose. He was a little thinner in person—either the TV really did add ten pounds or Nolan had lost weight in the year he'd been out of the public eye—and he had a few strands of silver in his hair. He had startling green eyes, as well. Grayson could have spent the whole day staring into them.

"As I mentioned when we met a couple of weeks ago," said Garrett, drawing Grayson's attention back to him, "we want a young, up-and-coming designer to work with Nolan on the show. So I wanted to bring you in today to do a screen test and have you meet Nolan. I think you're great, but Nolan and Helena have the final say. They're the ones you need to impress today."

"I believe I am up to the challenge," said Grayson, sounding more comfortable than he felt.

"Before we get to the screen test," said Nolan, "I'd love to hear more about your design aesthetic. Garrett gave me some photos. You seem to like color, but don't mind toning it down when the occasion calls for it."

"I love color. I love making patterns that shouldn't go together work in the same space. But, you know, you have to do what the client wants sometimes too. That wedding, for example. They wanted soft, muted colors, nothing that would distract too much from the venue itself."

"Sure, that makes sense," said Nolan.

"I'm kind of a minimalist when it comes to objects. It makes me crazy when designers over-accessorize."

"Sure. What kinds of clients do you have now? You do a lot of weddings?"

"Well, during the day, I work as an assistant to a design firm on the Upper West Side. Right now I mainly help out the senior designers, but that's changing. I've just started to find a few of my own clients, people who aren't friends." What Grayson didn't mention was that a couple of the photos in his portfolio were of his own apartment. He shared a place in Brooklyn with two roommates, and they'd let him go crazy designing the common areas. And his boss had let him design a few individual rooms in some of the houses they'd worked on as well, giving Grayson a lot of confidence in his own abilities. He knew he was young—he wasn't much past his twenty-fifth birthday—but he could do this job, and do it well. And he wanted the opportunity to work with his idol more than he wanted his next meal.

Unfortunately, that same idol was staring at him now as if he was not impressed. "So, your experience is limited."

Grayson didn't like Nolan's tone. "I mean, I went to design school."

"So did we all, kid." Nolan sighed. "I like the designs in your portfolio, so I'm willing to give this a shot, but I want to see how you do on camera, if that's all right."

This was the part that made Grayson nervous, but he said, "Yeah, of course."

TWO THINGS struck Nolan as he watched Grayson Woods's screen test.

First, Grayson was practically a fetus. He was young and wide-eyed and had an earnestness about him that told Nolan the kid hadn't been beaten down by life yet. And he had the arrogance of a recent design school grad who thought he was an expert at everything but hadn't been truly challenged yet.

Second, Grayson looked fucking fantastic on-screen. He had curly brown hair that was likely difficult to manage, cut short on the sides and long on top so that it fell over his forehead a bit. He had bright blue eyes and smooth skin. His clothing was a little eccentric for a job interview—worn skinny jeans, a purple-and-white plaid button-down, and a well-fitted leather jacket, with a pair of clunky motorcycle boots, odd choices for a kid who likely got here by subway—and he had the sort of fit body that showed he had enough vanity to go to the gym regularly.

That was… interesting. Nolan never gave much thought to how attractive men were anymore. After Ricky passed, something in Nolan had died with him, and everything had gone hollow and dormant. He could see a man and think, *He's objectively handsome*, but nothing really stirred in him.

Until he set eyes on Grayson Woods.

Even then, it was a gradual realization. In fact, it wasn't until he and Helena were staring at the monitor, watching the playback of Grayson's screen test, that he noticed the particular way Grayson gesticulated as he talked, the way he tossed his head to knock his hair out of his eyes, the resonant quality of his voice. Well, also that ass in those pants. He stared at the monitor and suddenly recognized the feeling. It wasn't just that Grayson was good-looking; Nolan was *attracted* to him.

That was bad news if they were going to work together, although if Nolan was doing the math right, there was also a fifteen-year age gap that was a pretty big impediment. Nolan had no desire to date a twenty-five-year-old. What kind of terrible cliché was that anyway?

He sighed.

"The kid's good, no?" said Helena.

"Yeah, he's great. I mean, he's an infant, but the camera loves him. He's so inexperienced, though…."

"That's the point. Garrett and I decided we wanted someone to work with you who was young and had fresh ideas. I love you, honey, but your recent work has been a little uninspired."

Nolan balked, although Helena was right. The last collection of home goods he'd designed had been very beige. There was a place for beige, of course, but even he could tell he was playing it too safe.

"I can do this on my own," Nolan said.

"I know. And you're definitely the star. The families that have applied for the show all addressed their audition videos to you. You're the one they're going to scream about when you turn up on their doorstep. I just think we need some new blood too, and this is an excellent opportunity for an up-and-coming designer. And I should tell you, this kid idolizes you. He almost passed out when he walked into the conference room earlier. Garrett said he wouldn't shut up about you at their first meetings. This kid wants the job, and I think he'd be good at it."

Nolan sighed. "All right. I can probably teach him some things."

Helena laughed. "There you go."

They reconvened in the conference room a half hour later. Garrett was all smiles, which meant he wanted this kid for the show. Nolan didn't know Garrett very well, but in the three months they'd spent developing *Residential Rehab*, Nolan had figured out his facial expressions.

"I think I've talked Nolan into it," Helena said as they sat down.

"Really?" said Grayson.

"I… sure." Nolan sighed. "Let's do it."

The kid shot out of his seat and jumped. "Oh my God. Thank you so much. I can't…. I'm so grateful. I promise you will not regret this."

Nolan already regretted it a little, but he nodded and stood, intending to shake Grayson's hand.

Grayson gave him a hug instead. It surprised Nolan; he was shocked by how warm and friendly it felt, puzzled by the fact that the first man he'd been attracted to in over a year was now pressed against him, and he gave the kid a quick squeeze and then pulled away.

"Sorry," Grayson said. "I got excited."

"It's all right," Nolan said.

Helena clapped once. "This is so great. I'm excited to start filming."

But suddenly Nolan was nervous as hell.

Chapter Three

GRAYSON'S FIRST task as cohost—holy cow!—of *Residential Rehab* was to watch the audition tapes of the families who had applied to be on the show. He and Nolan had two tasks: pick families that would look good on TV and who could talk to a camera without fidgeting too much, and pick families that seemed like they could genuinely use help.

He and Nolan sat in a largely empty room in the high-rise owned by the Restoration Channel. Eventually the room would be their studio set, where they'd film the two of them making design decisions together, but for now it was an echo-y room with white walls and scarred wood floors. He and Nolan sat beside each other on an old, uncomfortable prop sofa, across from a TV. Nolan controlled the video from a tablet.

Grayson's heart pounded, and it took everything in him to pretend that this was all totally normal and he wasn't sitting next to *Nolan Hamlin*. *Nolan is just a regular guy*, Grayson tried to tell himself. Sure, he was handsome, but so were hundreds of other men in New York. Hell, last week Grayson had talked to an impossibly handsome guy at a bar and had held it together just fine. He and Nolan were coworkers now—he needed to get used to him.

Coworkers. Regular guy. Sure, that was totally believable.

"All right, here's the first family," said Nolan, clearly oblivious to Grayson's inner turmoil.

Trying to look like he was taking this seriously, Grayson sat poised on the edge of the sofa, a clipboard on his lap and a pen in his hand, ready to take notes.

The video started with a middle-aged couple on screen. "Hi. I'm Carol and this is my husband, George. Recently, we inherited my father's old house, and we decided that since it was paid for and we were renting, it was the perfect opportunity to become homeowners. But as soon as we got to the house, we realized it was in rough shape. Come with me."

Carol picked up the camera and panned it around the area. Grayson immediately recognized that the space had not been renovated since the seventies, probably. There was wood paneling on the walls, old appliances in the kitchen, a very marigold color palette. Then Carol and George took turns describing structural issues: they'd brought in a contractor to discuss taking down walls but had instead discovered rot and termite damage. And once they'd gotten all that fixed, they were basically out of money to make any other repairs.

"Anyone can see that the house is ridiculously out-of-date. It's not functional as it is. The kitchen is too small, the house doesn't flow well, there isn't enough storage for all of our things. Please, Nolan Hamlin, we could use your help."

Grayson bristled a little at the couple appealing to just Nolan, although of course they hadn't known

Grayson would be working on the show when they applied. And Nolan really was the star; Grayson was trying to be okay with his role as the sidekick. He was itching to do his own work and flex his design muscles.

Well, what he really wanted was to show off for Nolan, show what he could really do, and then be more of a cohost than a sidekick. But he supposed he'd have to settle for this role. At least for now.

"I like them," Nolan said, barely looking at Grayson. "And that house definitely needs help."

"What would you do with it?" Grayson asked, more out of curiosity than anything else.

"Well, I'd like to see it in person before making any commitments, but obviously that wood paneling has got to go. I'd also take down a wall and completely reconfigure the kitchen. Nobody wants a little kitchen like that anymore. That passthrough is very 1985. What would you do?"

"I agree, take down the wood, reconfigure the kitchen. I think I'd make the whole main area open concept. Take down all the walls."

"That'll depend a lot on budget. And not everyone likes open concept."

"Yeah, but they say themselves the space is not functional. But you're right, we should wait to decide until we see it." Grayson supposed picking a fight with Nolan wouldn't go very far to impress him.

Nolan nodded. "All right. Let's watch the next one."

They watched four more videos. One family was pretty easy to rule out. They were super awkward on camera, and their house wasn't all that bad. Grayson's apartment in Brooklyn looked worse. The other three were serious contenders. Grayson dutifully took notes as they watched and tried not to think about how hot Nolan was.

Nolan was a little unkempt today, probably because he knew they weren't going to be on camera. His hair was disheveled, he had a few days of beard growth on his face, and there were bags under his eyes, making him look as if he hadn't gotten a good night's sleep in a while. He wore jeans and a navy T-shirt, though both looked expensive. He had well-worn boat shoes on his feet.

And still, he was sexy. He smelled good, the disheveled quality of his hair made him look a little disreputable but in a good way, and he seemed unselfconscious.

Grayson had dressed up for today, in black jeans and a button-down, because he wanted to impress Nolan, even if they weren't filming. He tried to say smart things as they reviewed each tape. He wanted to prove that he belonged on the show.

But working next to a man Grayson had adored from afar for a long time, who was even more handsome in person, especially when he let his guard down, was going to be a particular challenge. Grayson had been following Nolan's career since he'd first appeared on Oprah's show a zillion years ago. He'd read articles about him and DVR'd all his TV appearances and bought magazines when his designs were featured. Grayson wanted Nolan's career, wanted to have that kind of success and fame. He'd even harbored a few fantasies about all the things he'd say and do if they were ever to meet, and he'd had plenty of more prurient fantasies too. He'd never imagined he'd actually be on TV *with* Nolan. It was like a surreal dream. He would have pinched himself, but he was legitimately worried he'd wake up.

And, fine, Grayson had lain awake the entire night before he'd met Nolan imagining that he had more courage than he did, dreaming he'd strolled right up to Nolan and propositioned him, and then they'd started a whirlwind romance that ended with them getting married at some idyllic refurbished farmhouse in the country somewhere and living happily ever after. That thought swirled around in his head whenever he looked at Nolan, who still barely knew his name.

Out here in the real world, Nolan was fifteen years older, now a coworker, and his husband had just died. Grayson knew a few things about loss and how it could wreck a person.

So of course he knew nothing would happen here. There was no way on earth a man like Nolan would ever be interested in Grayson. There was too much of an age gap, Nolan was still mourning, and Nolan also didn't appear to take Grayson very seriously. Grayson should instead focus on what a great opportunity this was. He'd be on TV, in front of millions of viewers, on a show that he knew would pull at people's heartstrings. The visibility alone would be great for his career. He should be glad to even be in Nolan's orbit.

But it wasn't that easy. He glanced at Nolan's profile as Nolan queued up the next video. It was hard not to notice how perfect Nolan's profile was. Well, not *perfect*. Nolan's nose was a little on the long side. Up close, his age was a little more obvious. Not that there was anything wrong with being forty, just… he had a lot more life experience than Grayson did—in terms of years, anyway.

"Shall we look at the next one?" Nolan asked.

Grayson had to blink a few times to rejoin the corporeal world. "Sure."

THE VIDEO with the newlywed couple got to Nolan.

They'd bought their dream house in the New Jersey suburbs, only to find out that it was a money pit.

It reminded Nolan of the house he'd bought with Ricky in the Hollywood Hills. It hadn't been to his taste at all, but it was this gorgeous old mansion built into a hill with a spectacular view of the valley. That view alone had made the price worth it. But they'd sunk even more money into molding the property into their vision. Ricky and Nolan had remarkably similar tastes—or maybe Ricky had just been deferring to Nolan's expertise, Nolan had never been sure—and it had been the first time Nolan had designed an entire house for himself. And he had to admit, he'd gone a little over-the-top. Neutral colors on everything permanent—the walls, the floors, cabinets, counters—but lots of bright, colorful accessories and textiles. And Nolan had loved that house deep in his soul… until Ricky died. Then he saw Ricky in it every time he turned a corner, and it became unbearable to live in. He'd never been very fond of LA anyway, so escaping the memories was what he'd done on his hiatus.

Well, he'd spent the first few months in a sad, dark haze, where he didn't really go anywhere. But once he was moderately functional again, he'd packed up the house, sold it and half his stuff, and moved to a loft in New York City.

But because this couple's story pulled at his heartstrings, he said, "These guys for sure," to Grayson.

"Yeah, I like them. I hate that they feel like they have to sell their house. They're going to lose money if they do that."

"It was definitely worth more before they started ripping stuff down."

"And the couple is cute."

Nolan glanced at Grayson. Nolan wasn't sure what the kid's deal was—gay or straight or what, although he assumed gay. He thought he'd caught Grayson giving him The Look a couple of times. And the kid really was very cute. Nolan expected the female viewership to love him. He was on the prettier side of sexy—long eyelashes, big eyes, jaunty hair, soft features. Nolan himself found it very appealing. Except this kid was, well, a kid.

"You ready to start filming?" Nolan asked, mostly to be conversational.

"Sure? I mean, I'm very nervous. I've never done anything like this before."

"I haven't really done a show like this either. I mean, obviously I've been on TV, but for, like, three-minute segments where I tell people to decorate with different textures, you know? We're going to be filming hours of footage." Truth be told, Nolan was a little worried he wasn't entertaining enough to keep the audience engaged for an entire forty-two-minute episode, no matter how much he wanted to do the show. "Garrett keeps telling me I should just ignore the cameras."

"But at least you've been on camera plenty of times. My only real screen experience is that I had a minor part in my college roommate's student film. And he only asked me because he knew I'd been in my high-school drama club. I didn't tell him it was because I'd had a crush on the guy who played Felix in our production of *The Odd Couple*. Most of my parts were, like, Man Number Three."

Well, Nolan supposed that answered some of his questions. "You'd never know it. Your screen test was very good."

Grayson grinned. "Yeah? Thanks. I mean, I did want to act for a hot minute when I was, like, fifteen, but I wasn't very good at it. But this is not really acting, right? I'm just being myself, but in front of a camera."

"That's true, more or less."

"No one has ever called me shy, at any rate."

Nolan laughed. "I can see that."

Nolan hadn't intended his laughter to sound condescending, but apparently Grayson heard it that way, because he frowned. "Look, I get that I'm young and maybe you don't take me that seriously yet or maybe you don't want a costar… but I really want this to work."

Nolan nodded. He knew he'd been dismissive, and obviously Grayson had sensed that. "Can I ask you why you wanted to do this?"

"I mean, it's a dream come true. And this all happened so fast. It's completely crazy. Like, one minute I was picking out linens for my friends' wedding, then I'm meeting Marla Greene, then she's introducing me to Garrett Harwood. And the thing is, I love design. I love making spaces eye-catching but functional. I think I'm pretty good at it. But I'll admit, my career hasn't exactly taken off the way I expected it to. Just to get a job working for a company like the Restoration Channel would have been enough, but then Garrett told me I could work with *the* Nolan Hamlin? I've admired your work for years."

Nolan wondered how many years that could have been. This kid had been a toddler when Nolan had designed his first room. "I appreciate that."

"I mean, this was too good an opportunity to pass up. And, you know, I thought it would bring attention to my business. I had to leave my firm to take this job. I'd like to build my own business, and you have to admit, this is excellent publicity."

Nolan chuckled. "Well, there is that."

"Also, you know, I love the premise of the show. I love the idea of being able to use my skills to help other people."

Nolan looked the kid over. Grayson was a lot, but he had an earnestness about him that Nolan found endearing. Nolan had been in Grayson's shoes once, anxious to prove himself and be successful doing something he loved. Grayson still had a bit of the entitlement complex that a lot of recent design school grads had, especially those who had done well academically but hadn't worked in real spaces very long. Nolan had been that way too, once upon a time. It was hard to be mad about it.

"I'm giving you a chance to prove yourself, aren't I?" Nolan sighed. "I'm sorry if I've acted dismissive. I'm not intentionally being rude. And you... seem like a good kid. I think we'll be fine working together. I've had a hard year, that's all, and it's been an adjustment getting back into the swing of doing this sort of thing. I'll try not to take it out on you."

Grayson smiled. "All right. I'll take it."

"Don't think you can just rest on pretty, though. This is going to take some hard work. Designing a house for a family is a different kind of project than picking out chairs at a wedding."

Grayson smiled slowly. "I know. I'm grateful for the opportunity, really. And I hope we can be friends."

"Yeah, me too." And Nolan meant it. It had been a lonely year, and he could use a few more friends. "Okay, we've got eight more of these to watch. Ready for the next one?"

Chapter Four

THE CAR the Restoration Channel provided Nolan and Grayson was a massive SUV that had several cameras installed to film segments in which the stars of the show had conversations while en route. A PA showed Nolan how to operate the cameras—a touchscreen on the dashboard powered the cameras on and off—but the car was parked on Ninth Avenue, where it was not exactly quiet.

Grayson stood nearby fidgeting, undoubtedly nervous about the first day of filming.

Nolan understood how he felt, although he was more nervous about the car ride into New Jersey with Grayson than about filming, per se.

He got in the driver's seat and tapped on the touch screen. "How do I know the camera is on?"

The PA leaned through the driver's side window and pointed to one of the cameras. "If the red light there comes on, it's recording. See?"

The main camera was above the mirror, installed into the ceiling of the car just above the windshield. There were also cameras just above each top corner of the windshield.

"Most of the time, we'll use the center camera, because both of you are in the shot, but all three of the cameras will record in case we want to focus on the person speaking when we splice it together."

"But if the light is off, it's not recording at all, right?"

"Right. To record, make sure you—"

"No, I got that. What I'm saying is, if I, for example, wanted to have a private conversation with Grayson, like if I'm giving him feedback or something, and I don't want it recorded, I just make sure the light is off. Then I can speak freely, right?"

The PA's expression registered the moment he understood what Nolan was asking. "Yes. No light, no recording."

"Cool. Thanks." Nolan rolled down the window on the passenger seat side. "Grayson? Let's go."

"Okay."

As Grayson climbed into the car, Nolan fiddled with the touchscreen, turning the camera on and trying not to look at it. He put his hands on the steering wheel and waited for Grayson to settle into his seat. After Grayson clicked his seat belt into place, Nolan said, "Ready to go?"

"Yeah, let's hit it."

Nolan laughed softly and turned off the camera.

Helena walked over to his window and handed him a piece of paper. "The first address is the staging area. I'll meet you there."

This all felt needlessly complicated. The staging area was the parking lot of a VFW hall about a quarter mile from the house they would be working on. Part of the crew had already left to set up the day's filming at the house. It wasn't clear to Nolan if the couple

knew that he and Grayson would be coming today or
not. Helena had wanted him to ambush the couple—she
said viewers loved that kind of thing—but Nolan hated
that idea. So he'd asked Helena to call all the families
he and Grayson had chosen, to let them know officially
they would be on the show… though it wouldn't surprise Nolan if she hadn't told the family he and Grayson
would be arriving *today*. Helena loved a gimmick.

Nolan punched the address into the GPS. Then he
paused, waiting for Helena to get into the car ahead of
him and pull out, before he got on the road himself.

As they drove toward the Holland Tunnel, Nolan
explained the situation with the cameras and assigned
Grayson the task of turning them on if their discussion
turned into something relevant to the show.

"Helena gave me kind of a dossier on the Roberts,"
said Grayson. "I could read from it while you drive and
film it so we have an intro to the couple."

"Okay. Wait until I get through the tunnel, then go
for it."

Grayson pulled a folder out of his messenger bag
and leafed through it. They sat in companionable silence in the traffic on Canal Street as they approached
the tunnel. Living in LA had made Nolan forget how
much he hated driving in and out of Manhattan. He
sighed. LA was no stranger to gridlock, but Canal
Street in Manhattan was a particular kind of hell.

"I've never gone through the Holland Tunnel before," Grayson said, peering out the window.

"No? Where are you from, kid?"

"Lowell, Massachusetts. I've been living in New
York for seven years, though. I've just never had
a reason to go to New Jersey. Well, except for, like,

Hoboken. And then I took the PATH train. I mean, I don't even own a car."

Since it looked like they'd be here for a while, Nolan decided to make small talk. "What brought you to New York?"

"College. I went to NYU. But also, like, I was kind of a black sheep. I come from this blue-collar New England family. My mom is a receptionist at a dentist's office and my dad is a handyman. It's all very *Manchester by the Sea*." Grayson waved his hand. "I mean, my family is not the most open-minded. And I'm the weirdo who wanted to be an artist, so I thought it would be good to put a little distance between us."

"Ah." Nolan's family had always been accepting, but he nodded, because he knew something of the need to be among people who understood him. "I don't love driving in and out of the city, but this is unfortunately the best way to get to the house. The Roberts family lives in a part of Jersey that is not really accessible any other way, and Helena thought it would be a good idea if we drove and chatted in the car."

Some of the gridlock broke up as they approached the tunnel, and finally they were moving. Once they hit the Turnpike on the other side, Nolan said, "Turn on the camera and then tell me about the Roberts family."

Grayson nodded once and tapped a few things on the touchscreen, and then he glanced at the papers in his lap. "George and Carol Roberts are empty nesters who live in Tenafly, New Jersey. They recently inherited Carol's father's house and decided to make it their retirement home, but it's a mess inside. According to their casting video, the house hasn't been updated except for necessary repairs since the mideighties, and it doesn't really work for their lifestyle. George and Carol knew they would have to fix up the place to make the house livable, but they've now realized they are in way over their heads."

"That's where we come in," Nolan said. The line sounded canned, but he smiled and went with it. "We've got a small budget, plus whatever the owners pitch in, to get the Roberts' house in working order."

There was still some debate over the budget. Management at the Restoration Channel kept changing their mind about how much they were willing to pitch in. Currently, it was twenty-five thousand dollars. As far as home renovation budgets went, it wasn't much; twenty-five thousand dollars would likely cover a kitchen, not a whole house. But Nolan understood that the chosen families had their own renovation budgets that had been precleared by the network, and he hoped it was a decent-sized chunk of change for this project. The audition video indicated that the house needed a lot of work.

"Their house has a lot of potential," said Grayson. "But it will take some work to get there." Grayson shut off the camera. "How was that?"

"Good. You ready to do this?"

"Not really, but I'll do my best."

THE GPS took them on a journey down a lot of short one-way streets, but they soon they found themselves in the parking lot rendezvous point. Helena was already there and ran up to the car before Nolan or Grayson had time to get out of it. "I sent a camera crew and my assistant to the house already. The situation is that this is a quasi-ambush. By that, I mean that the family knows they've been chosen for the show and that a TV production team is coming today to film. But they don't know you guys are coming today too. What we're hoping happens is that you surprise them, they're excited, and everyone exchanges hugs. The wife is a fan of yours, Nolan."

Grayson smiled at that. He was still a nobody, but of course the families who submitted tapes had done so hoping that Nolan Hamlin would be designing their home. Nolan was the expert they knew. Well, Grayson would just have to prove that he could do this job too, that he'd be an asset to the team.

"So we just barge in while filming is going on?" asked Nolan.

"Yep. The house is number 528, about a quarter mile down this road. You can't miss it—the camera crews are parked out front."

Two minutes later Nolan parked in front of a two-story Colonial deep in the New Jersey suburbs.

Before they got out of the car, Grayson turned the camera back on and said, "What do you think?"

Nolan looked at the house. "Not bad from the outside. A new coat of paint wouldn't hurt it, but the shutters are cute and the roof looks like it's in decent shape."

"Shall we go in?"

Nolan smiled, which nearly knocked Grayson over. Nolan had a tremendous smile, though he hardly ever showed it. Grayson knew he was probably smiling because he knew he was on camera, not because of anything Grayson was doing, although Grayson would take the scraps. His desire to impress—and attract— Nolan was overwhelming sometimes.

"Let's go," said Nolan.

A cameraman followed them as they walked through the unlocked front door and tiptoed through a small foyer, down a narrow hallway, and into a very retro living room, where the Robertses were being filmed as they talked about their house. Nolan paused in the doorway, then turned around to Grayson and held a single finger to his lips. He listened to the Robertses—still oblivious to Nolan and Grayson's presence—talk about the wood paneling in their den for a moment. Then Nolan stormed forward, so Grayson ran after him.

That got the Robertses' attention. Carol Roberts turned toward Nolan and her mouth fell open before she shrieked, ran toward him, and threw her arms around him.

So. Surprise, hug. Exactly what Helena was hoping for.

"You guys are here to help us!" said Carol.

"Yes!" said Nolan, his enthusiasm sounding genuine. "Let me introduce you to up-and-coming designer Grayson Woods." Nolan put a hand in the middle of Grayson's back and steered him forward. "We're going to work together to make this your forever home."

For what felt like the next three years but what was probably only ten minutes, Carol and George fell over themselves to thank Nolan for coming to help them. Grayson didn't quite know what to do with his hands while he stood there, waiting for some direction for what to do next. Finally Nolan said, "Do you want to show us the house?"

Carol smiled, still looking a bit starstruck. "Well, my father passed away two years ago and left me this house."

"Did you grow up here?" Nolan asked.

"No. Dad moved here after my mom died, when I was in my early twenties. But he got this place for a song, and when he passed, George and I decided that we should move in, since it's paid for and bigger than where we were living. So we gave up our rental. But this place wasn't quite ready for us—there's a lot that doesn't work."

"Show us," said Nolan.

So they spent the next half hour walking around the house with cameras trailing them as Carol and George took turns explaining what was wrong with the house. Grayson mentally cataloged everything, although the most offensive thing to him was that the design was so outdated. On top of the wood paneling and late-seventies color palette, most of the first floor was covered in hideous beige shag carpeting that had definitely seen better days.

When they got to the U-shaped kitchen, which wasn't really big enough for the four of them and a camera crew to be in, Nolan stood in the middle for a long moment and said, "This really is a terrible layout."

Grayson saw the aesthetics. The maple-colored cabinets and the ugly gray Formica countertop practically yelled that the space hadn't been updated in many decades. The appliances looked old and dirty too.

"I'd want to reconfigure this whole layout," Nolan said, obviously not as daunted as Grayson. "Take out a wall, maybe. I'd run the cabinets all along this wall into what is now the dining area and put a big island here with stools."

"That sounds amazing," said Carol.

Grayson mentally berated himself for not seeing that, of course—this kitchen was tiny and inefficiently laid out. They weren't just here to update the house's surface design. They had to actually make the space more functional.

And, well, considering the kitchen in Grayson's apartment had about a single square foot of counter space shoved in a corner, Grayson didn't have a ton of firsthand knowledge about how to make a kitchen functional. His roommates mostly used the oven to store pots and pans, which Grayson recognized was not a sign of people who cooked… ever.

Was he in over his head?

For the rest of the house tour, he mostly just went along with Nolan. When they finished, Nolan said, "Grayson and I are going to meet at our studio to hash this out. Then we'll present you with a few design plans and we'll take it from there. But before we do, we should talk numbers."

They had a brief discussion on camera. The Robertses had a healthy budget, and with the extra money the network would be providing, Nolan and Grayson could do some pretty amazing things in the house. So that was good at least.

Grayson took some photos with his phone while Nolan continued to chat with the Robertses. When they wrapped for the day and got back in the car, Grayson started tapping some notes on his phone.

"Am I really so boring?" Nolan asked as he fiddled with the GPS.

"What?"

Nolan pointed at Grayson's phone.

"Oh. No. I'm not, like, texting or whatever. I'm making some notes about what we just saw so I remember when we do the design."

"Ah, okay. What did you think?" Nolan pulled out of the driveway and onto the street.

"I liked the Robertses. I have some general ideas, but I'm still kind of sorting it out."

"What about a general theme? What kind of approach would you take with a house like that?"

Grayson glanced at the camera and saw that it was on. So they were filming, and this was Nolan's way of testing him about his design skills. Best not to admit that he didn't know jack about how to renovate a kitchen. "Well, for this couple, I wouldn't go super modern. Nothing too off the wall. I think something more classic and timeless would work. Warm and homey. Contemporary but traditional."

"Sure."

"I mean, the house has good bones. Except for the kitchen, the layout isn't bad. You could take down a wall or two to make the first floor more open and improve the flow between the spaces."

"I want to tackle that master bathroom too," Nolan added. "A retired couple doesn't need all four bedrooms. What do you think about stealing some space from the bedroom adjacent to the master? Actually, what we could do is create a huge suite. Combine those two rooms. Add a big master bath and a walk-in closet. There'd be space to make a little seating area with some big comfy chairs. Did you see all the books in the den? I'm guessing one or both of them are big readers and would like a little reading nook in the bedroom."

Grayson pressed his lips together, once again taken aback by the fact that he hadn't seen the potential Nolan had. The books in the den hadn't registered, but that was, of course, the sort of detail Grayson should have noticed, because it said a lot about the couple and what their needs would be. "That's a great idea," Grayson said.

"Before we finalize the design, I want to create a color story for the whole house. I like the idea of medium gray, dark blue, and maybe salmon pink. The opposite of the marigold colors there now."

"I like those colors." Grayson had no idea what to say. Nolan's mind was obviously running now.

"Just an idea. We'll have paint cards and all manner of tile and flooring samples at the studio." Nolan hit the camera button. The red light went off. "Helena wants a lot of the final reveal to be a surprise to the owners, but we're not the ones who will have to live in the house when it's done. So my thought was, you and I would brainstorm and come up with a theme and color story that the owners will sign off on, then we'll run with it. I mean, I'd hate to put salmon pink in the house if Carol Roberts hates it."

"Who hates salmon pink?"

"Oh, you'd be surprised. I worked with an actress once who hated purple. She would not allow it anywhere in her house. Color is not just subjective, it's polarizing. Personally, I hate red in interiors."

"Red? Really?"

"It blocks light. It makes everything seem macabre."

"I wouldn't paint a wall, like, blood red, but what about cherry red? A bright, vibrant red?"

"Fine colors for lipstick, evening gowns, and carpets at award shows. Terrible on walls."

Grayson nodded. "One of my roommates in college put up red sheer curtains in our dorm room."

"Did it feel like you lived in a brothel?"

Grayson laughed, but nerves crept in the more they talked. He'd felt confident in his ability to do this job until the past hour. Suddenly the breadth and depth of Nolan's experience was evident. He'd worked on a lot of homes, designed for a lot of people, knew how to make clients happy instead of just imposing his vision on everyone.

It was humbling, and also terrifying. Grayson knew he had blind spots and knowledge gaps, but he hadn't quite realized how much he still had to learn. A lot of the kids from his class at design school had entered the world knowing full well how they'd conquer it, but Grayson had crawled home to Massachusetts after graduation, and that had not gone well. He'd managed to land back on his feet in New York, but there was nothing like a family who didn't understand why he wanted to be an interior designer to make him want to be the best damn interior designer who ever lived. He hoped he'd be able to learn what he needed to from Nolan. But for the first time since signing onto the project, he felt like he was truly in over his head.

"What was your first big project?" he asked Nolan. "Like, the first space you ever designed by yourself?"

Nolan considered for a moment. "When I was about your age, I was working for a big design firm here in New York, and my boss had an account with a fashion designer with offices in the garment district. The designer proved to be a challenging client because he had very firm ideas about what he wanted, and he and my boss clashed. So my boss threw up his hands and sent me in. I think he suspected that working with a less experienced decorator would help this fashion designer see how unreasonable he was being. But when

I saw the space, I had a clear vision for what it should look like."

"How did the fashion designer react?"

"Oh, he hated it at first. But once I worked out that he'd worked for Halston, I understood what he wanted. Did you ever see photos of Halston's studio in the seventies?"

"No."

"Big open space. Huge windows on one side. Mirrors everywhere. Huge runway that went through the middle of the space. Halston had a very specific aesthetic that was simple and minimalist, but glamorous all the same. So I told the client I could take that idea but modernize it for the twenty-first century. He loved my drawings. My boss was pissed. So I quit the firm and started my own company, and the fashion designer was my first client. I finished his offices and redesigned his SoHo store next. Even better, he had a lot of celebrities in his orbit that he introduced me to. Things kind of took off for me from there."

"Wow."

"Success in this industry is half talent, half connections. And, look, some designers don't like celebrity clients. I have a design school buddy who designs rooms for high-end hotels now. He makes more money than I do. He told me he's allergic to anyone high-maintenance. But I kind of like the difficult clients. I like the challenge of figuring out how to give them what they want without them knowing they want it."

"Okay."

"One thing you will learn through this project is that a lot of people don't know the words for things. They don't have the vocabulary about design that you and I do. You ask any layperson about their design aesthetic and they'll stare at you blankly. So the real skill is to figure out what the person likes and elevate it. I mean, you heard Carol. She says she wants modern, but by 'modern' she just means new, not modern design. I think if we gave her a sleek, monotone interior, she'd hate it. She's not really so different from a celebrity client who flipped through an issue of *House Beautiful* and thinks she wants her house to look like this one photo she saw but can't describe."

"Right. Gotcha." And Grayson did understand. He liked to listen to Nolan talk too. Nolan was animated when he started discussing design in a way he wasn't otherwise. It was nice to see someone who was good at what they did talk about their passion.

"In college I had a job at a video rental store, back when those were still a thing. I mostly just ran people up at the register or put movies back on the shelves, but I worked with this guy who was the biggest movie buff I've ever met. Someone could come into the store and say, 'What's that movie with the blue poster?' And he would know exactly what movie they were talking about. It was like a superpower. I try to be like that with design. If someone says they like things simple or they like white kitchens or they just want a whole house designed around this blanket their grandmother crocheted thirty years ago, I can take that and translate it into a real design."

Grayson nodded, because while he understood Nolan's point, he knew he wasn't there yet. His head swam with everything the Robertses had told them, and he couldn't quite figure out how to translate everything Carol had said about her preferences and turn it into a design. There were so many decisions to make. What style of cabinet should be used in the kitchen? Should the same cabinets go in the bathrooms? What kind of floors should they use? Should they run the same floor throughout the house or use tile in the kitchen? How could they ensure the floor didn't clash with anything else they picked? What about appliances and paint colors and accessories? Suddenly Grayson's head felt like it might explode.

"The last job I worked on was an office interior," Grayson said. "We helped convert this cube farm at a book publisher into a fun, open-plan office. They publish kids' books, so they wanted this very elementary school color palette."

"So… red."

"We actually did lime green and sherbet orange. But only as accent colors. We designed this big common space for people to hold informal meetings and put orange chairs at the tables, or we used green on some of the signage. Everything else was kind of neutral."

"Okay. Not bad. Someone could do a brisk business modernizing offices."

"Yeah. But I'd rather do houses, personally. There's something a little depressing about designing spaces where people are just gonna sit all day."

Nolan laughed. "I take it you didn't like working in an office."

"Nope, hated it. I wasn't that broken up about quitting my job to come do this show."

"Designing for families may not be the biggest stretch of your creativity, but I think it will be fun. I've got a dozen ideas for the Roberts house already."

Hoping to deflect from the fact that he had nothing, Grayson said, "I can't wait to hear them."

Chapter Five

SOMEONE AT the Restoration Channel had an interesting sense of humor and had built the studio set to look a lot like Nolan's old studio in LA, where he'd filmed a handful of TV appearances. It *looked* like a design studio: white walls, a big work table, a half-dozen chairs, a row of cabinets for holding various supplies, and then over to the side, a sofa and a TV. But there was also a whole lot of camera equipment.

"Pretend the cameras aren't there," Helena told Grayson as Nolan ignored everything and unrolled the Roberts house floor plans on the big table. He picked up a box of erasable colored pencils he'd requested. He pulled out a blue one and stared at the floor plans.

"All right, let's get into it," Helena said. "Grayson, you and Nolan sit at the table and discuss your design plan."

Grayson nodded and pulled over one of the chairs. Nolan followed his lead and sat beside him. He moved the floor plan for the first floor in front of them.

"Action!" said the director.

"Let's start in the kitchen," said Grayson.

Nolan went through his plan for the first floor, crossing out the walls he wanted to take down and drawing over the existing kitchen with where he thought cabinets and appliances should go. Since Nolan and Grayson were designers and not contractors, the emphasis of the show would be on design, not renovation necessarily. Most of the renovation work would take place off camera, although Helena's idea to pull in viewers was to get a few guest contractors from other Restoration shows to take care of the renovation parts of the project.

So this was mostly for show. Once the Robertses signed off on the floor plan, a crew would finish construction mostly off camera, and then Nolan could run wild with the design.

He pulled over the floor plan for the second floor and drew in where he wanted the new master bathroom and closet to go. Grayson watched without saying much. In an effort to pull him into the conversation, Nolan asked, "What are you thinking in terms of materials?"

Grayson bit his lip. Nolan found that endearing. "Well, the kitchen doesn't get a lot of natural light, so I was thinking white cabinets and light counters."

Nolan nodded. Design 101 was that light colors made a space look bigger, and lighter materials could make up for a lack of windows. White kitchens were always a crowd-pleaser.

"I'd do flat-panel cabinets and quartz counters. Maybe the quartz could be marble-look to make it interesting. Then we put a pop of color in the backsplash so it's not too monotone."

"Solid plan. Here, I have some samples."

Nolan had gotten to the studio an hour before Grayson for just this reason. He'd already gone through the store of material samples Restoration had gotten from its various vendors and planted a few in one of the cabinets so he could whip them out at this moment. He completely agreed that light and bright was the way to go, but flat-panel cabinets were too modern for this family.

"I'm thinking Shaker or even craftsman cabinets," Nolan said, laying a white cabinet sample on the table. "Then I agree, marble-look quartz because it's pretty and practical." He put a square of white quartz with a gray streak in it on the table. "Then we should do the same floor throughout the first floor. I think a medium brown, but I kind of want to do something with gray tones to make it match with the paint colors I have in mind." Nolan pulled a piece of paper out of the cabinet. He'd already painted streaks on it. "This is the color story I have in mind. Soft and beachy."

"So is that our theme for the design?"

"Jersey Shore in the winter."

"I like it," said Grayson. He grabbed a purple pencil from the box and used it to point to the den on the main floor plan. "We're getting rid of the wood paneling, right?"

"Oh, yeah. Why someone would make the interior of that house so dark is a mystery. And I think we could do something really fun with the den, but I'm not totally sure what yet."

Grayson looked at the floor plan for a moment. Nolan was conscious of the camera, but he also couldn't take his eyes off Grayson. Even though his hair was styled in a jaunty way that made Nolan think he was trying too hard, it still hung over his eye in a sexy way, and Grayson's perfect skin almost glowed under the big lights of the studio. He wore a lot of layers—a T-shirt

and a jacket and a scarf today—and Nolan still wanted
to peel them all off.

But they were designing a house.

"They seem like fun people," Grayson said. "They
need entertaining spaces."

"Absolutely. What did you have in mind?"

Grayson hesitated. The pause went on for an un-
comfortably long time. Just before Nolan was about to
ask again, or come up with something to say to help
Grayson out, Helena said, "Cut!" Then she walked onto
the set and addressed Grayson directly. "It's fine, Gray.
Share your ideas, even if you think Nolan will disagree.
Your role here is to challenge him so that together, you
come up with the best design."

Grayson took a deep breath and nodded.

The director yelled, "Action!"

Grayson pointed his pencil at the den again.
"Okay, here's what I'd do. We have two living areas,
right? One of them is directly next to the kitchen and is
the main entertaining space. The other one is the den,
which is a little more private. I'd widen the doorway to
the den and make it an intimate space. Big, soft furniture, built-in bookcases, and lots of little homey touches. It should be a comfortable, everyday kind of room,
whereas the other living space is a little more formal.
Does that make sense?"

"It does. I don't know if the Roberts are really formal people, though."

Nolan realized that he was prepared to bulldoze
right over Grayson, but he had a very clear vision of
what this house should look like. And in principle, Nolan opposed formal rooms. The formal living room at
his favorite aunt's house was still the room at the front
of the house where the furniture was covered in plastic

because no one ever sat there. What was the point of having a room in your home that no one ever used? But on the other hand, he was impressed Grayson had stood up for him and wanted to keep the frown off Grayson's beautiful face.

"Formal is the wrong word," said Grayson. "I just mean, they could have one room where they host company and one room that is just for them. Carol mentioned their daughters come to visit a lot, so they should have a good space for that, but also a retreat."

It wasn't a terrible idea. Nolan had thought to make the den into a library or office, depending on what the Robertses needed, but keeping it as a den wasn't a bad idea.

In all, they filmed two hours of brainstorming that would probably be distilled down to a five-minute segment of the show. Grayson pitched some reasonable ideas but seemed a little timid throughout the whole discussion. As the crew packed up, Nolan felt a little guilty for dominating the discussion so thoroughly, even though he thought his ideas were right and most of Grayson's showed his inexperience.

Or was Nolan overcompensating? His attraction to Grayson was becoming like an itch he really wanted to scratch but knew he shouldn't. At first Nolan had figured that he'd been thinking about Grayson a lot, even when they weren't filming, because they'd been spending so much time together lately. But no. This was a full-fledged crush. Nolan had forgotten what that felt like.

Still, Nolan worried he'd bullied Grayson into some of his ideas, so once most of the crew had cleared out, he walked up to Grayson and said, "Sorry if I was too assertive."

Grayson smiled ruefully and nodded. "It's okay. You have more experience at this."

"I'm set in my ways. Your idea about turning the den into a comfy retreat is a good one. It's fine to challenge me. It probably makes better TV if we disagree on some things."

"Okay. I mean, in that case, I'd add mustard to your color story."

Nolan looked down at the paper he'd prepared with the colored streaks on it. "Mustard?" He couldn't help but wrinkle his nose. He hated mustard almost as much as he hated red.

"Lemon or sunny yellow will get washed out, but something a little stronger would complement the blue. Not a lot, but some pops of it, especially in the kitchen and bathrooms. I mean orangey yellow, like a sunset." Grayson hesitated just a second and then seemed to decide something and said, "I think this color story could use some more depth, is all I'm saying. You afraid of a little color?" He raised an eyebrow.

Well, that certainly seemed like a dare. Nolan had some little cans with paint samples in one of the cabinets, so he dug around and found an orangey yellow. The sticker on the can said *mango*. He grabbed a paintbrush and added it to the color story he'd prepared. It… wasn't bad. And it played well with the soft pink and the blue.

"Is that what you meant?"

"Yes, exactly," said Grayson. "See what I mean?"

"I'll think about it."

WHILE NOLAN talked to Helena, Grayson flipped through a little booklet of paint cards to find the exact yellow he wanted. It didn't ultimately matter and the cameras were off, but Grayson felt like he needed to do something to prove to Nolan he wasn't completely inept, especially after Nolan's not-really apology.

He should go home. There was no reason for Grayson to linger at the studio now that they were done for the day. He hoped to catch Nolan's attention, but there was something a little sad about waiting around for crumbs of Nolan's affection.

What had Grayson really thought would happen here? That Nolan would meet him, and Grayson would charm him, and then they'd fall in love? That was ridiculous; Nolan was closed off, thought Grayson was too young and silly, and was clearly not interested.

"Yeah, we can close this down," Nolan said to Helena. "Looks like Grayson is on to something, so we'll finish up the design proposal and I'll shut down the studio. Just the light switch by the door, right?"

"Yes," said Helena. "Stay as long as you need to. Consider this your studio for real, not just the set. Here are the keys." She handed Nolan a ring with three keys on it. "Come in whenever you want. Turn off the lights and lock the door on the way out, that's all the network asks."

"Sure."

Helena left with her assistant on her heels. And then Nolan and Grayson were alone.

"Yellow I'll give you," Nolan said, walking over and looking over Grayson's shoulder. "Maybe a vibrant, punchy yellow. Like… this one." Nolan reached around Grayson and stabbed at a paint card with his pointer finger. It was New York taxi yellow.

Grayson held the paint card against the color story sheet. "That's not quite it. *This* melon yellow is very on-trend, though. It's not subtle. But adding it makes the theme more 'Sunset on the Jersey Shore in Winter.'"

"Can't hurt to run it by the Robertses."

"I just think that you don't hire Nolan Hamlin to decorate your home if you want something bland and neutral."

"Hmm." Nolan stood right behind Grayson, close enough that Grayson felt Nolan's breath on his neck. Part of him wanted to jump away. The rest wanted to lean back, to know what it would be like to touch Nolan for a moment.

But those were crumbs. Grayson might be willing to take whatever Nolan wanted to give him, but he shouldn't just settle for crumbs.

Grayson set the paint cards aside and stepped away from Nolan. "Can I ask you something?"

"Sure."

What Grayson wanted to ask was if he even had a chance, but that was too forward. He decided to relate it back to the show. "How much of ourselves are we sharing with the audience?"

"What do you mean?"

"What do we show to the audience? Do they want to know about our personalities, our life stories? Does the audience care that I'm a gay kid who lives in Brooklyn? Are they interested in who I'm dating? Like, what am I sharing?"

"Are you dating someone?"

The question took Grayson so off guard, he asked, "What?"

Nolan shrugged. "My story's out there. What's yours? How do you want to be known?"

"Well, I'm not dating anyone right now. I'm basically every other creative person in Brooklyn at the moment, except I don't have a beard. I live in a tiny apartment with roommates. I want to be a great interior designer. Most of my money goes toward my wardrobe, and even then, I buy everything on clearance. I want to look the part, I guess." Grayson plucked at the lapel of his blazer. "Ralph Lauren, 70 percent off at Macy's, can you believe that? Last one in the store happened to be my size."

"I remember those days."

Grayson shook his head. This was so different from anything Nolan would have experienced. Grayson had moved to New York with nothing. Now he didn't need to scour the clearance racks. "This show is going to change my life. I don't think I fully appreciated how much until I got my first paycheck. Even if it flops, it's high-profile enough that I'll find other work. Assuming, that is, it doesn't look like I'm just second banana to the real designer."

Nolan frowned and leaned against the side of the table. "I'm sorry. I haven't worked on a team in a while. I'm used to making decisions unilaterally. And even then, I haven't really worked in more than a year. I'm rusty, I think. The sunset colors are great, and I think Carol Roberts would really like them. This yellow goes really well with the peachy pink I picked."

"I am kind of the second banana, though. If I have any good ideas, I feel like they're flukes. I mean, a broken clock is right twice a day, yeah? You have so much more experience than I do. You notice things that I don't. You're confident about your designs in ways that I'm not. I thought going into this, I'd walk through the Roberts house and know exactly what I'd do with it. But it was like being in my first year of design school again." Grayson swallowed, suddenly horrified that he'd confessed so much. "I shouldn't even have said all that, because I really want to impress you."

Nolan smiled in a soft way that Grayson couldn't interpret. Supportive? Patronizing? Amused? But then he said, "You're not so arrogant after all."

Had Nolan read Grayson as arrogant? Grayson supposed he did put on a brave front most of the time. He wanted people to think he knew what he was talking about. But then he'd gone and confessed what an insecure mess he really was. Ugh, had he really said all that? It had been honest, though. Nolan probably read it as him fishing for compliments. He decided to shove it aside.

"You didn't answer my question, by the way," said Grayson.

Nolan pushed off the table and paced a few feet away. "About how much to show of yourself? Show what you're comfortable with. Garrett is always telling me that people like to get to know the Restoration Channel hosts. Actually, the fact that we're both single is not ideal, because the viewership loves families. But just doing this show is already putting myself out there more than I feel ready for."

Grayson bit his lip. Such terrible timing. He kept forgetting that Nolan's husband had passed away only a year ago. He knew also that most of the Restoration Channel hosts were couples. The highest-rated show on the network right then was about a heterosexual couple who renovated old houses in Georgia and tended to their large flock of children.

"Who's to say two single gay guys can't make houses fabulous and rake in the viewers doing it?" said Grayson.

Nolan laughed. "Well, I think if we're going to be successful, we need to meet in the middle. I will try to be less stubborn when you volunteer ideas, and I'll mentor you on the rest. Deal?"

"Yeah, deal." Grayson held out his hand.

Nolan grasped it in both of his. Grayson was alarmed by how soft and warm Nolan's hands were. But he reveled in it too. He looked up and met Nolan's gaze. They stared at each other for a long moment.

It seemed possible for a fleeting second that Nolan Hamlin was attracted to Grayson, but there was so much in this situation that was not conducive to romance.

And yet.

Nolan smiled and took his hands away. "We're meeting the Robertses at a coffeehouse in New Jersey tomorrow to go over the plans. The car leaves at ten. Can you be here maybe a half hour before that, so we can make sure we've got everything ready before we leave?"

"Yeah, no problem." Grayson felt dazed. He packed up his things and slung his messenger bag over his shoulder as Nolan neatly stacked everything they'd need for the next day on the table. Then he followed Nolan out of the studio. They parted ways when they got to Ninth Avenue, which gave Grayson plenty of time to contemplate what had just happened.

A long moment of eye contact probably didn't mean anything. Or it could mean everything.

Chapter Six

FOR THE first episode of *Residential Rehab*, the show would be borrowing contractor Travis Rogers, who worked on a house-flipping show called *Domestic Do-Over*. Travis lived in Brooklyn and had some rough edges, but it became clear to Nolan fairly quickly that the guy knew his stuff.

Travis trailed Nolan and Grayson as they toured the house again for the cameras. The Robertses had signed off on Nolan's new floor plan and color story, so they were good there. The issue now was what it was going to cost, because any time Nolan suggested something, Travis said, "Are you sure that's in the budget?"

Now they stood back in the living room. Travis frowned at the kitchen entry. "This wall has to come down," he said, placing his hand on the wall between the kitchen and living room. "I'd like to get an engineer in here to verify, but I don't believe it's load-bearing. If we do cabinets along the opposite wall and put a big island where the wall is currently, I think we have a good kitchen layout. Are we replacing the floors?"

"I want to do the same flooring throughout the first floor," said Nolan.

Travis frowned. "Hardwood?"

"That's my preference. Nothing in the house is really salvageable. And the linoleum in the kitchen is hideous."

"Be smart about your materials choices and we can get it done within budget. If you do vinyl plank flooring instead of wood and prefab kitchen cabinets instead of custom, that's already a big savings."

"Can you price all that out for us? Give us some options?"

"No problem." Travis wrote some notes on his clipboard. "Unless you want to tear down more walls or we find anything scary, this job seems pretty straight-forward. I didn't see any mold or water damage, so that's good. The plumbing and electrical look up to code. Digging into a kitchen this old could unearth some nastiness, but we'll deal with that when we see it." Then he shook his head and chuckled. "It's almost refreshing to work on a house that's *not* over a hundred years old. The houses we've worked on for my show are all so ancient, I'm almost afraid to open up walls. You wouldn't believe the horrors I've discovered. This house was built, what, midseventies?"

"Yeah."

"So most of the work is aesthetic. And you guys, unlike my boyfriend, actually like designing with color, so this project should be fun."

"We're calling the theme 'Jersey Shore Sunset.'"

Travis grinned. "I like it, but say that five times fast."

Grayson held back through most of this conversa-tion. He seemed to be out of his depth with the actual process of renovating the house. Although renovation wasn't Nolan's area of expertise either, he'd picked up enough knowledge over the years that he could hold his own in a conversation with Travis.

"Anyway," said Travis, "try to keep your expectations in check. This is a retired couple in the suburbs, not one of your Hollywood clients. You're going to have to compromise your design for the sake of cost."

Nolan knew that intellectually, but he realized he'd been mentally designing the space as if he had an unlimited budget. He glanced at Grayson, who was looking around at the kitchen and typing on his phone. "All right. What do you think you can do within budget?"

Travis walked Nolan through what he thought they could do. Then Grayson walked over and asked for a piece of paper. After Travis gave him one, he wandered off. Nolan wondered if Grayson was aware the cameras were on. As Travis and Nolan finished, Grayson returned and handed Travis a sketch.

"I want to take ownership of the den. Here's what I'm thinking for the built-ins. The line on top is the wall with the window. I want to put built-ins on the wall across from it—shelves on top and cabinets on the bottom. Leave a space for a TV in the middle. Then we do built-ins on the opposite side too, same thing with shelves and cabinets, but no TV hole on this side. I'm thinking we put a big sofa in the middle, but we can talk about furniture later. And then the crazy idea is to replace the window with a door to the side yard, maybe a slider to let in more light. What do you think that will cost?"

Travis shrugged. "A few hundred dollars. I've got a door guy who owes me a favor, so I think I can get a good deal on a slider."

"Cool. Let's do that. What do you think, Nolan?"

Nolan liked the idea of adding a door, because the den had only one small window that didn't let in much light. He wasn't a fan of doing that many built-ins, though. Still, he knew he couldn't plow over Grayson, both because it would make their dynamic look problematic on the show and because he was starting to really like Grayson and didn't want to tear him down. "Sure, let's do it."

Grayson was quiet in the car on the way back to the studio. Nolan burned to ask what was going through his head, but refrained. Instead, he took a moment to reflect on his own thoughts and actions.

Grayson was sexy in a cute way, and open and vulnerable, something he probably wasn't putting out deliberately. He wanted to do this job well, he'd said he wanted to impress Nolan, and he had clearly put some thought into his ideas.

The thought entered Nolan's mind: what if?

Grayson was the first man to really attract his attention in more than a year. Something in Nolan was awake now in a way it hadn't been in a very long time. Because he wanted Grayson. He wanted that slim body, he wanted to run his hands through Grayson's curly hair, he wanted to know what those plump, pretty lips tasted like. A thrill zipped through Nolan whenever Grayson entered the room. So, there was that. But there was more too: Grayson was hungry for success, he had a good eye for color, he had some design talent even if Nolan didn't always agree, and he put up an arrogant front but was really unsure of himself under it.

So what if Nolan gave in to his attraction? What if Grayson returned it? What if they had an affair? What if they had a relationship? What if they just kept each other warm at night for the duration of filming the show?

Sure, getting involved with someone he worked with seemed like a stupid idea, and there were a hundred reasons for Nolan to tuck this away and never think on it again, but the fact that *this* man was the one to wake him up *had* to mean something.

He glanced over at Grayson, who was looking at his phone.

"What did you think of Travis?"

Grayson looked up and turned his head toward Nolan. Nolan's gaze was focused on the road, so he didn't turn to look, but he felt Grayson's gaze on him.

"He's very practical," Grayson said. "I figured that would be the case. I've been watching his show."

"Is it good?"

"Yeah. His boyfriend is Brandon Chase."

"I don't know who that is."

"Oh. Well, Brandon used to host a show on Restoration with his ex-wife. They flipped houses upstate, mostly. Now Brandon is with Travis, and they flip houses in Victorian Flatbush, in Brooklyn. So they work on these old, crumbling mansions, basically, and bring them back to life."

"Interesting."

"You should watch the pilot, at least. It's really good. Usually when they flip houses, Brandon tries to keep the design very neutral, like Travis said, but they ended up keeping the house they renovated in the pilot, and the kitchen design is one of the best I've ever seen. Also, rumor has it they started dating while filming the first season, and the sexual tension crackles between them in a delightful way the whole episode."

"All right, I'll check it out."

After a beat, Grayson said, "I hope I didn't overstep by showing my sketch of the den to Travis."

"It's fine. The idea for the slider is very good. It will allow a lot more light into the room. That house is really dark because of the size of the windows and how overgrown the landscaping is. I want to get the Robertses' permission to change the landscaping too, but only if there's money left in the budget."

"Okay."

"Listen, Grayson, I—" Nolan snapped his mouth closed, unsure of what he wanted to say. *I like you* seemed silly. How did one do this? Had it really been so long since Nolan had hit on a man?

"I was just trying to follow your advice and assert myself when I have an idea I feel strongly about," Grayson said, parroting something Nolan had told him on the drive to the house that morning.

"That was good. I'm not saying you shouldn't have done it."

"Because I don't really know that much about kitchens, to be honest. I know what components they need, but I've never even turned on the oven in my own apartment. I can boil pasta and microwave leftovers, and that's about it. So I know you need an oven and a fridge, but otherwise I don't really know what someone who actually cooks would need. So I figured I'd let you worry about the kitchen and I'd work on some of the easier rooms, at least in this house."

"You'll figure it out. The main thing with kitchen design is prep space and storage. You want to maximize both without creating any traps or blocks. Everything else is aesthetics."

"Traps or blocks?"

"I worked on this loft for an actress in LA who had hired a bad designer to do her kitchen. You couldn't open the oven or dishwasher all the way because there wasn't enough clearance around the island. And if you had the refrigerator open, the pantry was inaccessible. The whole thing was a nonfunctional mess and an electrical nightmare, because if any two appliances were running at the same time, it tripped the circuit. I had to basically rip the kitchen apart to fix it."

"Ah, okay. What about appliances?"

"Well, that comes down to aesthetics. Antique-looking appliances are on-trend right now, and you can find some really cool-looking mid-century modern, space-age design but paired with modern technology like digital displays. Or you can find appliances that are sleek and modern with, like, copper finishes or black stainless steel. It all depends on what kind of design the client wants and what the budget is. I think the Robertses probably just want something middle of the road. Carol likes to bake cookies with her grandkids, not cook restaurant-quality dinners. They don't need six burners or high-end design. Stainless for sure, but it doesn't have to be top-of-the-line."

"That makes sense."

"Especially if you have a tight budget, you have to consider what the client needs over what you think will look good."

"Right."

"Once we do a few houses for the show, you'll catch on. I'm sure you'll have opinions about kitchens soon enough."

Traffic in the Holland Tunnel on a weekday afternoon wasn't bad, and Nolan felt a bit of disappointment when he pulled the car onto Ninth Avenue and knew their time together in the little bubble of the car was coming to an end.

"What do we still need to do today?" Grayson asked.

"I want to finalize the materials for the Robertses and then talk a little about the Cruz house, since we're going to see that one next week."

"Okay."

Nolan glanced at Grayson as he stopped the car behind another driver headed into the underground garage below the Restoration Channel's headquarters.

He swallowed. Making a move would be foolish, right? Nolan wasn't really ready, they were still finding their footing as costars, and also there was the fact that Grayson had been born when Nolan had been in high school. It would be best to stick to business, no matter how much Nolan wanted it.

GRAYSON FELT a little paranoid. He and Nolan were alone in the studio, with no cameramen around, and yet he worried that a camera was secretly recording every time he looked at Nolan.

But they were finished for the day. Grayson thought about texting one of his friends about grabbing dinner, because the idea of going home alone tonight made him feel sad. Resigning himself to not ever being with Nolan had made him feel sad too, although that had clearly been a pipe dream to start with. What the hell had he been thinking? There was no way on earth that Nolan Hamlin would ever think of Grayson as more than the pain-in-the-ass kid he'd been forced to work with.

"You're doing a good job, you know," Nolan said.

"Thanks." Grayson shot Nolan a smile but then turned back to his phone.

"No, I'm serious. You were quiet today, and I worried it was because you didn't feel confident in the design, so I wanted to let you know, you *should* feel confident, because you're doing a good job."

Grayson looked up and met Nolan's gaze. When Nolan said things like that, it made Grayson hope that something *could* happen between them. That a relationship was possible. As Nolan walked closer to Grayson, his heart pounded in anticipation.

"Can I be honest about something?" Nolan asked.

"Of course."

Nolan looked at the table for a moment. Then he took a deep breath and said, "For most of the past year, I've felt that something in me died with Ricky, and that's probably true. I've been numb for a long time. But when Garrett approached me about doing this show, I thought, *It's been a year. It's time to move on.* I didn't feel ready to face the world again, but how long could I just sit at home not feeling anything? Ricky wouldn't have wanted me to live that way."

Grayson tried to guess where Nolan was going with this. Was he not ready to do the show? Did he have regrets? Was he going to back out?

"I'm so sorry," Grayson said. "I can't even imagine what you must be going through."

"Working has made me feel almost normal again. Working on these designs? That's what I do. I feel functional again. Sometimes I look at my phone and expect to see a text from Ricky, and sometimes late at night, it surprises me that I'll never see him again. But I think I've mostly gotten to the acceptance part of grief. It's… hard. I still miss him and will never stop. But I want to live again. I'm tired of feeling numb."

Grayson nodded slowly. He didn't know what to say. "Why are you—?"

"For the last few days, I have not been able to get you out of my head."

"What?" His heart pounded harder. Had he misheard? Could this really be it? Did Nolan really want him?

Nolan closed his eyes for a moment. He stood maybe a foot from Grayson now, close enough for Grayson to reach out and touch him. Then he said, "It's crazy. You're the first man I've been attracted to since Ricky died. The more I get to know you, the more I really like you. But I can think of a hundred reasons why us pursuing anything is a really stupid idea, not the least of which is that we work together and I'm, what, fifteen years older than you? I mean, just for saying that, I've given you grounds to sue me. God, I'm such an asshole for even thinking—"

Grayson cut him off with a kiss.

He didn't even think about it, just leaned forward and planted his lips against Nolan's. Then he put a hand on Nolan's shoulder to steady himself and felt Nolan sigh against him. So he rolled with it, leaning forward. Nolan's arms came around him.

Had any kiss in the history of mankind ever been this exciting? Grayson was kissing *Nolan Hamlin*, the most beautiful man in the world, a man he'd lusted after from a distance for years, his hero, his idol. And Nolan was attracted to him! Oh, Grayson had heard all of the reasons why they shouldn't be together, and he agreed. But he was not going to waste this moment.

He pulled away slightly and searched Nolan's gaze.

"I take it you like me back, then," said Nolan.

"I've been thinking about this moment since I got the callback for the show."

"It's really stupid for us to get involved."

"I've felt really stupid all week. Might as well lean in."

Nolan laughed. "I'm serious, though. I feel like an ass for even propositioning you."

"I want to be propositioned. And you aren't my boss. And the show has only been picked up for six episodes."

"So what I hear you saying is that you're into it."

Grayson backed off. He needed to catch his breath. "I mean, I assume we've both given this situation some thought, what with the age gap and the working together thing and the fact that you've been, um, out of the game for a minute. But we're both consenting adults, right?" Good gravy. Grayson was amazed that he managed to sound so calm, given how hard his heart was pounding. He still couldn't get over the fact that he'd just kissed Nolan.

"You, ah, wanna get dinner or something? I know a guy who can get us a table at Morimoto on short notice."

"Morimoto? Geez. My last boyfriend once hit me up for money to buy a slice of pizza."

"Yeah, this will be a little different." Nolan took his phone out of his pocket. "You like sushi? It's my treat. If you want, we can talk about this."

Grayson resisted the urge to pinch himself, because he was obviously dreaming. "Sure. I like sushi."

Chapter Seven

NOLAN SUPPOSED the cat was out of the bag.

He was aware of the power imbalance. If they got involved and things went sideways, the network would want to keep Nolan. They'd probably ditch Grayson on Nolan's say-so faster than he could snap his fingers.

"I want you to know," he said as Grayson shoved the last of his sushi roll into his mouth, then mumbled something about not be able to eat another bite, "that I would never try to get you fired. The truth is, Helena and Garrett saw something in you that I didn't, and I think you are probably a good foil for me. I mean, you can help me see when I'm being stubborn and wrong, and I can help mentor you on how to think critically as a designer. So in that way, we're helping each other. But I'm aware of the fact that I'm the bankable star and I could have you replaced if I really wanted to."

Grayson dropped one of his chopsticks. "Wait, do you want to replace me? I'm sorry for kissing you back at the studio, but I thought that you wanted—"

"I did. And no, what I'm saying is, I *won't* try to replace you. You earned your spot on the show. I'm just mentally playing out all the scenarios. I mean, I don't live that far from here. What would happen if I paid the bill and took you home? Would we be able to look at each other tomorrow? Could we keep working together?"

"Of course."

"You don't know how you'll feel. I could be bad in bed."

"Are you?"

"I've never had any complaints."

Grayson picked up the chopstick from where it had landed on his plate and took the last bite of tuna from Nolan's plate. He made eye contact as he closed his lips around it. "I'm not worried about that. Are you?"

"No, I just… worst-case scenario. If something goes wrong…."

"It won't."

"How can you be sure?"

Grayson shrugged. "I mean, I'm as sure about this as I am of anything. I'm sure they picked me for the show as much because I'm cute and have some chemistry with you as they did for my actual design skills. I say we should use that chemistry. Maybe even play it up for the cameras. Get the audience to go, 'Hey, wait, are they…?' I mean, what have we got to lose?"

The idea of them doing anything publicly made Nolan very anxious, although he could see why viewers would eat it up. Viewers were going to love Grayson. He was a little quirky, but he was very cute. Still, Nolan said, "I don't know about that."

"I mean, realistically, this show is not going to go on forever," Grayson added. "If we get more than a couple of seasons out of it, I'll be surprised. I was thrilled just for the opportunity to work with you, but now that you've told me that you're attracted to me and that I might have the opportunity to *be* with you? I'm over the moon. And you can't unring that bell. I can't unknow that fact."

"See, and that's where I worry that I'm manipulating the situation. It's not fair to you for me to act on my attraction. I shouldn't have said anything, I shouldn't have—"

"This is happening, Nolan. Accept it. Embrace it. You've reeled me in. It's too late to throw me back."

Nolan couldn't help but laugh at that. "Oh, is that how it is?"

"I will admit I'm a little nervous about this whole situation. But just a little. Let's evaluate. Before I got cast on the show, I was a barely employed interior designer, but I was getting by okay. What's the worst thing that could happen here? You and I get involved, it doesn't work out, you ditch me next season. If that happens, I still have a season of an interior design show on the Restoration Channel to put on my résumé and I'll have gotten to be with an incredibly sexy man. Or, hey, maybe it works out and we live happily ever after. I'm okay with either outcome at this point. This isn't like a corporate job where I'll have to work my way up the ladder. Our initial run of this show is only six episodes, so hey, if the ratings suck, we're both out of a job anyway. I intend to make the most of this opportunity."

These were all good points. Nolan couldn't believe how logical Grayson was being. But Nolan couldn't help reminding him of one important fact. "Still, if I lose this job, I have other avenues."

"Yeah, and how did you find those avenues?"

That was a fair point too. Part of it was just persistence. On top of his fashion designer client, Nolan had a college roommate who'd made a name for himself in Hollywood shortly after graduation—one of those stars who was so ubiquitous for a couple of years that it seemed like it wasn't possible to make a movie without him—and he'd helped Nolan get a few jobs with people who had reputations for being tastemakers out in California. He'd done enough celebrity homes that soon enough, he was giving advice to Oprah's viewers about how to liven up their living rooms, after which department stores started approaching him about doing home goods collections.

It helped that he was photogenic, and he knew it.

Then again, so was Grayson. He didn't have much experience or self-confidence yet, but he *did* have a good eye and strong instincts. Nolan could teach him the rest.

"These are very odd circumstances," said Nolan.

"If you don't want to do this, that's fine. I'll catch the subway back to Brooklyn and return to work tomorrow, acting as if we didn't have a nice dinner together and talk indirectly about sex. But you're the one who put this idea on the table."

Nolan wasn't sure what to do. Give in to his desire or put up walls? Having a fling with a hot young thing was a pretty cliché way of moving on from the death of one's spouse, but maybe it was exactly what he needed to start living again.

"I'm not young," Nolan said.

"You're not old either. Forty is hardly ancient. And I think you're hot. That's what matters, right?"

Nolan couldn't keep himself from frowning, so he looked at the table. He'd let personal maintenance go by the wayside in that year he'd been hiding away, and he could see for himself that he was a little less firm and a little more gray than he'd been a year ago. Grayson didn't have so much as a wrinkle; he was all smooth skin and bright colors.

"You have no reason to be self-conscious," Grayson said.

"You say that, but—"

"We all feel insecure sometimes, but I will not accept that as a reason not to do this. Try again."

Nolan laughed. Grayson was persistent, if nothing else. "Finish your cocktail. Then we'll see, okay?"

AND SO Nolan brought Grayson back to his loft.

"You want something to drink, or…?" Nolan asked, not at all sure what to do once they were inside.

"Nolan. Babe. I am not here for cocktails."

Nolan hated how nervous he was. Obviously it had been a while since he'd done anything like this, but it wasn't that he was nervous about… performing. It was more that this felt… important. The first guy in a year who had snagged his interest was now standing across from him, his eyebrow cocked, waiting for Nolan to make a move. That had to mean something, right? This wasn't just some random guy he'd picked up in a bar. It was Grayson.

Grayson, his coworker, who was fifteen years younger than he was.

But also Grayson, who was incredibly sexy and charming.

"Do *you* need a drink?" Grayson asked.

"I might," Nolan said. "I just need to… slow down. For a second. It's not that I don't want to do this…."

"You're freaking out."

"A little."

"This doesn't have to be a thing you freak out about. It's easy and casual. We're just two guys hooking up because we're attracted to each other."

"Okay."

Grayson stepped closer to Nolan and put his hands on Nolan's waist, pulling him closer, until their chests touched. Then he kissed him.

Some kind of muscle memory kicked in. Nolan at least knew how to do the physical stuff. He could kiss, he could touch, he could… well, not go through the motions, but he knew the moves to make. Or he had, when he'd been with Ricky. What if Grayson liked different things? What if Nolan didn't know how to do those things?

"Shh," Grayson said, pulling away slightly. Nolan felt Grayson's breath against his lips. "You're tensing up. Just relax."

"I haven't had sex in almost two years," Nolan blurted.

Grayson nodded as if it was common knowledge. "I figured. But hey, it's like… riding a bike, right?" He cracked up. "That's a dumb metaphor."

"Can I ask you something?" Nolan said, leading Grayson toward the corner of his loft where his bed was.

"Of course."

"I was pretty wild when I was twenty-five. I had a place here, in the Village, and I went out every night I could. My friends and I were regulars at this gay bar on West Fourth that closed down years ago. But, like, I had that moment in my life… and now I'm past it. Is it projecting for me to say that I think that's probably the point you're at now?"

"I go out some, I guess. But until I got this job, I was also pretty much always broke. And, like, not gonna lie, I've been on some Tinder dates more to get a meal than to hook up with someone."

"Oh. I didn't realize things were that bad for you."

Grayson shrugged. "I had to keep things lean when I first graduated college, that's all. You know, first job in New York. It pays peanuts. I live in Brooklyn with two roommates. Typical stuff."

"Sure." But Nolan sensed a bigger story. Something about Grayson's expression hinted that something bad had happened. Hopefully nothing too horrible. Now wasn't the time to press, though. "I don't mean to pry. It's just… I'm not in that place anymore. First of all, I'd look pretty silly in a gay bar."

"You would not! My friends and I go to this drag show on Friday nights at a bar on Bleecker, and the crowd there is seriously, like, all ages. One of the regulars is this burly guy with a huge beard who must be, like, fifty? Sweet guy. His husband is one of the performers, but still, he fits right in. You're not, like, ancient, Nolan. You always talk like your best years are behind you, but that can't possibly be true."

"I just turned forty. I guess I have a complex about it."

"Well, knock it off." Grayson sat on the bed and leaned back on his hands. "Have I hooked up with a random stranger here or there in my day? Maybe. Is that something I need? Not really. I'd rather be in a relationship. Not that I'm saying that's what should happen here, but just… you don't need to freak out, okay? This is only as big a deal as you want it to be."

"The thing I'm struggling with is whether I want it to be a big deal."

"You're thinking too hard." Grayson slid off the frilly scarf he was wearing and tossed it on a chair near the foot of the bed. Then he began unbuttoning his shirt.

Grayson was probably right. Nolan wished he could turn off his brain. Although Grayson was doing a good job helping him along. Who knew that just that sliver of exposed skin from Grayson's Adam's apple to his sternum could be so appealing? Nolan wanted to lick it.

Instead he stood there, a little awed as he watched Grayson take off his shirt while shooting him seductive looks. Grayson toed off his shoes, every one of his gestures easy and casual, which helped put Nolan more at ease. Yeah, Grayson had a point; this was only a big deal if they made it one.

Nolan took off his own shoes—awkwardly, because he was wearing oxfords that needed to be untied—and peeled off his socks, which he dropped in the hamper before sitting next to Grayson on the bed.

"You are a fastidious sort, aren't you?" said Grayson.

"What do you mean?"

Grayson tossed his shirt over his shoulder, and it flew over the foot of the bed and landed on the floor. "Does that bother you?"

"No."

"Because you put your socks in the hamper like someone who cares if clothes are on the floor."

"I mean, I care, but it's not a big deal."

Grayson raised an eyebrow and then wriggled out of his black skinny jeans. Then he tossed those on the floor too.

"It's fine," said Nolan. He pulled off his T-shirt and tossed it toward Grayson's clothes. "See?"

Grayson grinned as he slunk over to Nolan and ran his hands over Nolan's now-naked chest. Nolan felt suddenly self-conscious. Here was Grayson, a fine specimen of the male form, sitting beside Nolan and feeling him up. And he seemed to want *him*—Nolan—who was forty, wearing only his underwear, and hadn't been to the gym in a while.

Ugh, he had to knock this off. He wasn't *that* old. And Grayson was clearly attracted to him. What was his problem?

He kissed Grayson, hoping that would disable whatever part of his brain was holding him back. Grayson groaned softly and hooked his tongue into Nolan's mouth. Nolan reached over and ran his hands through Grayson's hair, surprised by how soft it was, considering the way it was always styled.

Grayson reached for Nolan's pants and undid the button. "These beige khakis are very you and also very boring," he said. "Let's just take those off."

Nolan couldn't do much more than watch as Grayson peeled off his khakis and tossed them in the clothes pile. Then Grayson pounced, pushing Nolan down on the bed and straddling his hips. Nolan had on black briefs that he expected Grayson to comment on, while Grayson was wearing gray boxer briefs, but suddenly Nolan was acutely aware that two thin bits of fabric were all that separated them. Nolan felt the heat and weight of Grayson against his hardening cock, and he almost laughed, delighted that his body was responding the way it was supposed to.

Two years was at once too long, and not long enough, for Nolan to have gone without this.

He bucked his hips against Grayson, who smiled and started writhing.

"Oh, did you want to get all the way naked?" asked Grayson, hooking his thumbs into his boxer briefs. "You should have said something!" He got up on his knees and, through some kind of magic, smoothly slipped his underwear off. Then he knelt above Nolan, looking triumphant, his cock hard and jutting away from his body.

Nolan groaned. He slid out of his briefs and then raised an eyebrow at Grayson, as if to say, *Is this what you wanted? Are you happy now?*

"Oh, babe," said Grayson. "You are *sexy*. More than I even expected."

"You gonna talk all night or...."

Grayson leaned down and kissed Nolan, then ground his hips against Nolan's so their cocks rubbed together. Arousal shot through Nolan's body, making his skin feel alive.

"So... how do you want to do this?" Nolan asked.

"Mmm. Well. Normally I prefer to bottom, but I don't know if I'm totally ready for that just yet. So I was thinking we could... oh, this. Let's just do this."

Nolan reached between them and wrapped his hand around both of their cocks. They bucked against each other and... okay, yeah, if they did just this, Nolan would....

Grayson kissed him. Nolan groaned into his mouth as Grayson thrust his fingers into Nolan's hair. They pressed their tongues together and writhed on the bed.

And then Nolan took over. He pushed at Grayson's shoulders and rolled them over so that he was on top and Grayson was beneath him. Grayson grinned, but Nolan kissed the grin off his face as Grayson rubbed their cocks together. Nolan grabbed them again and stroked. This felt incredible. Nolan's whole body was alive in a way that it hadn't in a very long time. He controlled the pace now to make it exactly what he needed.

"Holy shit, I'm gonna come," said Grayson, digging his nails into Nolan's back. He was breathless. "I can't believe I'm so close, so soon. Keep doing that."

Who was Nolan to argue? He thrust his hips against Grayson's and ran his fingers over both their cocks, stroking, touching, adding pressure where he most needed it.

And maybe because it had been such a very long time, the orgasm hit Nolan quite suddenly, and he shouted when he came, surprised by it. As he spilled all over Grayson's belly, he heard Grayson groan, and then Grayson was coming too.

It was messy. It was exciting. It was perfect.

Nolan rolled onto his back and took a moment to catch his breath. He grabbed a tissue from the nightstand, but when he moved to hand it to Grayson, Grayson was licking his fingers.

"That was hot," said Grayson.

"It was," said Nolan. He wiped the tissue over Grayson's belly anyway.

"I had this whole plan where I was going to lick you all over and blow you and really drag it out, but instead we did this. I regret nothing."

"Your way sounds good too. That was one of those good ideas you have that you should be more assertive about. Maybe we should try it your way a little later."

Grayson chuckled and rolled over to lean on Nolan's chest. "Yeah? I like the sound of that."

Chapter Eight

So, THAT had happened.

Grayson must have fallen asleep, because he woke up in Nolan's gorgeous apartment. There wasn't really a bedroom so much as a sleeping area separated from the rest of the huge open space by a couple of beautiful wooden screens that were probably antique. Grayson guessed that at some point in this building's life, this apartment had been a factory floor. He pictured it as a clothing factory, maybe, with rows and rows of women working at sewing machines.

The space pretty much screamed that it was designed by a professional. Nolan snored softly, so Grayson got out of bed to use the bathroom. Now that sun was streaming in through the huge windows at one end of the space, he could see the apartment in good lighting. The floors were polished concrete, the walls were mostly exposed brick, and Nolan had clearly decided to go in an industrial direction with his design. There was a lot of metal, a few upcycled pieces that looked like they had maybe once been part of some kind of machinery, and the occasional pop of color. The whole space was a bit brutal and masculine. Grayson wondered what that said about Nolan's mood when he'd designed the space; Nolan was generally known for a softer aesthetic. Or maybe he just was for his clients but liked something else for himself. The only thing in the room that felt even a little soft was a huge painting of an abstract purple flower hanging on one wall.

Grayson also couldn't help but wonder what one paid to live in a loft this big in Chelsea. He wasn't sure he wanted to know.

After leaving the bathroom, he did a lap around the kitchen area, one corner of the loft that looked like it had been renovated recently. The cabinets were dark wood and the counter was gray quartz with a little bit of sparkle. All of the hardware was black, including the sink and faucet. The appliances were brand-new charcoal gray stainless steel. It was a rather dark kitchen, actually, mitigated only by the white subway tile backsplash and the enormous amount of light from the adjacent window.

"You hungry?"

Grayson spun around and saw Nolan, clad in a pair of gray sweatpants, staring back at him. Grayson realized abruptly he was not wearing a stitch of clothing.

"Uh," Grayson said. "Sure. I was just admiring your home design. Do you cook?"

"Yeah, I cook. How do you feel about pancakes?"

"I love pancakes. Um. I should probably go put some pants on."

"Don't feel like you have to on my account." Nolan gave him a once-over as he walked to a cabinet.

Grayson compromised by putting his briefs back on. Then he sat at the cute little wrought iron table next to the refrigerator.

Nolan was whisking something in a big bowl as he eyed a griddle on his stove. He set the bowl aside for a moment and turned to him. "You have plans for today?"

"No, not really." It was a day off. Had Grayson just gone home from the studio last night, he probably would have slept in and spent the day lazily binging some trashy TV show.

"Just wanted to make sure I wasn't keeping you from something," said Nolan.

"Only a hot date with my TV and this bonkers reality dating show I've been watching."

"Bonkers in what way?"

"They threw a diverse group of singles at an island resort and let them sort themselves out, basically. There's one girl on the show who is basically my id. She's fussy and particular but really funny about it, and she spends most of every episode being snarky about the other people on the show. I love her. Also, there's this one gay guy who is *so* hot. Like if Jesse Williams and Michael B. Jordan somehow mated. He's having a little romance with a guy who is very sweet but a little socially awkward. I'm eating it up."

Nolan laughed. "Really, really not my thing, but it's good you're enjoying it."

"Hmm. You can't tell me you don't watch TV because I saw a very nice flat-screen over there. Does this mean you only really like erudite dramas or whatever?"

"I actually don't watch much TV. But I like movies."

"Okay. I guess I can accept that."

Nolan poured batter onto the griddle in neat circles. Grayson watched them fluff up as they cooked. He was impressed that Nolan had just whipped up pancakes from scratch without a recipe or anything. "Do you mind me watching you cook?"

"No. I like the company."

"Okay. I never know. My mom used to love it when I hung around the kitchen while she was cooking, but my dad always kicked me out, because me watching him made him self-conscious. I don't cook, so I don't know."

Nolan flipped each of the pancakes over and then got a plate down from a cabinet. "I like to cook. Well, really, I like to bake. I think if I hadn't become an interior designer, I'd be one of those bakers who makes really elaborate cakes."

"Really? 'Cause I've seen some of that Restoration Channel show where the bakers compete to make the fanciest cake, and I always wondered if those cakes even tasted good. Like, sure, you made a unicorn out of fondant and modeling chocolate, and it looks amazing, but neither of those things actually tastes very good. I'd rather have a delicious and plain cake than a fancy one that tastes like Styrofoam."

Nolan transferred the pancakes from the griddle to a plate and then started another batch. "You want some bacon?"

"Obviously."

Nolan didn't have the microwavable bacon Grayson usually bought but pulled out an honest-to-goodness rasher of bacon wrapped in white butcher paper out of the refrigerator. He carefully unwrapped it and tossed a few slices on the griddle. "Oh, I put coffee on. Looks like the pot's almost ready. Help yourself. Mugs are in the cabinet above the coffee maker."

"Bless you."

"Sugar's in the container next to the coffee maker, and there's half and half in the fridge."

Nolan, of course, had a little sugar bowl that perfectly coordinated with everything else in the kitchen. It matched the row of canisters near the coffee maker, all of them green with a swirly white pattern painted on. They looked handmade and probably were. Grayson got a mug down—there was a set in the same shade of green next to a few mismatched ones—dumped a spoonful of sugar into the cup, and then poured in some coffee.

He sat back down at the table, and thirty seconds later Nolan placed a plate loaded with pancakes and bacon before him. Somehow a little gravy boat full of warm syrup was already on the table. Grayson didn't totally understand this witchcraft, but he wasn't mad at it.

He was a few bites into his pancakes when Nolan joined him.

"So good," Grayson said with his mouth full.

Nolan smiled and sliced into his own pancakes with a fork. "Glad you like it."

"Do *you* have big plans for today?" Grayson asked.

"No, not particularly. I'm having dinner with a friend tonight, but otherwise the day's free for whatever."

"A friend?"

Nolan raised an eyebrow. "A lady friend." He ate a slice of bacon. "I just told you I haven't had any sexual desire for anyone in a year, and you still assume I'm seeing another man?"

"I'm not saying my jealousy is rational. I'm just saying, you're really hot and I like you a lot. But also, we only met, like, five minutes ago, so it's not *wrong* if you *are* seeing someone else."

"I'm not."

"I'm not either. Just, like, for the record."

"So do you want to do something together today?"

"Sure. What did you have in mind?"

Nolan tilted his head and ate a few more bites. "I hadn't really thought that through all the way yet. All I know is that the idea of you headed back to Brooklyn right away made me sad."

Who knew Nolan could be so cute? "Aw, babe. Well, I do have to go home eventually because that's where all my clothes are, and the staff at the Restoration Channel are gonna get real suspicious if I repeat an outfit. Did you know that Helena said my fashion showed I was creative and I should really go all out when dressing for filming?"

"Really?"

"Yeah. I'm guessing you have a whole closet of, like, dark T-shirts and khakis."

"Not quite, but I always preferred decorating rooms to decorating myself. So I guess my wardrobe is a bit... simple."

"Uh-huh."

"It works for me, though. Not everyone needs to wear color. When I launched the home goods line, I was trying to appeal to housewives in middle America. Even some of my celebrity clients are afraid of color. Well, except this one pop star I won't name, who loves animal prints. That was a rough project. I hate animal prints."

Grayson laughed. "Me too."

"But my point is, I guess I got used to looking a little more... safe."

"Ah, I see."

Nolan put his fork down. "What do you see?"

"When was the first time you appeared on TV?"

"I don't know. Probably about twelve years ago. I was, uh, twenty-eight or twenty-nine when I did *Oprah* the first time. Ish. Math, I don't know. It all blends together."

"Okay. And you were out then? It wasn't a secret that you bang dudes."

Nolan narrowed his eyes. "Yes, I was out. Where are you going with this?"

"If you were openly gay on TV twelve years ago, and on *Oprah* and the *Today Show* no less, then you had to be a safe gay. The sweet guy ladies go shopping with who tells them they look fabulous—not a guy who is in any way unusual or who has a sex drive."

"Okay. Sure. That was part of it. But I'm comfortable, I don't know. I like how I dress."

"You wore a nice black tux when you went to the Golden Globes with your actor husband and didn't pull a Billy Porter and wear hot pink or a skirt."

"I don't have a problem with that, though. People should feel free to express themselves however they wish. But I'm a black tux. I'm not a pink ballgown."

"Uh-huh. Not that we would, but, like, if I ever got nominated for an Emmy or something, I would *so* wear something over-the-top. Like, a gold brocade tux."

Nolan grimaced. "Okay."

"Not your thing, I get it. Just saying." Grayson returned to his breakfast. "I tried wearing a skirt once for, like, two days in college because I wanted to prove that gender is a construct and I'm here and queer and all that, but there was just so much... air. Under there, I mean. I didn't like it."

"So, wait…. Are you dressing up for the show to make some kind of statement?"

Grayson grinned. "Not exactly. But I'm not holding back either. I thought I might have to, for the housewives in flyover states, but Helena told me to dress however I wanted. So I'm being authentically myself."

"Okay."

"You can't tell right now because I'm just wearing my underwear."

Nolan snorted a laugh and went back to eating.

NOLAN DIDN'T want to think too hard about what a cliché it was for them to go shopping together, and yet he found himself in his favorite men's clothing shop, a little boutique in Chelsea, with Grayson.

"I *love* this," Grayson said, picking up a cabled cardigan from a rack.

Nolan perused the sweaters on a table without picking anything up. He was charmed by Grayson—who talked pretty much constantly—and the way he moved through the store, just grabbing whatever he wanted. Grayson had a great body and certainly wore clothes well; with his jaunty haircut, he could wear almost anything and still look like a model.

"Hey, Nolan."

Nolan turned and saw his friend Stephen. Stephen lived in the neighborhood and was an editor who had been trying to talk Nolan into writing a book on home design. Nolan had been putting him off—he was no great writer and also didn't understand why people were always trying to get him to do things outside his skillset when he was really good at one thing—but here he was in the store.

"Hi, Stephen. How are you?"

"Great. It's good to see you. That little chatterbox over there yours?"

Nolan bristled at the use of the possessive but also didn't feel like he needed to explain himself. "Yeah, sort of."

The expression on Stephen's face was approving, which grossed Nolan out a little. Sure, Grayson was a hot young thing, but that wasn't why Nolan was with him right now.

"He's *very* pretty," said Stephen.

"He's my costar on that Restoration Channel show I'm doing." Nolan didn't want to admit he was rebounding, and he didn't think that was what this was anyway. Not completely. "We're just… shopping."

"*Oh*. Because I thought—"

"Yeah, I know what you thought."

"It's been a year. No one would judge."

Nolan shoved his hands in his pockets so he wouldn't be tempted to punch Stephen.

He was glad there were people in this world who did not have the intimate relationship with grief that Nolan did. He was glad that there were people who didn't wake up and reach for spouses who weren't there. He was happy there were people who weren't sometimes struck out of nowhere with the pain of missing someone they would never see again. He was thrilled Stephen likely didn't spend his days off sobbing in his living room because he still missed someone every damned day. He didn't want Stephen to truly understand what he was going through, because he didn't wish that on anyone.

At the same time, Stephen needed to shut up *because* he did not understand.

Things weren't as bad now as they had been a year ago. Now Nolan could go for hours, days sometimes, without that ache in his chest.

And, okay, *maybe* part of his reticence to get involved with Grayson was less about Grayson's age and more about Ricky than anything else.

"It's not like that," Nolan said, trying to sound as neutral as possible.

He clearly failed, because Stephen held his hands up. "All right. Unclench. Sorry to imply anything. He's cute, that's all. If you wanted to tap that, I'd understand."

Well, there was that too. "How's the book publishing biz, Stephen?"

By the time Stephen moved on and left the store without buying anything, Nolan had lost track of Grayson. Figuring he was in a fitting room, Nolan walked to the back of the store. "Grayson?"

There were three large fitting rooms in the back, each with a black door. One of those doors opened and Grayson stuck his head out. "Hey, in here. Tell me what you think of these pants."

Nolan waited for a beat, but once he understood that he was supposed to go into the fitting room and not wait for Grayson to walk out, he sighed and followed Grayson inside.

"The pants appear to be invisible," said Nolan.

And then Grayson was on him, pressing him against a mirror, grinding his brief-clad hips against Nolan's, kissing Nolan like his life depended on it.

Nolan went with it for a moment, savoring the taste of Grayson and enjoying the press of Grayson's near-naked body against his clothed one. Then he slowly pushed Grayson away. "What are you doing?"

Grayson gave Nolan another quick kiss. "I dunno. Cheering you up? You've seemed sad all day."

"Oh. Thanks."

"I do want your take on this pair of pants, though." Grayson picked up a pair of black pants with zippers in strange places and pulled them on. "Who was that guy?"

"My friend Stephen. Are you just this jealous all the time?"

"When the guy I'm with is you? Yes."

"All right."

"I heard you tell him we were just coworkers. Which is totally cool, by the way. I don't need the world to know about our sex life. I just had a moment. What do you think?" Grayson modeled the pants by posing and then slowly turning in a circle.

"Your ass looks great, but I don't like the zippers."

"Oh. I think the zippers are cool."

"If you like the pants, buy the pants."

"Oh. Sure, right. I keep forgetting I have money now." Grayson picked up a blue button-down shirt with small white polka dots. "It doesn't really go with these pants, but do you like this shirt?" The shirt fit Grayson like a glove, showing out how surprisingly fit his thin body was.

"I do like the shirt."

"Cool. Well, that's something."

And so it went for the next few minutes. Grayson must have brought half the store into the fitting room with him. He swapped out pants and shirts and sweaters and asked Nolan's opinion. He seemed completely un-selfconscious, and why shouldn't he be? He was young and beautiful and had a great body. No gray hair, no visible scars. The only marking on his whole body was a black star about the size of a quarter tattooed on his abdomen that Nolan had been meaning to ask about.

And why not now? Grayson pulled a shirt off over his head, so Nolan stepped forward and touched the star. "What's this?"

"Oh. Stupid drunk bet when I was nineteen. I mean, I wanted a tattoo, but I couldn't decide what it would be, and then a friend plied me with tequila shots and took me to this place in the Village. I spent, like, an hour going through the design books and just couldn't decide. The tattooist must have been really fed up with me, because he said, 'What do you want to be when you grow up?' And I said, 'A star.' And that's how that happened." Grayson put the shirt he'd been wearing earlier back on. "I'm thinking about adding some more stars there just so it doesn't look so lonely and weird, but I keep chickening out. Not sure if you knew this, but they put tattoos on with needles."

"I did know that."

"You don't have any tattoos, so I will just say, it fucking hurts. And I'm a big wuss about pain."

"Good to know."

Grayson finished putting his regular clothes back on and then surveyed the damage. "Okay. I'm taking the pants, the blue shirt, and the sweater. I love this sweater. Feel how soft it is."

Nolan reached over and touched it. It was very soft. "Cashmere?"

Grayson looked at the label. "Merino. I'm gonna wear this sweater every day all winter."

Nolan walked with Grayson to the counter.

"Are you gonna buy anything?" Grayson asked as he placed his clothes on the counter.

"No, I'm good."

"Not enough black T-shirts, eh?"

"My wardrobe is not *that* boring."

"Sure, babe."

When they walked back outside, Nolan asked, "You want to get lunch?"

"Okay. But somewhere not super expensive so I can pay for myself. I don't like feeling like I'm your kept man."

"There's a little Italian place on Sixteenth Street I like. They make a good sandwich."

"Okay. Sounds good. But then I should probably go home."

"Yeah." Although Nolan was a little shaken by how sad that made him feel, despite having other plans later.

"Are you…? No, never mind."

"No, ask," said Nolan.

"Are you gonna be okay? I hate leaving you alone tonight if you're going to be sad."

Grayson could be astute sometimes. Nolan pointed to the corner so Grayson would start walking toward the restaurant. Then he said, "Yeah, I'll be okay," surprised he actually meant it.

Chapter Nine

LARA AND Jason Cruz had been married about eight months. They'd spent most of their engagement saving money to buy a fixer-upper on Long Island. Only they quickly got in over their heads and hired a couple of contractors who were not great at their jobs. Their budget ballooned as they tried to get the place up to code, and now their dream home had been stripped to the studs.

"It's a blank canvas," said Grayson.

Nolan thought he was being charitable. Because what he could see was… nothing. No walls. No flooring. No appliances or cabinets or sinks. Just studs and subfloor.

"The house had asbestos," Jason Cruz said. "So we hired a crew to do an abatement, and they took out the walls."

"The floors were hideous. There was this awful beige-y pink linoleum throughout," said Lara Cruz. "So that had to go."

"Linoleum on the whole first floor?" Grayson asked, aghast. "That's a crime."

Nolan agreed, but all he saw were dollar signs.

The Cruzes were a photogenic couple. She was a Puerto Rican girl from the Bronx, he was a first-generation Cuban American who'd grown up in Florida. They'd met in college and dated for ten years before getting married, so although they were newlyweds, they clearly knew each other very well.

Nolan asked them a series of leading questions to get them to explain their taste and style, but neither of them had the vocabulary to describe what they liked. Nolan gleaned that Jason liked sleek and modern, Lara a little more traditional. That was okay, he could work with that.

But, man, this was a big job.

"I have to admit," Nolan said, "I'm finding this a little overwhelming."

"If it helps, we have a floor plan," said Jason. He picked up a roll of paper that was leaning against one of the nearby studs. He unrolled it and held it out for Nolan to examine.

"This does help." Nolan peered at the blueprint. "Okay, three bedrooms in the back. I assume you want to keep those?"

"Yes," said Lara. "And the master has an en suite bathroom here. The plumbing has been updated. The house is actually up to code now. We had all the new stuff inspected and everything."

"Just… no walls," said Nolan.

Lara led them through every room of the one-story ranch. It was difficult to visualize the rooms because the lack of walls made everything just look like a sea of studs and temporary supports, but Nolan started to get an idea for the floor layout. Three bedrooms in the back of the house; the master had an en suite, and Lara wanted a walk-in closet. That was easy to do. The kitchen at the front of the house was small, but the fact that the main wall was nothing but a few narrow pillars of wood made it easy for Nolan to see that it wasn't really needed.

"What I'd do…," Nolan said, "is keep the living room where it is, but remove the wall between the kitchen and dining room. I'd just make it one huge eat-in kitchen. Do you need a formal dining room?"

"We've never had one," said Jason. "So I guess not?" He looked at his wife.

"I honestly don't care as long as there's room for a table. I inherited this antique one from my grandmother that I'd like to put in the house. It's pretty big."

Nolan made a mental note that he'd have to pull a large antique table into his design.

"You know what we could do," said Grayson. "What if we took the Cruzes on an inspiration tour? I saw some For Sale signs in the neighborhood. What if we look at finished houses and see what they like and what they don't like to get a better feel for their design aesthetic? And then, of course, we would take them shopping for finishes."

Not a bad idea. "Okay. That will help us come up with a coherent design theme for the house."

"Sounds great," said Lara.

There had to be an assistant or someone who could get on finding some houses to tour. When they ended filming for the day, Nolan asked Helena about that, and she said she had people she could set that up with.

"I really can't thank you enough," Lara said when Helena left to go to her car.

"Oh, you're welcome."

"I've admired your work for a long time. That's why we applied to the show. I saw that episode of

Celebrity House Tours with the house you decorated for that skier, whatshername?"

Nolan remembered that house. He'd decorated the Park City bungalow of a skier who had won a pile of Olympic medals. She was a beautiful woman and kind of a party girl on top of it, so she'd gained some notoriety off the ski slopes. *Celebrity House Tours* was a Restoration Channel show where B-list celebrities showed off their fancy houses, and though Nolan hadn't been on the show, several houses he'd decorated had been. He'd always been happy to let his work speak for itself. Funny how he was the one doing the talking now.

"Thanks," he said.

"I was sorry to hear about your husband."

"Thank you for that too." Nolan smiled, although he would've preferred if people didn't keep bringing it up.

Grayson, perhaps sensing Nolan's unease, skipped over and said, "Hey, we should probably get going."

So Nolan shook Lara's hand and said, "It was lovely to meet you. We'll be in touch with next steps soon."

Nolan followed Grayson to the car. He took a deep breath before he climbed in. Helena and the rest of the Restoration Channel staff were gone, and Lara and Jason Cruz were getting into their own car up the block, so Nolan felt reasonably safe turning to Grayson and planting a kiss on his lips.

Grayson sighed into it, snaking his hand up the side of Nolan's face and tangling it in the hair at the back of Nolan's head. Nolan wanted to melt into the kiss, wanted just this feeling to make the rest of the world fade away.

Unfortunately, when Grayson pulled away, Nolan was still in the Restoration Channel's SUV, parked in front of a house with no walls, and Ricky was still dead.

"Let's go back to the studio, shall we?" he said.

LATER, AT the studio, Grayson was browsing a real estate website for design ideas while Nolan was on the phone with one of the vendors, trying to charm him into a discount on flooring. When Nolan finally got off the phone, Grayson said, "I think 'open concept' has gone too far."

"How so?" said Nolan.

Grayson rotated his laptop and pointed to a photo he'd pulled up. "It's an open-concept bathroom." The photo showed a bathroom separated from the rest of the living space by a single glass panel no wider than a shower door. Which meant that anyone in the house could just stroll through the house and see someone peeing.

"Oh God," said Nolan.

"Even your place has a separate bathroom."

"The Cruz place basically has open-plan bathrooms right now."

Grayson laughed but then realized Nolan wasn't completely joking. "You're really terrified of this project."

Nolan sighed. "Not... exactly. It's just a lot of work with a fairly small budget."

"We're getting a different contractor for this project," Grayson said. "He's supposed to be really good. Some guy named Mike. He's an actual contractor in the city, not just a Restoration Channel guy."

"Okay."

"Have you never wanted to design a house from scratch?"

Nolan let out a sigh and scratched his chin. "Sure." He shook his head slightly. "There's something about this project that's bothering me. It's not even the lack of walls. I just need a hook that'll lead me into the project. I can't really begin to think about colors or accessories until I better understand what they like." He paused. "I just don't know where to start with this one."

"Did you get the flooring discount, at least?"

"Yes. He's willing to knock a couple hundred dollars off the total price in exchange for finding a way to advertise his place on the show. I figured we could do a segment where we take the family to the store to look at samples and get a nice shot of the exterior."

"Sounds good."

Grayson looked around. They were basically done for the day. The cameras had recorded them making some final decisions about materials for the Roberts house; then the crew had left for the day. They were mostly still milling about because they were waiting for Helena to call up and tell them about house tours for the Cruzes. So no one was around right now. He leaned over and kissed Nolan. Nolan accepted the kiss, but Grayson could feel he was troubled.

"Is this okay?" Grayson asked. "You and me?"

"Yeah, it's okay. Sorry. I'm just distracted today."

Grayson worried maybe Nolan wasn't ready for a relationship, but every time he'd brought it up in the past week, Nolan assured him that wasn't the problem. Of course, that implied that there *was* a problem.

Whatever was happening here probably wouldn't last past the end of the series—or this season, if Nolan decided to have Grayson put out to pasture after all—but as long as Nolan was willing, Grayson would take it.

Chapter Ten

NOLAN HAD been at one of those holiday parties ten years ago, where an odd assortment of people Nolan never would have expected to know each other all mingled as if it were normal. Nolan had spotted Ricardo Vega from across the room and just floated right over to him, as if pulled like a magnet. He knew Ricky vaguely, which was to say he'd never watched that show, but he lived in the world, so he knew Ricky was the star of it.

Ricky was just… beautiful. Tall, athletic. Dark hair, dark eyes, a long face and a long thin nose. He had the most beautiful lips, and he smiled easily, revealing perfectly white teeth. He was Hollywood attractive, in other words, but there was a softness to him, a realness that Nolan appreciated.

Nolan introduced himself. Ricky took his hand. Then he just… didn't let go.

They dated for four years and were married for five. They weren't exactly a Hollywood power couple but instead preferred to fly just below the radar, especially as Ricky's star began to fade.

Ricky had been a sweet soul. He was frustrated by his struggle to find work he found rewarding, but he never resented Nolan for his success and had only ever been supportive.

Ricky had been Nolan's favorite person, his best friend, his partner. Their love had been deep and intense and comforting. They'd built a beautiful home together.

They'd been working on the nursery when Ricky got his diagnosis.

Kids had been Ricky's dream more than Nolan's, but the more Ricky talked about being a father, the more Nolan wanted it too. The idea of the two of them as dads, doting on a child, was something Nolan hadn't been able to get out of his head ever since. They'd wanted to adopt because they could give a child a wonderful home, one filled with love.

And then cancer had taken Ricky.

Nolan knew he would never recover. He'd miss Ricky for the rest of his days. He'd remember their anniversary even if he didn't celebrate it anymore. Ricky was his great love, and nobody got two of those.

Or did they?

He was forty years old, successful beyond what he'd ever imagined, and he had a good life. The romantic part of his life was over—or at least, he'd assumed it was.

"What if you lived to be a hundred?" Stacey Lewis had asked him once.

Her point was that he still had a lot of life to live. Did he want to spend the rest of his time on earth alone?

He didn't.

He and Grayson were eating sandwiches on a bench on the High Line, a quick lunch break because Nolan had looked at so many material samples in the studio that morning that he'd lost all sense of what colors and textures even went together. Grayson was chattering about the house tours they'd done with the Cruzes the day before and what things had stood out to Jason and Lara, who had nearly diametrically opposed tastes. Jason seemed to like sleek and modern, minimalist, black and white. Lara liked softer, more traditional elements and was open to bright colors. Grayson talked about how to reconcile these things, as if trying to solve a math problem.

Nolan just sat there watching him, only hearing half of what he said. Grayson was so different from Ricky. It wasn't just his youth. Ricky had often been taciturn, only speaking when he had something important to say, but Grayson just rambled on all the time. Ricky had been patient and calm; Grayson was constantly moving. In a way, the contrast wasn't so different from Jason and Lara Cruz. Ricky had been soft, traditional, comforting like a warm blanket; Grayson was edgy and hard, clomping around in those ridiculous motorcycle boots. Today he had on a gray-and-white-striped scarf draped around the collar of his leather jacket and those damned pants with the zippers in weird places.

But maybe what Nolan really needed right now was not so much a warm blanket as a bucket of ice water. He'd been asleep for a year. And Grayson seemed unknowingly determined to wake him up.

Grayson sat there now and pulled a roasted red pepper off his sandwich. "Ugh. Why does everyone put roasted red peppers on *everything*."

"Do you not like them?"

"I like them in moderation. This is a lot. I feel like all I taste are red peppers and not the good stuff on the sandwich. Anyway, my thought is, anything too pink or floral is a nonstarter, but maybe we could do a two-tone kitchen with white uppers and gray lowers and light counters, and we carry that through to the bathrooms. Flat-panel cabinets. But we soften it up with accessories. Put cushiony stools at the kitchen island, maybe add a banquette in that little nook by the window, soft curtains, that kind of thing. Something geometric for the backsplash but more interesting than subway tile."

Nolan nodded because he wasn't even sure which house they were talking about anymore.

The thing with Grayson, though, was that he drew Nolan in. He was a talker, sure, but his voice had a strange, soothing quality on Nolan. It was sort of like Grayson was worrying about all these little challenges so Nolan didn't have to. And not even in a facetious way, but actually because Grayson cared about this stuff and Nolan wasn't actually ready to be back at work and functioning at full capacity.

And Grayson was *alive*. He was so alive, constantly moving, constantly talking, soaking everything in, moving through the world like he belonged there. It was refreshing, in a way, to be with someone who lived so loudly.

"Oh, so, I saw this documentary," Grayson said, apparently making a left turn in the conversation. "I think you would like it. It was about…."

And Nolan just stared, because how could he not? He nodded when appropriate and continued to eat his lunch, but mostly he just watched Grayson talk and move and go on about whatever he was going on about.

It wasn't the same as falling in love with Ricky. Well, maybe it was a little. It had that same instant quality. The same lightning-bolt attraction. The same desire to spend as much time with this person as possible. But it was different too, because Nolan was different now. He wasn't even sure he wanted to fall in love again, because going through a loss like that again would kill him.

Maybe it wasn't fair to think this would be the same thing. For now, he and Grayson were just having fun; they could break up in two weeks. They might never fall in love.

But in a way, it was reassuring to know maybe Nolan still could.

"Are you even listening?" Grayson asked.

"Sure."

"Uh-huh."

"You're pretty."

Grayson laughed. "Okay, you're forgiven. You ready to head back to the studio?"

"Ugh, no. What's a paint card? I don't even know anymore."

"All right. We can people watch a little more. There's a girl walking a poodle at eleven o'clock who has a fox tail attached to her belt."

Nolan looked and spotted the woman. She looked like she was in her midthirties. She wore a cute black-and-white dress. And, indeed, there was a fox tail hanging over her butt.

"It's a look," Nolan said.

"I have questions."

"Best not to ask. Cute dog, though."

"Man, I would love to get a dog. We had a big dumb black Lab when I was a kid. I loved that dog. My current landlord won't allow pets, though."

"Ricky had a collie mix when we first met. Sweet dog, but he got hair all over everything. After he passed, Ricky didn't want to get another dog right away, and then we just... didn't."

"Yeah, I get it. And dogs are a lot. Tough to have one in a New York City apartment. I know people do it, but...."

"I'm still kind of adjusting to being back in an apartment. I love this city in a way I never loved LA, but I'm still getting used to living here again." He'd lived in New York for most of his twenties, only moving to LA because he'd started getting design clients there.

"I've never been to LA."

"It has some charm. It never snows, which I appreciated. The culture is different. I don't know. I needed a change in scenery when I moved out there, and I was getting more clients on the West Coast, so LA seemed like a smart place to be. But I never quite acclimated, I guess."

"I've actually only been on a plane once. Well, twice, since I went and came back. Family vacation to Disney World when I was ten. That's the one and only time."

That surprised Nolan. Grayson was young but seemed worldly. Nolan again had the sense that there was something ugly lurking in Grayson's backstory, something that contradicted the happy-go-lucky facade Grayson put on most of the time. He figured Grayson would tell him when he was ready. No need to push now, even though Nolan was curious.

"I've actually never been to Disney World," said Nolan. "Although Ricky and I used to go to Disneyland all the time. He loved roller coasters."

"Me too. When I was a kid, we went out to Six Flags New England once a summer."

"Cool." Nolan closed his eyes for a long moment. When he opened them again, a smoking-hot guy who looked a little like Ricky went by. The man was jogging in just a pair of very tiny shorts.

"Hello," said Grayson, his gaze following the man. "People watching here is the best."

Nolan laughed. "All right. I'm ready to go back now."

"Perfect." Grayson leaned across the table and gave Nolan a kiss on the cheek. "Let's go, babe."

NOLAN DROVE them out to the Cruz house in New Jersey to meet with the contractor. A camera crew trailed them just in case anything interesting happened.

A very handsome man wearing a navy-blue hoodie and a well-worn pair of jeans with a tool belt slung around his hips was standing out front, examining the house's exterior, when Nolan pulled into the driveway. Grayson hopped out of the car. "Are you Mike?"

The man turned. "Yes, hello."

"I'm Grayson, the cohost. That guy getting out of the car is Nolan."

Grayson and Mike shook hands while they waited for Nolan to walk over. Nolan introduced himself as he and Mike shook hands.

"Yeah, I've seen you on TV." Mike looked back at the house. "The exterior could use a coat of paint. It looks a little rough."

"You think this is rough, wait until we get inside," said Nolan.

The front door had a keypad lock, so Nolan punched in the code and let everyone inside.

"Uh," said Mike. "This place has no walls."

"Yeah," Nolan said. "My understanding is that they started updating the plumbing and electricity and then discovered there was asbestos. So the good news is that this place has no more asbestos nor any pests, and allegedly the plumbing and electric are up to code."

"I'll double-check that," said Mike.

"And the bad news," said Nolan, "is that there aren't any walls."

Mike grimaced.

Grayson ended up leading the walk-through, because he seemed to have a better sense of the floor plan than Nolan did. Nolan struggled to visualize what the space could be; when he walked into the house, all he could see was a jumble of wood, not a series of rooms. Grayson had made copies of the floor plan, though, and he handed one to Mike now. Mike put it on his clipboard and pulled a pencil from his tool belt. He scribbled notes on it as they walked through the house.

"Are you taking any walls down?" Mike asked.

"This is a young couple who don't really need a formal dining room," said Nolan. "Here's my thought. I think the front of the house should be one big open space. So...." He pointed to the floor plan Mike had on the clipboard. "We basically destroy the entryway and take down the walls on either side of the staircase. Then we also take down the wall between the dining room and the kitchen. As a result, we have a huge eat-in kitchen that flows right into the living room. Both Lara and Jason have big families, so this will give them plenty of space to have everyone over and have them all interacting together."

Mike nodded and looked around the front of the house. "Well, the good news is that I can see right up to the roof because this house has no ceilings." He looked up. "Okay. There are joists going this way." He gestured. "That means the wall between the kitchen and dining room can come down, no sweat. Actually, it looks like the wall between the living room and the vestibule could come down too. But this wall between the vestibule and the kitchen is load-bearing. So either we get creative with your budget, or we have to keep at least part of it."

Nolan nodded slowly. "Okay. I'll think about that. Let's go look at the bedrooms."

Mike examined all the plumbing and poked at the electric. "This looks up to code, but I'd want to get a plumber and electrician in here to verify."

"The only wall I've thought about," Nolan said when they were in the master bedroom, "is adding one about here, and creating a walk-in closet." He traced what he was thinking with a finger on Mike's floorplan.

"Sure. Like this?" Mike sketched a wall on the floorplan.

"Exactly."

He nodded. "I have a teenage daughter, so I have some sympathy for wanting a walk-in closet. We're running out of places to put all her clothes. When they aren't on the floor, I mean. Unfortunately I live in a small Manhattan apartment and can't invent space for a huge closet." He sighed. "But, yes, wall here, no problem. This is a big bedroom, so they'll still have plenty of space."

As they walked back outside fifteen minutes later, Mike said, "I'm guessing if they stripped the house and then ran out of money, the budget for this project is small."

"Yes. Restoration is offering up some money, and this couple is basically giving us their life savings to finish it. But, yeah. Money for drywall and paint, not so much for engineered beams to take out load-bearing walls."

Mike gave them a ballpark figure for what he thought it would cost with midrange finishings. "Add a few thousand if you want to take out that one wall, and add a few more thousands if you want to do anything fancy with the finishings."

"Oof," said Grayson. Their budget was a good ten thousand short of what they'd need.

"Okay," said Nolan. "I don't think we're getting any more money out of this couple, but I'll talk to the powers that be at Restoration, then call in some favors and see what we can do."

"Awesome. Just let me know what you want and I'll get the crew started on Monday." Mike looked at his watch. "Oh, geez. I have an appointment in the city. I gotta run. Here's my number, though." He handed Nolan a business card. "Call me anytime."

He jogged to his car, leaving Nolan, Grayson, and the camera crew on the front lawn of the house. The camera guys started to pack up and head toward their van.

"Let's go back to the city, shall we?" Grayson said.

Nolan took one last long look at the house and nodded before heading toward the car.

When they were on their way to the city, Nolan said, "Do you want to get dinner somewhere? I don't feel up to cooking tonight."

"Sure."

"You want to come back to my place after?"

"Of course."

Nolan nodded.

They had dinner at a Spanish restaurant on Twenty-Third, and though Nolan kept up his end of the conversation, he seemed very sad. As they walked back to his loft, Grayson asked about that.

"Sorry. I'm really trying not to be, but—"

"It's okay to be sad. I'm not telling you not to be. But it's also okay to talk to me if you need to."

"You don't want to hear about how much I miss my dead husband."

"Maybe I do."

Nolan sighed. "Our wedding anniversary is tomorrow, and I can't stop thinking about it. This is the second anniversary I've spent without him, and I should be over this by now, but I can't seem to move past this ache I feel. Is that what you want me to say?"

Grayson's heart went out to Nolan, but his tone was combative. Grayson wanted to get him off the defensive. "Say whatever you need to say."

"I don't want to feel this way. I'm so tired of feeling this way. And every time I think I'm getting better, there's some significant date or anniversary or I see some social media post about his old TV show, and I'm right back where I was a year ago, aching and inconsolable."

Grayson reached over and took Nolan's hand. This seemed to startle Nolan, who stopped walking and stared at Grayson.

"Is this not okay?" Grayson asked, squeezing Nolan's hand.

"It's okay," said Nolan. "You just startled me, that's all."

"Do you want to talk about Ricky, or do you want to be distracted?"

Nolan resumed walking, so Grayson fell into step with him, and they continued to hold hands as they headed toward Nolan's building.

"I want to be distracted," said Nolan.

When they arrived at Nolan's apartment, Nolan didn't waste any time. He grabbed Grayson by the ears and crashed their lips together.

Grayson rolled with it, giving as good as he got, dragging Nolan through the middle of the loft. Nolan wanted a distraction? Grayson would give him one.

Grayson heard Nolan's bag hit the floor, so he let go of his own near the sofa, then continued pulling Nolan toward the corner of the loft. Nolan maneuvered them around the screen and toward the bed.

"Get naked," Grayson said.

Nolan didn't even pause before peeling off his clothes. Grayson mirrored his movements, unbuttoning and taking off his shirt, shucking his pants, pulling off his shoes. As if to call back to the first time Grayson had been in this space, Nolan raised an eyebrow and tossed his clothes on the floor.

Grayson laughed. "You're a rebel."

Nolan smiled, which was good. They were both down to just their briefs now. Grayson ran his hands over Nolan's chest and linked his fingers behind Nolan's neck and said, "If I could take your pain away, I would."

"I believe you."

"I can't do that, but I *can* try really hard to make you forget about it for a while."

"Kiss me."

Who was Grayson to turn down a command like that?

As they kissed, Grayson steered Nolan toward the bed. Since the last time Grayson had been here, Nolan had put blush pink bedding on the bed, and Grayson spared a thought for whatever thought process had gone through Nolan's head when he'd picked it—it added softness to the otherwise industrial vibe of the whole loft—but then he pushed all of that aside and pushed Nolan on the bed.

Nolan laughed when his back hit the mattress. His hair was disheveled now, and when his mouth was open in a smile like that, his whole face seemed to glow. Nolan's body betrayed his beauty regimen; he was the kind of high-maintenance guy who wanted you to *think* he was low-maintenance, so he wore expensive T-shirts and often had a little scruffy beard growth on his face. But his chest had been waxed recently, and he clearly used good moisturizers. Grayson was growing to love all the little contradictions that made up Nolan. He had taken to teasing Nolan about his beige taste on set, but Nolan was really anything but beige.

"Stay put," Grayson ordered.

Nolan disobeyed and shifted around on the bed until he was perpendicular to the custom wrought iron headboard. He stripped off his briefs, so he was now beautifully, perfectly naked.

He wasn't very aroused, though. Grayson would have to work on that.

Grayson danced a little, moving to a random hip-hop beat from a song that had been stuck in his head all day. Then he turned around and showed Nolan all the goods. Grayson obviously couldn't see his own ass, but he'd received many compliments on it in the past. So he hooked his thumbs into his briefs and shimmied them down his hips.

Nolan whistled.

Grayson tried not to laugh because he was going for sexy, not funny, but he appreciated that Nolan was getting into this. Grayson twirled his briefs around his finger before flipping them toward the pile of clothes. Then he danced over to the nightstand and pulled a condom out of the drawer. He showed it to Nolan, who nodded.

So, yeah, they were doing this.

Nolan had his hand on his own cock, which had clearly taken an interest in the proceedings. Grayson swatted his hands out of the way and then swallowed him. Nolan groaned. Grayson continued to blow him until he was good and hard and writhing on the bed. Then he turned around and shoved his ass in Nolan's face.

"Get me ready," Grayson said.

"Somebody's bossy."

"You want it too."

"You're right."

Nolan wasn't shy. He gave Grayson's balls a squeeze and then shoved two lubed-up fingers inside Grayson. It hurt, but in a startling, delightful way, and Grayson moaned around Nolan's cock.

Nolan's mouth was getting into some interesting places—Grayson was glad he'd showered very thoroughly before he'd left for the set, but he was probably a little sweaty now—and he continued to stretch Grayson.

Grayson had thought this would be kind of a wham, bam, thank you, man encounter, meant to blow Nolan's mind. But now Nolan was running his hands almost reverently over Grayson's backside, and the kisses he planted on Grayson's skin felt almost worshipful. Was *that* how he wanted to play this?

Grayson wasn't sure if he could handle a deep, emotional moment without completely melting, so he shifted the mood again by rotating his body until he knelt over Nolan's hips.

"You ready?" Grayson asked.

"Are you?"

"Babe, I've been ready all day."

Grayson grabbed Nolan's hard cock and rolled the condom on it. Then he lowered himself onto Nolan, loving the burn as Nolan entered him. He went slowly at first, and Nolan reached up and pinched his nipples, sending electric arousal to all corners of Grayson's body.

And then Grayson was fully seated, so he began to ride.

Nolan threw his head back and groaned. Yeah, that was what Grayson wanted. He wanted Nolan out of his mind, so overwhelmed by the physical that he forgot about whatever was in his head.

But then Nolan surprised Grayson by lifting up and kissing him.

Grayson kissed him back, which required some weight shifting. Nolan canted his hips up so he could have more control over the pace and sent Grayson colliding forward. Grayson propped himself up on his hands and bent down to kiss Nolan.

"This is testing all of my flexibility," Grayson said.

"Too much talking." Nolan shut him up with another kiss.

Grayson shifted back up so he could ride Nolan. Nolan grabbed Grayson's cock and started to stroke, which completely overwhelmed Grayson. He felt it all, suddenly, Nolan's wandering hands, Nolan inside him, this strange connection between them, even though they didn't have much in common other than their occupation. He rode Nolan, watched the ecstasy play out over Nolan's face, and felt that himself as his own body started to roar.

"Look at me, look at me," Nolan said, out of breath.

"Wha—?"

"I want to know it's you."

Something in Grayson went all mushy then, but his desire did not abate, so he kept riding and pushing them forward. But then he looked at Nolan—his face was flushed with arousal, his eyes a little watery—and something in Grayson utterly collapsed.

Lord, this man. So hurt, but wanting so much to live again. It was a heavy burden, being the person to steer a ghost back into the land of the living, but Nolan was certainly alive now. His skin was hot, his lips were swollen from all the kissing, and he looked like he might be about to fall apart. Grayson felt that facial expression deep in his chest.

"Nolan, I—"

But whatever Grayson was about to say was quickly lost as Nolan's fingers pressed into some spot on Grayson that made him nearly explode. So instead of trying to reason with what was happening, instead of trying to make sense of it, he surrendered to it. Just as he was riding Nolan with the hopes of giving him everything, Nolan was doing the same.

"Oh, I'm gonna come," said Grayson.

"Yes, come for me, baby."

It hit Grayson suddenly. He was almost there… almost there… and then pow! With a gasp, he was coming ribbons all over Nolan's chest, and Nolan just kept stroking him, until he was rendered motionless as an orgasm rocked his body too. Grayson reveled in Nolan's body jerking and vibrating beneath him, as much as he could be conscious of it while his own orgasm surged his body.

A few minutes later, he lay beside Nolan on the bed. He wanted to ask about that *I want to know it's you* comment but decided it was better to let it go. Whatever Nolan had meant by that had made Grayson feel special, and he wanted to hold on to that.

"That was great," Nolan said. "I forgot my own name for a minute there."

"Who are you? Where am I?"

"Exactly."

Grayson laughed and snuggled against Nolan's side. Nolan put an arm around Grayson's shoulders.

"Mmm," said Nolan.

Grayson didn't want to read too much into this. Nolan probably still thought he was too young, still thought this was just a fling. Grayson's heart was starting to get ensnared. Maybe holding out hope that this could really be something was a risk, but it could be worth it too. Or this might blow up in his face.

It was hard to say.

Chapter Eleven

LATE THAT Friday night, Nolan was staring at samples, still trying to come up with a theme for the Cruz house. Grayson had plans with his friends in Brooklyn and had left an hour ago, so it was just Nolan and the damned samples in the studio. He decided to give up for the day and was about to leave when his cell phone rang. He didn't recognize the number, but it was a California area code. On the off chance it was a client, he answered.

"Mr. Hamlin?"

"Yes."

"Hi, this is Hilda from the Abbott Agency."

It took Nolan a moment to figure out what the Abbott Agency was. A design firm? A literary or entertainment agency?

No. It was an adoption agency. It was the agency he and Ricky had gone to almost two years ago, before Ricky's cancer diagnosis.

"Hi, Hilda," Nolan said, suddenly nervous. There was no way…. After all this time, was the agency coming through? Didn't they know Ricky had died?

"I have good news. We have a woman who chose you and Ricardo. Her baby is due in two months."

Nolan and Ricky had wanted an open adoption so that the birth mother could check in with her child any time she wanted. But they'd wanted privacy too, so they'd gone with an agency that had anonymized their application. The birth mother could then peruse profiles without the names, although probably there were only so many interior designer/actor gay couples. Then again, in LA, anything was possible.

"Two months is soon," said Nolan. "Also, my circumstances have changed somewhat."

"Do you not still want to adopt?"

Did he? He and Ricky had talked about this so much, and they'd had a solid plan. Ricky had been struggling to find work, so he'd planned to stay home with the baby while Nolan kept up with his design clients. Now Nolan was in the middle of filming a TV show and getting his life back on track. In LA, they'd started decorating the nursery. Nolan's loft in New York was hardly ready for a baby.

"It's not that. I'm…. I mean, it was pretty public, but Ricky died a little over a year ago."

"Oh, gosh. I'm so sorry."

"I would have called to tell you, but I suppose it slipped my mind. And so much time has gone by that it seemed unlikely anyone would pick us, and I guess I thought—"

"No, I completely understand."

He was about to tell Hilda *Thanks, but no thanks* when he realized that he didn't want to say no. The whole time he'd been on the phone, he'd been mentally picturing how to rearrange furniture in the loft to make space for a baby. He could put up a screen and buy a vintage crib that worked with the space's modern design, as well as build in some storage for clothes and toys. At some point, while Ricky had been trying to persuade Nolan that he wanted to be a father, Nolan had realized he *did* want to be a father. And he still did. And given that it had taken two years to get to this point, it might be his last chance.

"I can't even believe I'm about to ask this," he said to Hilda, "but could you go back to the mom and explain the situation? I'm still interested in adopting, but I'd be a single dad now, and also, I live in New York, not LA."

"Hmm. Well, the reason I'm calling you is because I wanted to invite you into the office to meet the mother." Hilda's chipper tone hadn't changed. "So let's keep that appointment. Can you fly out here? Meet with the mom, let her meet you, explain the situation, see if you both agree this is a good idea."

"I... sure. I can do that. I assume sooner is better than later?" Nolan's heart started pounding. This was really happening. His mind rapidly cycled through all the many ways it could go wrong, but it could go right too. And if it did, Nolan's life was about to change in a huge way.

"Yes, definitely soon. The mother lives locally, so I can have her come in next weekend. Can you get away then?"

He'd have to shuffle the filming schedule around, but he said, "Yes, I can do that."

"Great. I'll send you an email and let you set up an appointment through our online system."

Nolan got off the phone and plopped down on the sofa. It was profoundly uncomfortable, likely ported around various sets over the years, and the cushions were worn and flat. But it didn't matter. His knees had gone rubbery.

He didn't know much, but he *did* know in that moment, that there was a very good chance he'd become a father—and he wanted that a great deal. He was at a stage in his life when he wanted things settled. He could offer a good home to a child, a loving home where the child could have all of their needs met, with a father who loved that child fiercely.

He took a deep breath and got up. As he shut down the studio, he saw that Grayson had left his scarf behind.

It was only then that he realized that he was in a relationship. Maybe it wasn't a serious one, but it would have to change now. Once Nolan had a baby, he couldn't have flings with young men anymore. He'd have to focus on this new person in his life.

So he'd have to have a difficult conversation with Grayson. The idea of it made him feel like he'd swallowed a rock. The truth was, he was enjoying his time with Grayson. They had fun together, and Grayson had a way of making Nolan feel a lot less lonely. He didn't *want* to end their relationship; he wanted to see where it would go. But he also knew better than to think he could carry on a relationship *and* bring a baby home. Grayson wouldn't want to play dad; he was young and had friends to see and parties to go to and clothes to buy.

But maybe Nolan didn't have to have that difficult conversation just yet. It was very possible this mother would find out Nolan was a single man now and change her mind about the adoption. No need to end the affair, in that case.

But if she said yes, Nolan would have a lot to think about.

GRAYSON WAS grinding against a shirtless guy in a club, and somehow didn't feel weird about it until the guy moved to kiss him. It was too loud for Grayson to explain that he was kinda sorta seeing a guy he really liked, so instead he just shook his head. The guy shrugged and went back to molesting Grayson's ass, but now that Nolan was on his mind, this all felt very inappropriate. When the song ended, Grayson gave the guy a pat on the shoulder and slunk off the dance floor and over to the bar. He ordered a vodka soda, more for something to do than because he wanted to drink, and took a long breath while he waited for the bartender to mix it.

His friend Danny sidled up to him and ordered a martini. "Extra dirty," he purred to the bartender. While he waited, he turned to Grayson and said, "I saw you dancing with that dark-haired guy. *Smoking* hot. You get his number?"

"No."

"Really? Why? Does he have bad breath?"

Grayson laughed. "No. It's just…. I've been kind of seeing someone?"

"Yeah? That's awesome. You should have brought him!"

Grayson could not picture Nolan in a club like this. He'd probably complain about how loud it was. "Oh, no. This is not really his scene."

"Are you going monogamous on me?"

Grayson was reluctant to explain what was going on with Nolan, because it still felt fragile. He figured Nolan wouldn't mind if he told his friends about the relationship, but there was also something comforting about keeping it just between the two of them, as if they existed in their own little bubble. "Not… exactly," he said. "We haven't had a conversation about exclusivity yet. We've only been seeing each other for a few weeks." Although *seeing each other* felt inaccurate. They'd been working and fucking and eating the occasional meal out. It didn't feel like dating so much as falling into a pattern, and they hadn't had a serious conversation about what it was or where it was going.

Grayson wanted that to change. He cared about Nolan and enjoyed the time they spent together. He'd tried to give up on his expectations and see Nolan for the man he was and not who Grayson wanted him to be. Grayson had practically worshipped at the altar of Nolan Hamlin before they'd met in person. Grayson felt like he *had* gotten to know the real Nolan, at least a little.

Nolan had some deep wounds that needed to heal. Grayson was not so delusional as to think he could make Nolan all better, but he thought he could help, and he wanted to. Nolan had hidden himself away from the world for a year, and Grayson wanted to show him how to live again. And, well, he'd started fantasizing about them hosting the show as a couple instead of two random designers the Restoration Channel had put together. It would be like that new show, *Domestic Do-Over*, the one that their contractor Travis was on. Travis and his boyfriend Brandon flipped houses together. Nolan and Grayson could run their show like that.

Grayson had some wounds, too. He wasn't ready to talk about them with Nolan, but if they were a couple, he'd probably have to explain why he didn't talk to his family anymore. His loss hadn't been permanent the way Nolan's had—they were all still living beige lives in Lowell, as far as Grayson knew—but he'd lost something important just the same. He also put a lot of energy into not thinking about his family—ever—and maybe that was a bigger part of his personality than he'd realized. He strove to seem confident and competent in public, but he was anything but. Maybe TV was turning him into a successful actor, after all.

That thought grossed Grayson out. And anyway, it was too soon to be making any decisions. Grayson didn't want to rush Nolan.

"Do you *want* to see this guy exclusively?" Danny asked.

"Yes." Not even a question. "That's why I kind of freaked out there. That guy was super hot." Grayson hooked his thumb back toward the dance floor. "But when he tried to kiss me, it felt like I was cheating."

"Interesting," said Danny, taking a sip of the martini that had appeared on the bar in front of him.

"What is?"

"You must really like this guy."

"I do."

Danny looked like he was going to ask a question, but he was stopped by Aiden, who rambled over and crashed their conversation. Danny, Aiden, and Grayson had been a trio since college. Aiden was straight but loved dancing. Danny was gay, but he and Grayson had never been interested in each other. So here they were, at a club in the Village that was known for being open to whoever wanted to dance with anyone, drinking and dancing the night away.

"I'm not here," Aiden said.

Grayson poked at him. "Uh, you seem to be here."

"I'm just getting a cosmo for the redhead by that pillar over there." Aiden gestured with his head. "Her name is Janelle. She's a retired gymnast!"

"It's fine. Grayson has gone and fallen in love, and thus is no fun," said Danny.

"In love? With that guy you were dancing with?"

"No," said Grayson. "I'm seeing someone. I was just telling Danny that it felt like cheating when that guy tried to make out with me."

"Hmm. Do you think the guy you're seeing would mind?"

"I don't know. We haven't been seeing each other very long. We haven't talked about it. I'm not *actually* in love, I just really like this guy."

"Obviously we have to meet him," said Aiden. He slid the bartender a ten-dollar bill and picked up the cosmo. "I'd love to stay and chat, but this girl is a *gymnast*."

Danny laughed and watched him go. "You want to stay?"

"I'm having fun dancing." Grayson couldn't keep the smile off his face. These guys, Danny and Aiden, they were his real family. They were the people who loved and accepted him just as he was. He loved them back so much, he didn't want the night to end.

"Okay," said Danny, his eyes narrowed, as if skeptical of Grayson's sudden good mood.

Grayson downed the rest of his drink. "You wanna dance some more?"

"Yes. And if you aren't gonna go home with that hot guy, I might."

Chapter Twelve

NOLAN HAD told Grayson only that he had some business in LA. Restoration had agreed not to film anything that weekend. So by the time Nolan boarded the plane, he had freed his schedule.

When he landed in LA, he mostly wanted to retreat to his hotel room and hide from the world, but he'd made dinner plans with an old friend. Stepping back into the life he'd essentially abandoned felt surreal. The restaurant his friend had picked in West Hollywood was just the sort of place he'd eaten at with Ricky all the time. Good food, on the noisy side, lots of beautiful male servers. He enjoyed dinner but was happy to get back to his hotel that night. He took a sleeping pill and passed out.

He was anxious, so he arrived twenty minutes early for his appointment at the adoption agency the next day but had been left to cool his heels in the waiting room until, five minutes after his apartment was supposed to start, a large, bald man with a kind smile called him back.

"I'm Clyde MacDonald," the bald man said. "I oversee some of our accounts. I believe we spoke on the phone last year?"

"Yes, probably." The name seemed familiar. "Should I have brought in my lawyer? I called him this morning and he said he'd be reachable by phone, just in case."

"That's good, but try to relax. This is more of an informal meeting."

"Relax, sure. You have clearly never spent two years on an adoption waitlist."

"True. But we genuinely want to help find the best homes for these children. You've already been through the vetting process, and I know your home situation is different now, but also that you can still offer a good home. If this isn't your child, one is still out there."

It had been Ricky's idea to go through a private, pro-LGBT adoption agency, but it still seemed odd that, with so many homeless children in the world, this Clyde fellow was feeding Nolan platitudes about his future son or daughter being "out there" somewhere. But then again, this wasn't a sure thing. The way it worked was that the birth mother got to choose the family who adopted her child. And there was apparently no shortage of affluent gay couples in California competing for those children.

Clyde led him into a conference room. A very young pregnant woman sat there. She was nineteen, max, which likely explained why she was here. She stood when Nolan walked in.

"Mr. Hamlin," she said. "It's nice to finally meet you. I'm Angela."

Nolan shook her hand and took stock. She had a strikingly pretty face with big eyes and plump lips and thick black hair that hung loose to the middle of her back.

"Nice to meet you, Angela."

"I was sorry to hear about your husband."

"Thank you."

"And Mr. MacDonald said you moved to New York?"

"Yes, I—" Nolan sighed and decided to let go of the formality. "It was too hard to stay in LA after my husband died. I'm not really meant for SoCal anyway. I grew up in the New York area, so I decided to go back there. I live in a loft apartment in Chelsea."

"I've never been to New York," said Angela. "Is that a nice neighborhood?"

"Yes, it's great. It's in Manhattan. I'm working at the Restoration Channel now, and their offices are just a quick walk from my loft, which is part of the reason I bought it."

Angela giggled nervously. "That is very different from my life."

"I'm sorry."

"No, it's all right. I live with my mama in an apartment in Huntington Park. Do you know where that is?"

"I do, yes." Nolan's recollection was that it was a working-class, mostly Latinx neighborhood.

"Well, anyway. I was dating this guy, and I got pregnant, and he freaked out and left me. I can't afford to keep the baby, but I want to make sure she's well taken care of. Um. It's a girl, by the way."

A girl. "Oh, wow. Okay."

"I was hoping you'd be willing to tell me a little about why you want to adopt her."

Nolan didn't know how to talk to this woman. He was intimidated by the fact that she was carrying a child that could potentially go home with him. He wanted to impress her and make her like him so she'd choose him ultimately, which was an odd thing to think about. He wanted this baby who wasn't even born yet, without even knowing anything about the child. The moment was… surreal.

But he closed his eyes for a moment, trying to pull himself together. Why *did* he want to adopt? He dug deep and decided to speak from the heart. "My late husband came from a big family and loved children. When he first brought up having a child, I was skeptical. I was happy with our life the way it was. We loved each other, we had good jobs, we were happy. Why complicate that? But the more he talked about it, the more I got on board. The way he used to talk." And oh fuck, here came the tears. Nolan blinked a few times to keep that stinging feeling away. "He wanted children so badly. He wanted to raise them, to teach them how to be good people, to play with them at the playground in the park near our old house, to do the whole thing with the PTA and Little League and all of it. And the more we talked, the more it felt like our life would be incomplete if we *didn't* have a child. So we got a lawyer and started the process. And we began designing the nursery in our old house."

Nolan lost the battle here. The tears were coming whether he wanted them to or not. He thought he'd gotten past this phase, but apparently not.

He wiped at his eyes and said, "I'm sorry."

"It's okay," said Clyde. "Keep going."

Nolan nodded. "We were designing the nursery. And Ricky, he was so excited about having a child. And then he got sick. And now he's gone." He took a shaky breath. "At some point, his dream became mine and I wanted to be a father. I have so much love to give. I have a good income and can provide a good home. I know I'd be a single dad, but I'm in a good place in my life, evidence to the contrary." He gestured at his face. "And I want to do this."

Clyde pushed a box of tissues toward Nolan and Nolan took one.

"Sorry," he said again. "That's all."

Angela nodded. "I believe you," she said. "I believe you would love and care for a child." She reached across the table and put her hand over Nolan's. "I picked you and Ricky because I read your profile and I thought, these are two professional men in a loving, committed relationship who want a child but can't have one the natural way. That's really what you want in adoptive parents, no? People who really *want* a child. And I think you do."

"I do," said Nolan, nodding.

"My only worry is that I'd been hoping the parents would stay in LA."

Well, there it was. Nolan's stomach sank. He nodded. "I'm sorry about that. LA's not my home anymore."

"I'm not saying no, I just need to think about it."

"If it helps, I'd be happy to fly you out to New York whenever you want to visit, and I can make sure you see the baby whenever I'm in LA, which is bound to happen now and then because I still have a lot of clients here."

Angela patted her belly. "I'm still deciding how much of a role I want to play in the kid's life. Part of me just wants to know she's all right, you know? I feel like if I saw her a lot, it might be too painful."

"I understand," said Nolan, mostly because it was the thing people wanted to hear more than something he could fully relate to.

Angela sighed. "Thank you for meeting with me. I think this helped. But I need a little time to make a final decision."

"Absolutely," said Nolan. "It's your child. You have to pick someone you trust. But I... I could take could care of her. So I hope you'll consider me."

"I definitely will." Angela smiled. "I had a hunch when I saw your profile that you'd be someone famous. I've seen you on *The Stacey Lewis Show*. And, of course, I watched Ricardo Vega in everything. He was *so* fine."

Nolan laughed softly, warm suddenly. God, he missed Ricky. "He was." He cleared his throat. "I have to fly back to New York tomorrow, but if you want to ask me any questions, the agency has my number. Right, Clyde?"

"Sure, with your authorization, I can give Angela your phone number."

"Please do, yes. Okay." Nolan took a deep breath, still overwhelmed. "Let me know when you make a decision."

Clyde showed Nolan out a few minutes later. Nolan still felt off-kilter, not used to crying in front of other people. He did all of his crying in private; that was part of why he'd gone underground for a year.

"What are you doing at the Restoration Channel?" Clyde asked. "My wife is a big fan. It's on in my house almost constantly. She can't get enough of those house-flipping shows."

Nolan smiled. "I'm filming a new show, actually."

"Oh, neat. Does that take a lot of time?"

"Less than you'd think." It felt like a loaded question. Nolan didn't want to give Clyde any reason to sway Angela into not choosing Nolan. "I have quite a bit of downtime."

"The agency wants to do another home visit at your place in the city. We have an office in Manhattan too, so I can arrange for someone local to drop by."

"Not a problem, although I'm not currently set up for a baby."

"That's all right. I'll call you to set that up."

They shook hands and Nolan left. He walked outside into the hot LA sun and was glad he didn't live here anymore. The air was stifling. New York wasn't the cleanest city, but it didn't have the heavy air LA did. Nor did it have the heavy memories of Nolan's old life. He'd made the right choice in leaving.

He wasn't at all sure he was doing the right thing here, but he wanted it. More than he'd ever dreamed.

Chapter Thirteen

GRAYSON WALKED into the studio and held up his phone. "Nolan, I have an audition video you have to see."

They'd been looking for another couple to round out the season but hadn't liked any of the audition tapes they'd seen lately. So Nolan was game. He put his pencil down. "Give me the highlights."

"Another pair of newlyweds, but with a bit of a twist this time. I mean, their love story made me cry. They were best friends as kids and then were separated when one of their fathers got a job in another state, and then they found each other again, and it's just...." Grayson let out a little squeal.

Nolan laughed. "Well, show me, then."

Grayson pulled the video up on his phone, pressed Play, and passed the phone to Nolan.

The video began with a zoom in on a nice house in a wooded area. Then the camera panned to two men. The one on the left said, "I'm Justin, and this is my husband, Peter, and we're in over our heads."

He went on to explain that he and Peter had been kids together in the Jersey suburbs, but Peter had moved away when they were fourteen and they'd lost track of each other. Then one day, when they were both about twenty-five, they'd run into each other at a mall. They immediately rekindled their friendship, and then it turned out they were both gay and had been in love with each other since they were teenagers. They'd been together ever since. The previous year, they'd gotten married and bought this fixer-upper, but it turned out neither was as handy as they thought, and the house had a zillion issues. And now their life was on hold while they figured out how to deal with it.

"Aren't they the cutest?" Grayson asked.

"It's a gay couple."

Grayson rolled his eyes. "Thanks, genius. I never would have noticed."

Nolan sighed. He wasn't sure why this had surprised him, but the Restoration Channel was pretty heterosexual. Still, Garrett Harwood was clearly working on changing that. Maybe this was an opportunity to help. He cleared his throat. "I mean, this house…. Where is it?"

"Upstate. In the Catskills. Did you see how beautiful the scenery is? All I want to do is put a huge window on the back of that house so they can look at the mountains all the time."

"Well, they are certainly photogenic. And it might be fun to do a project in the woods instead of doing another ranch house in the suburbs."

Grayson let out another little squeal. "Yes. I'll tell Helena when she's back in the office tomorrow." He pocketed his phone and walked around the big drafting table where Nolan currently sat as he stared at blueprints.

The previous day they'd ambushed a single mom with a teenage daughter—two of the sweetest people

Nolan had ever met. Their house was a big nonfunctional mess with busted flooring and faulty electrical
in the kitchen, so it needed some expensive repairs, but
Nolan was still determined to find a way to fix their
place within the budget they had. He just had to figure
out how. He was hoping that if he stared at the floor
plans long enough, something would come to him.

Grayson sidled up to Nolan and kissed his cheek.
"I missed you this weekend. I think those three days
were the longest we've gone without seeing each other
since we met."

Nolan felt guilty for not telling Grayson about
the potential adoption situation, but he also didn't feel
like it was worth the consequences to his relationship
with Grayson if Angela ultimately said no. He'd been
back in New York for two entire days and still hadn't
heard anything. And the longer he waited, the less
hope he had.

"LA sucks," Nolan said. He turned his head and
kissed Grayson. "I'm glad to be back."

"Mmm." Grayson leaned in and kissed Nolan
again, *really* kissed him this time, snaking his tongue
into Nolan's mouth. "I missed you last night too."

"Sorry. I wasn't up for company. LA brought up a
lot of memories. I just needed to be by myself for a bit."
Well, and he'd called his mother because he needed to
talk to someone.

"You don't like being emotional in front of people."

Nolan balked and pushed the floor plans to the
side. "That's a weird thing to say."

"It's true, though. I never really noticed it before,
but you have this persona that you put on for the TV
cameras. The more you and I get to know each other, the more you let go of it when the cameras aren't

around. But when things get sticky emotionally, you tend to clam up and retreat."

"Are you my shrink now?" Nolan pushed away from the table and crossed the room to the little cube fridge in the corner. He grabbed a Diet Coke just for something to do. He didn't have to have this conversation.

"No, I'm just trying to get a read on you. And, like, fine. You need some alone time, I get it. We've been dating a few weeks. It's probably better if we *don't* spend every minute together. I just happened to notice that you get wiggy when you start to feel things when other people are around."

Nolan wasn't aware that he had a different persona in front of the camera, although Grayson's observation didn't surprise him. He purposely tried to seem more optimistic when they were filming. Fighting through the fog was easier on some days than others, and sometimes it was all he could do to hold out until filming ended. So, yeah, he didn't like crying in front of people. Who did? But maybe that extended more broadly to any deep emotion and Nolan just hadn't realized it.

He shook his head and opened the soda can. "Well, since we didn't talk much yesterday, what did you end up doing this weekend?"

"I went dancing on Friday." Grayson shot Nolan a cheeky grin. "A very handsome man tried to kiss me, but I put him off because it felt like I was cheating on you, which is nuts because we haven't even had a conversation about being exclusive. But still… that happened."

"Oh." Was Grayson saying he wanted to be exclusive? Was Nolan ready for that? "I mean, okay. I appreciate that. But I don't know if I'm ready for—"

"Say no more. You're still fairly new to the land of the living. If you want to cut a swath across the sexy men of Manhattan, I won't stop you."

"It's not that." God, there really was a lot he hadn't told Grayson. This hardly seemed like the right venue, though. "I'm not interested in being with anyone else. But saying I want to be exclusive implies a… certain level of commitment. And I'm just not ready for that. Are you okay with keeping things casual for now?"

"Sure. I don't need a ring or anything. We've barely just started seeing each other." Grayson rocked on his heels. "Would you be upset if I slept with somebody else?"

"Are you asking permission?"

"Posing a hypothetical."

Nolan considered. He didn't have the same jealous streak Grayson did. Would it bother him? No, because this relationship wasn't serious. Was it? No, it wasn't. "Do what you need to."

Grayson leaned close. "So if I'd gone home with that guy I met at the club Friday, it wouldn't bother you?"

"No. Not if it was a one-night thing. As long as you come back to me, do what you want."

"Ah, there it is."

"What?"

Grayson gave Nolan a peck on the nose. "A little bit of possessiveness."

Nolan grunted. He hadn't meant to sound possessive, but he couldn't deny that he really liked Grayson. "Okay, fine. You're great. I like you. I want to be with you. I'm just not in a position right now to make any long-term promises, okay?" Because even if Angela picked some other adoptive parents, there could still be another child down the line. And then he'd have to call things off with Grayson. Because there was no way he'd saddle a young guy who liked to go out with a family.

"Okay," Grayson said. He smiled. "I gotcha."

"Do you?"

Grayson patted Nolan's chest. "I know you better than you think I do. I see what's going on here. You don't actually want me to sleep with other people, but you don't feel like you can tell me not to. That's fine. I don't want to sleep with other people. But I'm not asking for some big commitment either. This is just... what we're doing for now. Yeah?"

Nolan sighed, feeling a little relieved. "Yeah. Although if you did, I don't know, fall into bed with some other guy, it's not a deal-breaker."

"Okay. Good to know."

THEY DROVE out to Maria Dunlop's house the next morning to meet up with Sandy, the contractor for this project. Maria was the single-mom client they'd seen on Monday. They had a plan to turn Maria's unfinished basement into a space that could double as a gym for her gymnast daughter and convert her den into a suite for her aging father, who was coming to live with her, as well as some other little projects around the house. Unlike their other clients, most of the first floor of her house was fine. The kitchen had been redone about ten years ago, but it was functional. The budget didn't allow for anything major in the living areas, although Grayson itched to update the design.

They were mostly silent on the drive. Grayson was still turning over the conversation they'd had the previous evening. They'd gone back to Nolan's place after that, ordered in Thai food, and had sex well into the wee hours of the morning, so Grayson wasn't worried about the status of their relationship as such. But he felt like Nolan was keeping something from him—something big. But he didn't think he was in much of a position to make demands after Nolan said he wasn't willing to make a big commitment.

So, fine. This was all good for now, but if Grayson continued to fall for Nolan, they'd have to have a serious talk about what was really going on. Part of Grayson wanted the whole thing—the white picket fence, the 2.5 children, the loving supportive family he'd never had—but it was probably too soon to admit that.

In the meantime, they were driving out to Long Island to see the Dunlop house.

"You okay?" Nolan said as he took the exit off the Northern State. "You're uncharacteristically quiet."

"Yeah, I'm fine. Just thinking."

"Okay. About interior design?"

Grayson laughed. "Sure, if you like."

They beat Sandy to the house. Nolan went inside to take another look at the den while Grayson waited outside for Sandy.

He was not going to freak out.

Something had happened when Nolan was in LA. Grayson was sure of it. Nolan had been distant the past few days. Sometimes he let his guard down—that was especially true in bed—but most of the time he had all his walls up. Grayson was very determined to tear those walls down. He was willing to invest the time—sort of like investing in an engineered beam to tear down the wall of a house—if it would open up Nolan.

Because at some point Grayson's feelings had turned a corner from "willing to roll with this and see what happens because I worship Nolan" to "I'm starting to get to know the real Nolan and I really like him and I'm falling more in love with him by the day." Unfortunately, Nolan seemed to be pulling in the other direction.

A black sedan with the logo of Mike's renovation company—Mike and Sandy were business partners—pulled up to the curb, and a middle-aged blond guy hopped out.

"Hey, I'm Sandy," the man said as he approached the house. "Are you Grayson?"

"Yes. How'd you guess?"

"My husband is kind of obsessed with home decor, so I already knew who Nolan Hamlin is. All Everett wanted for Christmas was this set of throw pillows from the Nolan Hamlin collection. I heard all about these pillows for weeks, so now my sofa has these damned purple pillows on it *and* a matching purple throw. Personally, I don't really care, but they make my husband happy, so here we are." Sandy shrugged.

Grayson laughed. "Okay."

"You look young, so I'm guessing you're not married. One day you'll see. If the person you love is happy, few other things matter. A couple of overpriced throw pillows is a small cost in the long run."

"I'll keep that in mind. You want to see the house?"

"Yeah, give me the tour."

When they went inside, Sandy introduced himself to Nolan and told the throw-pillow story again, but made it sound a little less judgmental. Nolan smiled. "The purple ones? Those were the worst sellers in that collection."

"Really? I guess they are a rather vibrant shade of purple."

"The color palette I have in mind for this house is mostly off-white and beige, because Maria, the homeowner, seems particularly allergic to color. I pitched the idea of blue accents to her and she almost passed out."

Sandy laughed. "Yes, I'm familiar with this. I do a lot of kitchens in my untelevised life, and good Lord, white kitchens are *so* dull, but that's all anyone wants. I just did a white kitchen with white counters in a brownstone in Brooklyn Heights, and getting the owner to pick one of five basically identical white quartz slabs for the counter was exquisite torture. The gray veining in the beautiful slab of Carrara marble I had originally wanted to use was too much color for her. I almost accidentally on purpose installed blue cabinets because the stuff she picked was so boring."

Nolan smiled. "Okay. I can see we're going to get along just fine."

"Show me what you want to do in this beige house."

Sandy took notes on his phone as they toured the den and the basement. He grimaced when they got downstairs. "Oh God. This is the sort of basement kids have nightmares about," he said.

"I know," said Nolan. "The only light comes from that bald light bulb near the foot of the stairs and two tiny windows. That's it. I do actually want to paint everything white in here and do very light flooring to maximize what little light there is. And I think we need to add some lights in the ceiling too. What do you think?"

"Sure."

"Do you not have an opinion?"

"I'm just here to install what you want me to install. We'll definitely need to do some electrical work down here. And plumbing too, if you want to add a bathroom. But I don't care if you paint the walls white or lime green. Hand me a can of paint, I'll see that it gets done."

Nolan nodded. "Okay."

As they walked back up the admittedly rickety staircase, Sandy said, "You know, you guys don't talk like designers. I mean, you obviously know what you're doing, but I've worked with some design guys who have such weird vocabularies."

"What do you mean?" Grayson asked.

"I worked with a guy on a house last month who kept describing things as 'moments.' We put slate tiles at the front entrance to the house and he called it a 'tile moment.' We put a sofa in the middle of a room instead of against a wall, and he described the furniture as 'floating like islands' and then said that we had a little 'floating moment' in the living room. And, like, sure, but also, it's not like placing a sofa facing a TV is really turning interior design on its head, you know?"

Grayson had probably used the word "moment" in that context a few times in his life, but he made a mental note never to do it again.

Nolan seemed somewhat revived on the drive back to the city. He was chatty, talking about design ideas and some fabric he'd seen at a shop in LA that he thought would make pretty curtains for the Cruz house. He'd apparently bought twenty yards and had it shipped to the Restoration offices. Grayson hoped somebody there knew how to sew curtains, because Grayson sure didn't.

In the end, he decided not to push Nolan on anything. Soon they would have to have a conversation about what was going on between them. But not just yet.

Chapter Fourteen

CONSTRUCTION AT the Roberts house was set to wrap five weeks after it started, which to Grayson seemed like some kind of land-speed record for a renovation this extensive.

Most of the work happened off-camera. There were cameras in the house so that the episode could include a time-lapse view of the work done, but actual construction was neither Nolan's nor Grayson's strong suit, so they weren't directly involved in that.

They did need to pick out materials and finishes, though. The Robertses had pretty much deferred to Nolan and Grayson, which was how Grayson found himself standing in the kitchen one day, midconstruction, staring at cabinet and counter samples. Well, that and the fact that Nolan had changed his mind again.

Nolan pointed at the white Shaker cabinets with his foot. "Those, obviously."

Grayson couldn't find it in himself to care that much about cabinets. White cabinets made sense for the space. Where he'd get involved, though, was with the countertops. Nolan had picked out a dark granite that was absolutely not going to work.

"Nolan. Sweetheart. No." Grayson put his hands on his hips.

Nolan stared at it for a long moment. "I just wanted to see how I liked it in the space."

"Our theme is Jersey Shore in Winter, right? There is nothing beachy about dark granite. But this blueish-gray quartz is *perfect*. Doesn't the color make you think of, like, rocks on the shore?"

Nolan pressed his lips together. Travis stood off to the side, looking like he was trying not to laugh.

"Fine. Gray quartz," Nolan said. He pulled something that clanged out of his pocket and lay some black metal drawer pulls on the sawhorse that they'd set up to approximate where the kitchen island would be. "This is our hardware."

"Where did you get these?" Grayson asked.

Nolan waved his hand as if it was of no consequence. "I love these, so we're using them. White cabinets, black hardware, gray countertops. Same vinyl plank flooring we're doing throughout the house. Done and done."

"What about the backsplash?" asked Grayson. "'Cause I found these tiles online, and it's a *little* bit of a risk, but what do you think?"

Grayson got out his phone, pulled up the photo he saved, and showed it to Nolan. He'd found subway tile that came in a soft salmon that went perfectly with the color story of the house.

"Pink? For a *backsplash*?" Nolan said.

"Salmon. And yes, because it goes with the design. It's the same pink as your color story."

"No. I pictured the salmon for throw pillows. Maybe curtains. We're doing white subway for the backsplash. Remember, we're designing for the Robertses, not for ourselves. Pink is too… specific."

"White subway is too boring."

"Are we really—?"

"If I can intervene for a sec," said Travis. "Not pink. But maybe the compromise here is a pattern. We just used these tiles on a house I did in Brooklyn that were white with a gray pattern on them. I'm not a designer, so I don't know what the pattern is called, but it was kind of… French? Swirly? I dunno. But they would tie the cabinets with the counters." Travis pulled out his phone and found the photo he wanted, then showed it to them.

"Perfect," said Nolan. "Let's do that."

"I just think the kitchen needs a pop of color," said Grayson.

"So we do it in staging. You can buy some pink dishes if it will make you feel better."

Grayson crossed his arms. "Yeah, fine."

"So, wait," said Travis. "Your name is Gray, but—"

"Yeah, haha, my name is Gray, but I love color. Like nobody told me that every day of design school."

Travis cracked up, clearly enjoying this tiff between Grayson and Nolan.

Once they settled on materials and finishes, everything took another ten days to install.

That left Grayson and Nolan with a week to stage the house. The way it worked was that they would do a full design on the house—or at least the rooms they'd worked on; they were leaving the bedrooms alone— and then the family had the option to keep or return whatever furniture they used. Furnishings were baked into the budget, and they had a pretty generous amount of money to work with, primarily because this was what they both did well.

On Monday of that week, a camera crew followed them around furniture stores while they picked things out. They went to a big chain place that Grayson found overwhelming. They found a sofa they could agree on—and they also agreed that the Robertses' current sofa was hideous—but it quickly became clear to Grayson that Nolan's tastes leaned more traditional and Grayson's more edgy.

"The Robertses are retirees," Nolan argued. "They don't want new and different. They want safe and traditional."

"Sure, but you don't hire professional designers to do something you could do yourself. Anyone could put a gray sofa in a living room. The blue sofa, at least, has some character."

"Hmm," said Nolan.

Their next stop was an antique shop—Nolan kept calling it a "vintage store" and Grayson didn't have the heart to tell him it made him sound pretentious—but they found a bunch of really cool accessories to put in the house. Grayson's favorite finds were some antique picture frames. He planned to email Carol and ask her to send him some digital photos he could print out at the Restoration Channel offices on good paper and frame them.

They wrapped up at a trendy lighting shop because Nolan wanted a cool overhead fixture for the kitchen. That, too, created a little bit of conflict when Grayson fell in love with a really cool chandelier made of glass balls that looked so light, they could have been bubbles. But Nolan said, "Absolutely not. Way too modern.

Doesn't work with the theme at all." The camera guys seemed to be eating this up.

Their "load in day" happened the following day. In addition to what they'd picked out, they had access to a truck full of stuff from one of the Restoration Channel's sponsors. In exchange for dropping the name of the company into casual conversation several times in the episode, they could take pretty much anything they wanted from the truck at no cost. Was anything in the truck cutting-edge? No. But Grayson spent some time browsing and picked up a cool ottoman and lots of textiles: throw-pillow cases, throw blankets, curtains, sheets, towels. There were also boxes of dishes, picture frames, wicker baskets, ceramic animals, storage boxes, all kinds of things. He was determined to leave an impression on this house, and if that meant he only picked the throw pillows because Nolan was a control freak who kept nixing his ideas, well, they would be *fabulous* throw pillows.

He carried his finds into the house, where he found Nolan staring intently at a line of mismatched wicker baskets sitting on the kitchen island.

"Do you like any of these?" Nolan asked.

"I like the black one with the white trim."

"Sure, okay."

Grayson ignored whatever basket crisis Nolan was having as he found a good spot for the ottoman and then placed the throw pillows where he wanted them. He gave each pillow a karate chop and then tossed a pretty cabled throw over the back of the sofa he and Nolan had picked out.

Nolan held up a sea green ceramic vase. "What do you think of this?"

"It's nice."

"You say that like you don't want to tell me you hate it."

"It's a little plain, but the color goes with the rest of the design well. Are you going to put flowers in it?"

"Sure. I figured we could buy some on the way here on reveal day."

"Cool. Do you think the sofa needs more pillows?"

Nolan walked over and looked at what Grayson had done. "Any more pillows and there won't be anywhere to sit."

Grayson nodded and decided he was satisfied with the living room. Then he looked at the bookshelves.

"Oh, no. Absolutely not."

"What?" Nolan said.

"I know that turning books with their spines toward the wall creates this nice off-white color palette for stuff on the shelves. But I hate it. A lot. It's totally impractical. How is the home owner supposed to tell what's on the shelf?"

"So put them back."

"I will."

The camera got all of this. They got every little tiff about design Grayson and Nolan had all day. When they finally finished to Nolan's satisfaction, Helena said, "I've been watching the dailies. You guys are already arguing like an old married couple. I love it."

"Oh, boy," said Nolan.

"Viewers love this sort of thing. Little conflicts. Compromises. It's great."

"Are we done?" Nolan asked, seeming annoyed.

"Yes," said Helena. "The house looks great. We'll all come back tomorrow for the reveal. The Robertses are scheduled to arrive back at the house at eleven, so I want to get here at ten to get some footage of you guys doing some final tinkering."

In the car a half hour later, Grayson asked, "So are you actually annoyed with me?"

Nolan let out a sigh. "No. I'm just not used to designing with a partner. And our aesthetics are different."

"I think I've landed on how to define us. I'm more modern, but a little quirky. You're surprisingly more traditional. The furniture you picked for the den all looks kind of antique. But I don't really care for that look."

"Uh-huh."

"I don't have a point, I'm just observing. Well, and I wanted to make sure you weren't actually annoyed, because we just spent all day bickering."

"It was constructive. I'm happy with the design. It reflects both of us, don't you think?"

"Yeah, I think so." Although Grayson also recognized he was still finding his voice as a designer. He definitely knew, in his gut, what looked good, and he had preferences in terms of colors and textures, but he wasn't sure if he could define what he liked as a coherent style. "Modern" was the closest description for it, but he also loved colors and patterns.

"I'm not upset with you," Nolan said. "I'm… stuck in my ways. Comes with age, I guess."

"I hear what you're saying, but it translates as 'stubborn.' And I think what you really need is to have your old ways shaken up."

"Oh, is that what I need?"

"Yes." And Grayson realized he meant it. Not that he had any issue with Nolan's year of hibernation. Grayson had never lost anyone that close to him, and he imagined it must be completely devastating. Nolan should take as much time as he needed. But now that he was back living in the world, Grayson intended to show him how to live again. And that meant reminding him what he was passionate about.

Nolan's whole adult life had been dedicated to interior design. He *should* get worked up about colors and vases and throw pillows.

"I gotta go home tonight," Grayson said. "The shirt I want to wear for our first reveal day is there, and I don't trust my roommates to water my plants. But tomorrow we should celebrate. I'm thinking a nice bottle of champagne followed by sex on your couch."

Nolan laughed. "Okay. Reasonable plan. Should we have something to eat?"

"Food, schmood. Who needs it when your boyfriend is hot?"

"So noted."

NOLAN THOUGHT he might throw up.

Hopefully future reveals would not trigger his nerves quite to this level. Although, in his defense, he had a lot on his mind. Angela had called the previous night.

He spent probably twenty minutes finding the perfect place for a ceramic hippo on a floating shelf in the den because he didn't know what to do with his hands.

Grayson was popping around between the rooms they'd renovated, checking everything and second-guessing his pillow placement, so he was clearly nervous too.

"Fair warning," said Grayson. "I'm probably gonna cry."

Nolan glanced at him. "Really?" That seemed out of character.

"It's a thing, I don't know. You were there when that dog commercial came on the other day."

Nolan nodded, because he had indeed witnessed Grayson crying at a commercial for... well, Nolan couldn't remember now. But it had involved someone narrating over a video of a soldier being reunited with a very excited golden retriever. Nolan had reached for the bowl of popcorn on the coffee table and noticed Grayson wiping away tears. When Nolan had asked about it, Grayson just said that sometimes sad movies and weddings and commercials with cute dogs got to him. Nolan found the fact that he seemed completely unselfconscious about this admirable. Grayson felt emotions deeply sometimes. He didn't try to defend himself or have a crisis of masculinity about it. A lot of people saw tears as a sign of weakness, but Grayson was unbothered. It was part of his boldness.

"I mean," Grayson said now, "especially if Carol cries. Watching other people cry is like turning a spigot for me."

"The Robertses just pulled into the driveway!" called Helena from the front of the house.

As they'd discussed in advance, Nolan and Grayson jogged to the front door. "Big smiles," Nolan said. Then he opened the door.

"Welcome to your new home!" Nolan said.

He hadn't been this nervous about showing a design to a client... maybe ever. Part of it was just first-project-after-a-long-hiatus jitters, probably, plus the presence of the cameras. But he also really wanted this family to like what they'd done. Whether Nolan liked the design was really beside the point; the Robertses were the ones who would have to stay in the house.

As the camera rolled, Nolan instructed the couple to close their eyes. Then he led them into their new entryway, which was part of the new open floor plan on the first floor. On the left was their brand-new kitchen, and on the right, their new living room area, with a new TV and plenty of seating for guests.

"Open your eyes!"

Carol and George Roberts both gasped. Carol said, "Oh, my God!" Nolan couldn't tell at first if the reaction was good or bad, but then Carol smiled and added, "I love it so much!"

"Let's show you the features of your new kitchen," said Grayson. He led her by the elbow into the space. Helena had made some suggestions for what he should say on camera, so he played right along. "Do you remember the old kitchen?"

"Of course, but this doesn't even look like the same house. It's so beautiful! Look how bright this room is!"

This was, in a lot of ways, part of a script. Nolan gave a brief rundown of the changes they'd made and his reasoning for the finishes he chose.

"These counters...." Carol shook her head, though she was smiling. "I never thought I was the sort of person who would say, 'these counters and cabinets are beautiful,' but they really are! I always thought I could just operate in any kitchen I had, but this is so much better than the old kitchen."

"The sink at the island faces the living room," said Grayson, "so one of you can be in here prepping and still interact with whoever else is around. Getting rid of the walls made the flow much better and let in a lot more natural light."

"It's really spectacular."

They continued into the den and one of the first-floor bathrooms. In each room, Carol and George seemed to genuinely love everything Nolan and Grayson had done. When they reconvened in the living room, things got a little dicey, though.

"You know, I was worried," said Carol. "This was my dad's house, and after he died, part of me wanted to keep everything as-is, in his honor. But I really think changing it to make this house work better is what he would have wanted. I don't want to hold on to the past. And by making this home work for us, for making it our forever home, I think that… that would have made Dad happy."

George blinked a few times and put an arm around his wife. Carol's voice was watery, and she dabbed under her eyes with her finger. Grayson pulled a handkerchief out of his pocket and dabbed at his own eyes.

"I'm so happy we could do this for you," said Grayson.

And Nolan felt… nothing. Well, not *nothing*, because he was glad his clients were happy and he felt some pride in a job well done. But it was like his body just had no more capacity for grief. He looked on this tableau of mostly happy tears and couldn't bring forth much emotion at all.

Or maybe he was just… drained. Angela had decided that she wanted him to have the baby, so it looked very much like he was going to have a daughter in about two months. On the one hand, he was thrilled, but on the other… he was terrified. He'd called his mother with the news right after he'd gotten off the phone with

Angela, and she'd cried so effusively with joy he could hear it through the phone, which had made his own eyes sting. So he'd already experienced every possible emotion this week and just had no more capacity for anything else.

"Sorry," said Grayson to the Robertses. "I really tried not to cry." He fanned his face with his hand.

They all exchanged hugs; then they split a bottle of cheap champagne in the new kitchen before they wrapped filming. George and Carol seemed genuinely thrilled with how their house had turned out. Further negotiations about what they'd keep and return would happen directly with Helena and the production staff. Helena wanted them to send in some video after they'd been in the house about a month, so they could talk about the difference the renovations had made in their lives at the end of the episode. But that was out of Nolan and Grayson's hands. On to the next house!

"You good to drive?" Grayson asked as they walked out to the car.

"I had, like, three sips of champagne. I'm fine."

"Okay. Just checking." Grayson climbed into the car.

"You weren't wrong about crying."

Grayson laughed. "I know, I know."

Helena ran over to the car as Nolan was about to start it. "Can I just say," she said, "that was an excellent reveal. A little schmoopy, but exactly the kind of thing our viewers will eat up."

Nolan took that to mean viewers would eat up Grayson getting emotional. "So you thought it went okay?" he asked, although he knew it had.

"It went spectacularly. Great job, guys. See you tomorrow."

Nolan took a long breath as he watched Helena walk over to her car. Grayson reached over and patted Nolan's arm where it rested on the console.

"We're gonna be TV stars, aren't we?" said Grayson.

"Afraid so," Nolan said, putting the car in gear.

Chapter Fifteen

ON THE ride home that night, Grayson finally gathered the courage to ask, "Okay. So what aren't you telling me?"

"Gray."

"I've been patient all week because I wanted to make sure everything with this reveal went okay, but I think that the fact that we've been fighting on camera is less about our design differences and possibly about something else. You've been acting very weird ever since you got back from LA. I think something happened that you're not telling me, and I want to know what it is…."

"I can promise you, it's not whatever you're thinking."

"You don't know what I'm thinking." Although of course Grayson was thinking Nolan had hooked up with some old flame in LA. Nolan felt guilty and that was why he was tiptoeing around Grayson. Part of him recognized how absurd that was, and he found it unlikely that Nolan had slept with anyone else, but he couldn't imagine what else would make Nolan act so out of character.

"The car is not the place to talk about this," said Nolan. "What we're going to do right now while I drive is record a nice little bit where we talk about how happy we are that we could make a true home for the Roberts. Then, I promise, I'll take you back to my place and tell you everything. I can't avoid talking to you about this much longer anyway. But you have to promise not to bring it up until I'm not behind the wheel."

"All right."

But that was not at all comforting. Whatever Nolan had to say was going to be big, and it was going to have an impact on their relationship. If it was something trivial, Nolan could have explained now.

So Grayson smiled and filmed the little car talk segment and then spent the next hour completely losing his mind, wondering what Nolan had to tell him.

When they finally got to Nolan's place, Nolan asked, "You want a beer or—?"

"I want you to just tell me whatever you have to tell me so that I can figure out how to deal with it. Because whatever it is has to be better than the DEFCON One situation I've got going on in my head."

Nolan sighed. "Let's sit down."

They settled into the living room area, next to each other on the big sofa.

"I need you to know something before I tell you everything," Nolan said.

"Okay."

"I really, genuinely like you, a lot more than I ever expected to. These last, what, six weeks? They've been amazing. I enjoy your company, you make me laugh, but more than that, you've made me feel things I didn't know I could feel anymore. And that's really not nothing. When Ricky died, it was like I totally shut down, body and soul. But now, finally, it's starting to come back online."

"Okay." Grayson didn't know what to do with that. It sure sounded like the prelude to a breakup. "I really like you too. And not only because I admired and lusted after you before we met. Getting to know you as a real person has been really great too."

Nolan smiled. "I appreciate that. But let me talk, because this is hard, and I want to make sure you understand the whole situation."

"Okay."

"Before Ricky got his cancer diagnosis, we applied to be adoptive parents through an agency in LA."

Grayson stared. Where was Nolan going with this? Did he want kids? Was this some kind of "where is this going?" relationship talk? He opened his mouth to ask, but Nolan held up his hand and kept talking.

"A lot of time passed and nothing happened. Apparently that's normal, and sometimes it takes a few years for agencies to pair the right child with the right parents, and it's harder for gay parents, but blah, blah.... Long story short, when Ricky got sick, I completely forgot about almost all of that. Well, not completely. We'd started designing the nursery in our house in LA. But I haven't thought about it all since I moved to New York."

"Okay," said Grayson. It hit him that Nolan and Ricky had the sort of relationship in which they had big future plans. What must it have been like to have those kinds of big plans together and then abruptly have it all taken away? Grayson had never given the depth of Nolan's mourning much thought beyond "it must suck to lose your husband." But it wasn't just losing someone close to him; it was losing a vision for what your life was supposed to be like. No wonder Nolan had taken a year off to mourn. Grayson wanted to take Nolan into his arms and do whatever he could to comfort him, but he opted to wait for Nolan to finish saying whatever it was he had to say.

Nolan took a deep breath. "Two weeks ago, I got a call from the agency that a mom had picked us to adopt her child. Except now Ricky is gone." Nolan took a deep breath and let it out. "When I told the agency that my family status had changed, they invited me to come out to LA and meet this expectant mom, so that's what I did."

Nolan was right. This was not what Grayson had expected. "So... wait. You're adopting a baby? That's why you went to LA?" Of all things, this wasn't even in the same universe as what Grayson had been imagining Nolan would say. A baby? Holy shit!

"Yes, it looks that way. I mean, the mother, Angela, took a few days to think about it, but I guess whatever I told her about wanting to be a father really got to her, because she picked me. The baby's due in about seven weeks. I still have to talk to Helena about it, because it's going to mess with our schedule a little. But the Cruz and Dunlop houses should be done by then. And that just leaves Justin and Peter's house, out of the episodes we've committed to so far. So maybe we could take a little break in the middle of filming. Of course, I'll hire a nanny, but—"

"You're adopting a baby."

"Yes. It's a girl, by the way."

Well, damn. Nolan's words charmed Grayson— how could they not?—especially the way Nolan smiled when he said it. He *wanted* this. The timing might not be ideal, but he really wanted to be a dad. He spoke about the whole situation in kind of a detached way, but Grayson had gotten good at reading Nolan. He could tell by Nolan's facial expressions that this meant a lot to him.

Grayson couldn't believe he'd be dating a single dad. How weird was that?

"Congratulations," said Grayson.

"The thing that really sucks is… I don't want to stop seeing you."

"Who says you have to?"

Nolan sighed and rolled his eyes. "I can't possibly ask you to stay involved with me once I become a parent. You never signed on to be a dad too."

"No, but…. Wait, *are* you breaking up with me? Because I won't accept that."

"What do you mean, you won't accept it?"

Grayson stood because sitting next to Nolan was making him nervous. "You can't say all those things about how awesome I am and how I helped you wake up from the stupor you've been in the last year and then tell me I have to leave because your home situation is changing. If we care about each other and are still compatible, we shouldn't break up."

"Come on, Gray, think about this logically. I'm about to become a father. Do you understand how much my life will change? And you're… you're young. You have so much ahead of you. I'm at the point in my life where if I don't do this now, I'll soon be too old. And I don't want my life to pass me by like that. So I'm doing this. But you, you should be young and have fun and do stupid things and, God, just be twenty-five. You don't want to be saddled with an old man and a kid."

Well, now Nolan was just pissing him off. "Okay, first of all, forty is not old."

Nolan sighed.

"Second, it is not up to you what I choose to do with my life. It's up to me. And right now, I am on my way to becoming an interior designer with his own TV show. And I've been slowly falling in love with the most amazing man. I will not have you tell me that we can't be together just because you're forty and about to be a dad and I'm twenty-five. That's not fair to me at all."

"You're falling—"

"I don't know." Grayson would die on the spot if Nolan made fun of him for saying that, so he plowed right over it. "Maybe. I do care about you a lot. I think that working together, we're creating some really great homes for people, and spending time together off camera is creating something really special between us as well. Is it going to last forever? Who knows? Maybe it won't last until the end of filming. But I will not let you just cut me out of your life. Not when I know that deep down, you care about me as much as I care about you."

Nolan stared at him for a long moment, not saying anything. Grayson had paced as he talked, but now he stood right in front of Nolan.

"Are you done?" Nolan asked.

Grayson wanted to run screaming from this apartment, actually, but he held his ground. "Yes."

Nolan stood. "It's not that I want to break up, because I don't. But I think you'll see, when the baby arrives, that our relationship will change. And that baby is going to have to be my first priority. I just thought that maybe if we parted ways romantically now, we could survive the pain and disappointment and continue to do the show together. But in two months, when we're in deeper? It'll suck a lot more."

"Maybe. Or maybe everything will work out."

Nolan raised an eyebrow. "How? Are you saying you want to co-parent this baby with me?"

Well, there was a terrifying thought. Grayson had been compartmentalizing this as "my boyfriend will have a baby," not "we will parent this child together." He wasn't actually eager to be a father; he hadn't thought about kids, not really. He supposed he'd have to give some thought to what it would mean to stay with Nolan, if there was some future for them. But this information was too new, and Grayson couldn't process it.

"Not necessarily," said Grayson. "But rather than having you tell me how I feel or what I want to do, I want to be able to make those decisions for myself. And right now, I say I don't want to break up."

"You're delusional if you think this will work."

"So are you breaking up with me anyway?"

Nolan sighed again. He seemed tired. But he put his hands on Grayson's shoulders and said, "I guess not."

"'Cause we could be one of those cutesy Restoration Channel couples that live in, like, Arkansas and have two cute little babies that run around the construction site in tiny hard hats while their parents renovate homes. Except we're gay and live in New York City."

Nolan laughed at that. "Gray, my life is about to change so much."

That was starting to sink in. Grayson nodded. "I don't know about this whole fatherhood thing, but you have come to mean a lot to me, and I want to help you in any way that I can. If that means listening or if that means just fucking your brains out, I am here for either option. Or anything else in between."

"All right. I hear you."

Grayson put his hands on Nolan's waist. "Where are you gonna put the crib and all that?"

"I was thinking between my bed and the kitchen. I could buy another privacy screen. But she won't really care about privacy until some years in the future, and maybe I'll decide living in a loft is not conducive to…. What?"

"I love listening to you talk about this. It's clear you're very excited about it."

"Yeah, well. Two years. It took them two years to call me."

Grayson nodded. "Maybe I'm not thinking straight because you just gave me a lot of information, but I think this could all work out."

"Yeah?"

"Yeah." Grayson kissed Nolan.

Nolan immediately pressed against Grayson. This was good. They were about the same height—well, Nolan was slightly taller—but when they kissed like this, when Nolan reached for Grayson, it felt like they were on equal footing. Nolan was no longer the expert and Grayson the apprentice. Nolan wasn't the one with fifteen years more life experience. They were just two people who desired each other, who needed each other.

"Take me to bed," Grayson whispered.

"Yes. Come on."

Chapter Sixteen

THREE DAYS later, Grayson could tell that something had changed between them. Nolan had clearly wanted to talk about his impending fatherhood. Apparently being so secretive about it meant he hadn't had anyone to talk to. But Grayson's stubborn refusal to let Nolan push him away had opened the floodgates. Grayson didn't have regrets—not really—but he had to admit, he could happily go a whole day without discussing how to put a baby to sleep in a crib or what brand of diapers was best.

Now Nolan had thirty paint chips laid down in a geometric array on the big table in the studio and was staring at them as if they might magically move around and reveal the right color story to him.

The Cruzes had proved to be the sort of indecisive couple who would look at a bunch of samples and become crippled with indecision, overwhelmed by the choices. Whenever they were presented with more than one option, they froze. It was like when Grayson scrolled through Netflix if he was home alone at night and couldn't decide what to watch. Grayson had essentially asked them to tell him what they did *not* like and then declared he and Nolan would do the choosing. The only things they didn't like were tile floors, anything that looked too industrial, like polished concrete, and Jason had a weird thing about wallpaper.

"I think we should do a feature wall in the living room, but I can't settle on which color I like for it."

Nolan frowned at the paint samples. He'd also clearly become overwhelmed by the many choices. Grayson half wondered if—like Grayson choosing to watch a show he'd seen for the fourth time because he couldn't decide on which new thing to watch—Nolan would just revert back to beige. During his heyday as a designer, Nolan had been known for bold colors, but in the past couple of years, his designs had gotten very neutral. He seemed interested in colors again now, but sometimes he rejected Grayson's color ideas in favor of neutrals. Beige was Nolan's safe space, his comfort zone. But these clients didn't want beige. They wanted the old Nolan Hamlin.

"What's the theme again?" Grayson asked.

"Urban Islands, I'm calling it. Caribbean meets Manhattan. So the kitchen color scheme is very urban, but I thought we could go a little more tropical everywhere else."

"What about this pink? It would look really good with the dark brown flooring you picked."

Nolan pressed his lips together. "Yeah, I think you're right. Pops of yellow and blue in the furnishings would make it look very tropical. This pink helps too. But I want it to look chic, not like a cheap hotel in Miami." He picked up a blue paint chip. "You think the lighter shade or the middle shade?"

"Middle. It's brighter. Makes me think of the color of the ocean in mid-century travel posters."

Nolan chuckled. "That's very specific. You're right, though. I've been to Puerto Rico because Ricky had family there. So I can verify that the ocean is close to this color in the Caribbean."

"See that? Decision made. Was that so hard?"

Nolan was cleaning up the paint chips when Helena came in. "Hey, guys, I want to pitch you an idea."

Nolan shot Grayson a look that told him he dreaded whatever Helena was about to say.

She stood at the head of the big table and smiled. "So, we have a six-episode order for the first season. So far we've got the Robertses, the Cruzes, the Dunlops, and the gay couple in the Catskills. They're on board, by the way. I talked to them this morning. So we'll set up a time to go look at their house soon. But we need one more couple."

"I'm no math whiz," said Grayson, "but that still only adds up to five."

"That's why I wanted to pitch something to you. A friend of mine is on the board of Rainbow House. It's a homeless shelter for LGBTQ teens in Manhattan. They have a common room that has been pretty much the same since the nineties. The shelter has been raising money to renovate it, but obviously feeding and clothing these kids is their main priority. So I talked my higher-ups at the Restoration Channel into donating some money, and I thought it would be fun for us to makeover the place. Have it be kind of a special episode."

"Sure," said Nolan. "How big is the space?"

"It's massive. I don't know the exact measurements, but the shelter is built into an old building that used to be a school, and the common room was once a cafeteria. I think it's a job we could do in a week or so, maybe? And rather than hiring labor, we could get the kids to help out with basic stuff like painting. If you want to do any construction, I can talk to Travis. He's actually a carpenter, so he could build cabinets or tables or whatever you want. But we're not, like, messing with plumbing or electrical, I don't think. We'll just be giving the room a facelift."

"So, wait," said Grayson. He felt like there was an angle to this project he wasn't seeing. "Would the kids be on TV? Is the point to highlight the plight of homeless LGBTQ kids?"

"Yes. I mean, I'd like to get this shelter more money in donations because they do such good work and a lot of LGBTQ kids come to New York for all kinds of reasons. We've done charity projects like this on other shows. We just redid a couple of elementary school cafeterias on *House Flippers*, and we renovated a women's shelter on another show last year. Viewers love this kind of thing, and it generates a lot of income for them. And I thought—and I hope you don't mind this—we've got two gay interior designers right here who could help be models to the kids about how things can get better, right?"

"Sure," said Nolan, although now he sounded doubtful.

Grayson thought this was objectively a good idea, but he felt unsettled. His own experience moving to New York had been a bit of a challenge. He worried that talking to homeless kids would bring up a lot of old stuff that he'd rather leave buried.

"It'll be great," said Helena. "I see you guys hesitating, but I think it will be fun. Taking a big room and redesigning it to be more functional while also bring attention to a good cause? *I* think it's a no-brainer. Please say you'll do it."

Nolan looked at Grayson. Grayson understood that he was supposed to say yes here, so he did. "Okay."

Nolan nodded. "Good. Let's do it."

It wasn't that Grayson thought this was a bad idea. Making a better space for some homeless teenagers was obviously a great thing to do. But he knew it might also make him confront some things he'd rather avoid. On the other hand, he could be an adult about this and separate his feelings from the task at hand. It was a project. Nothing more.

Grayson kind of tuned out while Helena and Nolan discussed the best time to go see the shelter. He pretended to study the paint chips Nolan had left out so his face wouldn't betray him. Nolan and Helena seemed to agree on something, and then she said good night and walked toward the door.

"You okay?" Nolan asked after Helena left.

"I'm... yeah. I'm fine." Grayson smiled. "Where do you want to eat tonight?"

SINCE CONSTRUCTION was still going on at the Cruz and Dunlop homes, Nolan and Helena decided there was no time like the present, so he, Grayson, and the whole camera crew drove over to Rainbow House.

The executive director of the shelter knew they were coming, but they'd be ambushing the kids. Nolan had been told that there were seventeen kids currently living at the shelter, and some of them were attending nearby Harvey Milk High School, so they wouldn't be around during the day to help out. He'd seen a couple of photos of the space, and he guessed the bulk of the work would be painting and deciding on new furniture. The project was being sponsored by an online furniture store that would ship anything he wanted for the room in short order.

On the drive over, Nolan said, "Are these kids even going to know who I am? I don't see the point in ambushing them."

Grayson shrugged. He'd been quiet all morning. Something about this project was bothering him, but every time Nolan asked, Grayson said he was fine. Nolan supposed Grayson didn't exactly owe it to Nolan to tell him all of his secrets, especially given the strange limbo status of their relationship—Grayson insisted he wanted to stay, but Nolan suspected he'd bolt as soon as the baby showed up.

But that was a problem for another day. He pulled into the tiny parking lot next to the shelter and parked in the back, careful to stay clear of the basketball court drawn on the blacktop.

A tall man ran out into the parking lot as Nolan was getting out of the car.

"Hello!" the man said. "I'm Marcus Jackson, the executive director of Rainbow House. I'm such a big fan, Mr. Hamlin. It's thrilling to meet you."

Nolan shook his hand. "Nice to meet you too. Do the kids know what's going on?"

"I told them we're filming something for a TV show, but that's really it. So everyone who was around this afternoon is in the common room right now. I figured once your cameras were set up, you could walk in and surprise everyone."

"Are they gonna know who I am?" Nolan said.

"A few of them will. I like to watch Stacey Lewis's show with whoever is around in the common room on weekday mornings."

Helena walked over. "I'll get the cameras set up. You guys chill in the parking lot and I'll come get you when we're ready."

Helena followed Marcus into the building.

"You okay with this?" Nolan asked.

Grayson seemed agitated. He chewed on his thumbnail while they stood there. "Yeah."

Nolan started mentally designing the space rather than trying to force Grayson into conversation. Marcus and Helena came back out about ten minutes later.

"I figured Marcus could bring you in and introduce you to the kids," said Helena. "They're waiting."

"Game face on," Nolan told Grayson.

Grayson managed to pull it together for the ambush. He grinned when he and Nolan entered the common room, which was indeed a huge space. It was also an eyesore. The walls were painted dark blue and chipped in many places, the furniture was all beat up and threadbare, and the whole area felt more like an elementary school cafeteria than a nice common room where teenagers would want to hang out. There were even a couple of cafeteria tables—the long ones with bench seating attached that could be folded up—on one side of the room.

The kids seemed excited. There were ten teenagers in the room who all hopped up and yelled when Nolan and Grayson walked in.

Since Grayson was still being weird, Nolan took the lead. "We're here," he explained, "to make this space fabulous!"

The kids all cheered.

At Helena's suggestion, they all sat down on the sad old sofas in one corner of the room, and Nolan started peppering the kids with questions about what wasn't working about the space.

A girl with long, dark hair who introduced herself as Marisol said, "Well, the furniture sucks. It's not comfortable. It's old. It's ugly."

"Right," said Nolan. "Easy fix."

"It's so dark," said a boy with purple hair named Ander. "It's not bad during the day when we open the curtains, but at night it can be hard to see in here."

"Okay. We can fix that too. I mean, the color on the walls is contributing to that."

"It would be cool," said a nonbinary kid named Sam, "if we could have, like, zones? Like, we've got all these books that were donated, but they're in those bins in the corner, and I hate trying to sort through them. I was thinking it would be cool if they were all in book-cases in one corner and there were some nice chairs for reading."

"Maybe we could put a game table over there," said a skinny boy named Ben. "Carlos and I play table-top games sometimes."

"Sure, we can do that," Nolan said.

And they went around like that. Grayson dutifully took notes on his phone. When one of the kids asked him if he was texting someone, he said he wasn't, just that he was writing down everything they said so he'd remember it later.

Once Nolan had a fuzzy idea of what he wanted to do—new paint, new floors, bookshelves, storage cabinets, and the whole space divided into zones—he decided he wanted to chat with the kids a little to solidify his ideas for what they'd find useful. "Why don't you each tell us a little about yourselves. It doesn't have to be anything personal, but I'd like to get to know you all a little to help us finalize what we want to do with the space."

It started off innocently enough. Marisol was sixteen and a sophomore in high school. She wanted to be an engineer and seemed excited about the plans for any construction work they might do. Sam loved to read but added that they were living in Rainbow House because their parents didn't understand their gender. Ben had been kicked out of his house when he'd gotten in trouble at school for kissing a boy. But the kicker was poor Ander, whose single mom was an evangelical preacher at a big church upstate and who had disowned Ander when he came out.

Nolan hadn't been looking at Grayson as each kid started telling their sob story, so he was surprised when Grayson stood and said, "Would you excuse me for a moment?" Then he left the room.

They were basically done with all the information they needed. Nolan wanted to finalize a few things with Marcus, but he wondered if he should go after Grayson.

"It was really great to meet all of you," Nolan said. "We're gonna ask you guys to help us out with a few tasks to save some money, but we'll get professionals in here for most of the hard work. I don't want you guys to take time away from school or whatever else you've got going on, so just come by the common room when you're available and I'll put you to work. Sound good?"

"Can I ask you a question?" asked a really big kid named Brian.

"Sure."

"You're queer, right?"

"As a three-dollar bill," said Nolan.

"You still in touch with your parents?"

"I am. They live upstate. My mom and I are pretty close."

Brian took this in. "My mami, she lives in the Bronx. She says she still loves me, but I wore a dress one time, and she says I can't stay at the apartment anymore because it's a bad influence on my brothers and sisters." Brian rolled his eyes. "You got kids?"

"No."

"You married?"

"I was. He… died."

"Oh. I'm sorry." Brian frowned. "That sucks."

Nolan let out a surprised laugh. "Yeah. It does."

"This house is really important to us, so make it look good, okay?"

"Of course."

Nolan moved to find Grayson. When Marcus approached, he put out his hand. "Hey, Marcus, can you wait like two minutes? I need to find out what happened to Grayson. Once I make sure he's okay, I'll come back and we can work out a work schedule."

"Yes, absolutely. Go find him."

Nolan retraced his steps to the parking lot and found Grayson leaning against the exterior wall of the building.

He was sobbing.

Nolan ran to him and pulled him into his arms. "Oh, Gray, oh, honey, what is wrong?"

Grayson didn't say anything at first. He just clung to Nolan's shirt and continued to cry into his shoulder.

"If I had known, I would have come sooner," Nolan said. "I didn't realize—"

"My parents kicked me out three years ago," said Grayson.

Nolan held Grayson closer and stroked his hair. He hadn't even had a clue. Grayson rarely talked about his family and seemed so happy-go-lucky all the time. It had never occurred to Nolan that he might have this kind of trauma in his background. Then again, when he thought about it, Grayson *had* said a few things that made Nolan think his New England upbringing was not always good or healthy. He'd never been explicit or said he was unhappy, he'd just dropped comments here or there. But Nolan hadn't ever imagined it was this bad.

He held Grayson for a few minutes and felt it when Grayson started to calm down.

"You don't have to talk about it," Nolan said, "but you can if you want to."

Grayson pulled away slightly. He leaned against the wall again but didn't go far from Nolan. He took a deep breath and started to talk. He spoke slowly and kept having to stop to catch his breath.

"I came to New York for college, and I had this life-changing experience where I had the freedom to be myself and meet people like me. I found this whole new family here. But I graduated from design school and I was broke, so I went back home. Only by then, I couldn't go back in the closet."

He gasped, his breath shaky. Nolan reached over and took his hand, but Grayson kept going. "My dad never liked that I wanted to do anything artistic. He didn't like that he was spending all this money on a school where I learned to be a designer. I mean, what value does decorating a room even have?"

Nolan understood the question to be rhetorical, so he didn't interrupt to argue in defense of his profession. Instead, he squeezed Grayson's hand.

"I think my being queer was the last straw for them. And, I don't know. I wanted them to know me, the real me, and I thought they loved me and it would be okay. But it wasn't." Grayson's voice shook. "I didn't have a job lined up when I graduated. I figured I'd go back home, wait tables for a bit, save some money, and then come back to New York and find work. But my parents said I couldn't stay there anymore. I had, like, three hundred dollars to my name. I was driving this old junker of a car that I'd gotten as a gift for my eighteenth birthday, so I loaded everything that would fit into it and drove to New York. So basically I spent the next six months couch surfing. And when I couldn't find a couch to sleep on, I slept in my car."

Nolan put a hand over his mouth. He couldn't imagine being young and sleeping in a car in New York City. "That must have been scary."

"Terrifying. I kept worrying someone would steal my car and I'd lose everything."

Nolan's heart broke for Grayson. Seeing Grayson open and vulnerable like this… it did something to Nolan. He'd never expected that Grayson had this kind of depth. That all he wanted to do was make it better surprised Nolan. He wanted to make a home for Grayson, one he'd never be thrown out of, full of love and empty of judgment. Realizing this was astonishing.

Grayson squeezed Nolan's hand. "I finally got a job as an apprentice at a big design agency, and it paid peanuts, but at least I had money to rent a room in my current apartment. I had to sell my car to make rent one month, but still. I can't tell you what it means for me that you picked *me* to help you out with this show. I hope you know that you changed my life. Even if things with us don't work out, even if the show only has one season, this has opened so many doors for me and, hell, just the regular paycheck itself is life-changing."

Nolan took Grayson into his arms and hugged him close. "I had no idea."

"The only people that do are my parents and the friends whose couches I crashed on. I don't like to talk about it."

"I won't push you to say more than you're comfortable with, but you can tell me anything. If you need to talk about it, I'm here."

Grayson shot Nolan a watery smile. "I like to think I've made my peace with it. My parents didn't want me? Fine. I'll make my own way in the world."

"And you have. You have." That Grayson had learned how to survive in New York with nothing impressed Nolan. Nolan didn't think he could have done it.

"So, okay." Grayson sniffed and wiped at his eyes. "I'm sorry. I fudged some of my credentials. I *did* design that wedding, and I did do some work for a big agency. But I only really have two years of experience, and I—"

"You're a great designer, Gray. You have good instincts. I don't care if you fudged anything."

Grayson sighed into Nolan's shoulder. "I'm really sorry about walking out of there, but this is so fucking hard. Listening to those kids talk, it just brought up every terrible thing I've ever thought about myself. About how I disappointed my parents, how I wasn't good enough for them, how deep down, I'm still just this fucked-up queer kid who nobody wants. All of that came back and I felt overwhelmed."

"Your parents are fools for not wanting you. You're amazing."

"Yeah, well." Grayson pulled away and wiped at his eyes again. "I know I've been quiet all day, but I had a feeling this would be hard. I was worried I'd freak out, and I sure enough, I did, right on cue. I thought I could compartmentalize everything, but being confronted with it… I don't know. It's so hard. And, at least I was twenty-two. I can't imagine what it's like being a teenager and getting tossed out of the house."

"That's why places like this exist."

"Yeah."

"You know, it might be cathartic for you to put some work into this space. Make a good home for these kids so that nobody has to go through what you did again."

"Yeah. I think I'd like that." Grayson took a deep breath and wiped his eyes. "I must look a mess."

"You're fine. I have a couple of things to work out with Marcus before we can leave, but then I'll take you home, okay?"

"Yeah. Do you mind if I sit in the car? I need a few minutes to myself."

"Sure, no problem." Nolan handed Grayson the keys.

Nolan then leaned over and kissed Grayson. He wondered if the move was inappropriate under the circumstances, but then Grayson hooked his hand behind Nolan's head and held him there. They kissed for a long moment, but the longer they stood here, the later they'd get home. So Nolan pulled away and said, "I'll only be a few minutes."

It wasn't until he was walking back into the building that he realized he'd told Grayson he was taking him "home," and that he'd meant his loft, as if Grayson belonged there. And maybe he did. Except that soon, there'd be a baby.

Lord, what was Nolan getting himself into?

Chapter Seventeen

AFTER THE waterworks outside the night before, Grayson felt somewhat embarrassed to be walking back into Rainbow House, but he was here, he was queer, and he was ready to get rolling on this redesign.

He hated that he'd broken down in front of Nolan, but Nolan had been so sweet to him the rest of the night. They'd gotten dinner delivered and then snuggled on the sofa to watch the dumb primetime soap Grayson was really into. Then they'd made love in Nolan's bed for what felt like half the night, and Nolan had held him tightly afterward.

Finally Nolan had decided it was time to talk. "My life is open. You probably know everything there is to know about me. The great pain of my life is Ricky. And I guess I kept you at arm's length because I didn't want to get you tangled up in the dark ugliness of my grief, because you seemed so, I don't know, young and happy—as if nothing ever bothered you. But now that I see your pain, I don't know. I want to take it from you and make it better."

"I feel the same way about you. I don't want you to hurt anymore," Grayson said.

Nolan had cried a little then too, but rather than finding it off-putting, Grayson thought it beautiful.

Maybe the lesson here was that intimacy came from vulnerability—Nolan would never truly understand him without knowing where he came from. And now Nolan knew about all his demons and hadn't, for one moment, hesitated to take Grayson in and hold him close.

They'd crossed some kind of line now, and Grayson didn't think there was any going back.

He knew he'd cry again, probably with a camera rolling, while they worked on this project, but he also thought he'd gotten the worst of it out of his system.

He surveyed the common room now and took it all in. "It's even more hideous in the daylight."

"I know," said Nolan. He turned to Marcus. "Okay. First order of business is to get everything out of here. There's a dumpster in the parking lot, so let's get the kids in here and unload it all. What are we keeping?"

"Well, the books, we should keep," said Marcus. "You can put the bins in my office. Pretty much everything else can go."

There were six kids available, so they teamed up and unloaded everything. Happily, the old, cheap furniture wasn't very heavy. None of it was salvageable, so it all went in the dumpster. Then Nolan got some of the kids to help him roll up the old carpet, which was stained with God only knew what. That, too, went in the dumpster.

Brian, the big kid Grayson had met the day before, came over to him. "So, Marcus said that probably everyone from the show working on this project would be queer. Does that mean you too?"

"Yup," said Grayson. He didn't love how forward this kid was, but he wanted Brian and all the shelter residents to feel comfortable with him and Nolan. "And Travis, our contractor, is dating a guy too. Maybe that's the unexpected one. I don't know if anyone is really shocked when interior designers are gay."

"I guess not. And Nolan is *hot*." Brian pronounced the *T* hard.

Grayson wanted to snap that Nolan was taken, but no one on the show knew they were a couple. So instead he said, "Nolan *is* hot, but I think he's seeing someone. He's also, like, twenty-five years older than you are."

"Sure, I know. Just saying."

In the end, they were left with a giant room with high ceilings and an echo, now that the carpet and furniture were gone. Nolan stood in the middle of it and looked around.

"This is going to be so great, guys," Nolan said. "Travis is coming tomorrow, and I'm going to put him to work building some shelving and other things. I called in a favor, and we've got flooring coming on Thursday. But tomorrow, if any of you are available, I want to get this place painted. That's going to be our main task. And then after Thursday, I'm kicking you all out. No peeking until we finish the design, which will probably be Sunday night."

The kids all nodded.

Before the meeting—Marcus, Helena, and eight kids standing in a circle looking at Grayson and Nolan—broke, Grayson took a step forward. "I just wanted to apologize for walking out yesterday. I freaked out a little, but it's because I was homeless myself for about six months when I was twenty-two. And like a lot of you, it was because my parents kicked me out for being gay. So I want you to know I understand what a lot of you are living through right now, but this place!" Grayson looked around. "If I had known places like this existed, it would have made such a difference in my life. So I give you my promise that this is not just a job for me. For either of us."

He looked at Nolan. Nolan nodded.

"This is personal," Grayson continued. "I want to make this place a space where you'll be able to come and feel like you're at home. Yeah?"

"Yeah," the kids all murmured.

They went back to the studio after that. Nolan fiddled with the floor plan while Grayson worked the phones to see about getting furniture delivered by the weekend. The sponsor who was donating it had a warehouse in New Jersey, and to save time and shipping costs, he offered to let them just take whatever they wanted if they could get a truck down there. "I think we should be able to arrange that," said Grayson, hoping it was true. His next call was to Helena, who said that a truck could definitely be arranged.

That settled, Grayson went over to Nolan, who had actually penciled a lot of things into the room.

"So here are my thoughts," Nolan said. "We basically divide the space into five zones. This corner here is the reading nook. I'm gonna ask Travis to build some custom bookcases so we can put all those books on display. Maybe even see if we can get some more donated. It'd be nice if they had books with queer characters and not just, like, *Moby Dick* and *The Scarlet Letter*. I have a friend in publishing. I'll give him a call, and maybe we can pull something together. At least maybe he'll give me some titles and I can buy them myself."

"Cool. Sounds good."

"Okay. This area over here is for the tabletop gamers. I figured we could maybe put in some high tops and stools. And more shelving to store games. Then over here, the lounge. Big comfy seating and a smart TV so they can stream stuff. Maybe a video game console too. Depends on what we can get in donations. And then over here will just be a hangout space, basically. Couches, room for people to sit and chat. Maybe a mini fridge for snacks and beverages. In the middle, I want to put a huge table. I'll ask Travis for help with that too. Marcus said they eat most of their meals in the kitchen, but the table could still be a communal meal spot or just a place to sit and do homework or study together or whatever. What do you think?"

"I think it's a great plan. What are we doing for colors?"

"Not a hundred percent, but I was thinking light walls and floors. Maybe off-white or cream paint. Did you know the Restoration Channel has its own paint line? I can use whatever I want from the store room on the fourteenth floor as long as I flash the label at the camera when we're filming. What do you think of cream or off-white for the walls?"

"I think that's fine. You don't want anything too dark or it will absorb light."

"Right, exactly. The windows aren't very big when you consider the size of the space. I want to replace those heinous fluorescent lights with some more modern light fixtures too. Nothing fancy, they can be fairly utilitarian."

"This sounds like a great plan."

"I want it to be a space that teenagers actually want to hang out in. It shouldn't feel so prison cafeteria, you know? And Marcus said they do a lot of programming for LGBTQ kids in the region, so the space is used by more than just the kids who live in the shelter. We'll have to pick durable materials for the floor and the furniture. Speaking of which, how'd it go with the furniture guy?"

Grayson explained about the warehouse and the truck.

"Okay. Cool. Good. This might actually come together." Nolan rolled up the floor plan and slid it into a tube so he could take it with him to the site the next day. "How are you doing?"

"I'm… okay. It actually felt good to talk to those kids today. Well, Brian is a lot."

Nolan laughed. "He is, yes."

"It feels good to be doing this for them. It's a shame that any of them have to be homeless at all, but at least they have a place like Rainbow House to go to. So I want to make the space look amazing." And Grayson felt that deep in his gut. He'd meant everything he'd said to the kids earlier.

"Good. I think it will be." Nolan leaned over and kissed Grayson. "Fun fact. I did your laundry a couple of nights ago. So you've probably got enough clean clothes at my place that you don't have to go home tonight if you don't want to."

Wow. How great was Nolan? "I really don't want to go home. I'll have to, at some point this week, but the clothes help."

At this point, Grayson *was* keeping a lot of stuff at Nolan's. Partly, it was convenient. Nolan lived within walking distance of the Restoration Channel studios, so it was easier to walk home with him than go back to Brooklyn sometimes. Grayson had started bringing

overnight bags when he knew he'd want to stay at Nolan's and then just… leaving clothes behind. But now
Nolan's loft was starting to feel like home much more
than the room in Grayson's apartment had ever done.

Still, though, Grayson knew better than to invite
himself to move in with Nolan. Nolan probably wasn't
ready for that, especially considering all the changes
that would have to happen when the new arrival showed
up. Though he didn't like it, Grayson knew it was smart
to wait to make any decisions until after the baby came.
That was what Nolan would tell him.

And besides, Grayson really did have to decide
if living with a baby was what he wanted. Because
moving into Nolan's home, being his partner, meant
Grayson would have to be a father too. Otherwise, there
was no way to make it work. He couldn't just be fun
Uncle Grayson.

But that decision was still six weeks away.

Nolan yawned. "Well, now that we've sorted that,
I'm tired. Also, I've been wanting pizza all day. Is that
weird?"

"One of the kids mentioned it and I've been wanting pizza every minute since."

"That must be why. I'm gonna call the place on
Sixteenth and we can pick it up on the way home."

EVERYTHING IN the Rainbow House common room
came together more easily than Nolan had expected.
He'd picked a slightly boring but neutral cream col-
or for the walls, and the kids had spent an entire day
painting. But on the wall at the end of the room, he and
his crew had decided to do something different. He let
Grayson pick the color, and they'd painted it vibrant

electric blue, just for fun. Grayson suggested that the kids could add a mural there at some point in the future if they wanted. Though some of the kids seemed game, there wasn't enough time to squeeze it into this week.

Travis got his boyfriend Brandon to come to the site, and together they got four bookcases and the big table built with remarkable speed. Travis and Brandon also did most of the flooring install themselves. While they were doing that, Nolan and Grayson drove a rental truck to a warehouse in Elizabeth, where they picked out some plush bluish-gray sofas in a durable fabric that was machine washable. They also got some matching chairs and end tables and a mess of accessories—pillows, blankets, ottomans—and loaded it all into the truck.

Then they spent all day Saturday pulling it all together. Travis and Brandon had done a tremendous job on the bookcases. Grayson put all the books on shelves, and Nolan's friend Stephen came by with a box of books donated by the publisher he worked for. They also got a TV donated from the electronics store where one of Grayson's roommates worked *and* the hottest new gaming console and a few games. Nolan took a break to walk to a department store near Union Square and bought a bunch of board games that he carried back to set up in the gaming area.

Overall, Nolan was pleased with the design. Timeless, clean, durable, functional. It was so much brighter and warmer now. He thought the kids would be thrilled.

In lieu of the mural, each of the kids had also made a drawing, so Nolan framed them and hung them on the blue wall.

After they finished decorating that night, Nolan took Grayson home. Grayson seemed mildly irritated that the purple shirt he wanted to wear for the reveal was in Brooklyn, but he found clothes he was willing to wear on television the next morning, partly by raiding Nolan's closet.

"So you *do* own things that aren't T-shirts," he said, trying on one of Nolan's more formal button-down shirts.

"A few things," said Nolan, who was currently wearing a maroon T-shirt.

"You could at least wear a scarf or something. We gotta impress these kids with how successful you are."

"I like to be comfortable."

"Mm-hmm." Grayson had a cotton scarf that he threw over Nolan's head and draped around his shoulders. "Yes, I like that."

"Okay, fine."

Grayson grinned at him. And, okay, Nolan liked putting that expression on Grayson's face.

They walked the few blocks down to the Restoration Offices hand-in-hand, which helped Nolan realize two things. First, he was still the sort of celebrity that people generally ignored. He got a few "Do I know you from somewhere?" looks from passersby whenever he was out in public, but no one had stopped him to ask for an autograph since he'd moved to New York City. That hadn't happened in LA, where he'd been ambushed at least once a week. At first he'd thought it was just because he'd been out of the spotlight for so long, but he was lately realizing that celebrity culture was just different in New York City. He and Grayson had even eaten at a café near the loft and sat two tables away from Sarah Jessica Parker, and no one had so much as batted an eyelash at her.

Second, he realized he didn't care who knew he and Grayson were together. They'd crossed some kind of line, and he'd stopped treating their relationship as if it were a secret. Nolan wasn't sure when exactly the line had been crossed—maybe when Grayson had finally opened up to him about his past—but it was definitely in the rearview mirror now. If Helena discovered they were together, so be it.

When they arrived at the front of the building, Helena did indeed give them a hairy eyeball.

"Arriving together, are you?" she said.

Nolan shrugged as if it wasn't a big deal, although it very much was. Something had definitely changed. He couldn't quite define it yet, but he didn't feel he needed to either.

Talk to him in six weeks, though.

They all piled into the company SUVs and arrived at Rainbow House twenty minutes later. When Marcus let them in, he told them that the kids hadn't been allowed to see the room yet, so they were all wound up and excited to see it. The camera crew followed Nolan and Grayson in, and they both did some last-minute tweaking, primarily for show. Nolan looked around, thinking they'd done a pretty good job. The room was bright and colorful—definitely more to Grayson's taste aesthetically, but appealing to Nolan as well.

"We use this room for community events as well," Marcus said as they stood outside the room, waiting for the kids to arrive. "We have a club that meets here once a month, and sometimes we bring in guest speakers. We'd love to have you two back sometime.

Maybe you can talk about some of the choices you made in the space."

"Sure," said Nolan.

Marcus nodded. "I think it's helpful for the kids to see successful LGBTQ people. And, actually, before we let everyone in, I want to introduce you to Ellen, who doesn't want to be on camera."

"Okay," said Grayson.

Marcus called down the hall. "Ellen?"

A thin, pretty girl with long brown hair appeared. She walked forward and held out a hand. "Nice to meet you," she said.

"Hi," said Nolan. "Nice to meet you, too."

Ellen smiled slowly. "It's my dream to be an interior designer when I graduate. The kids here tease me about how much Restoration Channel I watch. But I don't even care, because I love it so much. Did you go to design school?"

"We both did, yes," said Nolan. "Me much longer ago than Grayson."

Grayson rolled his eyes. "Stop acting like you're an old man. You're not that old."

Ellen smiled and nodded. "I go to Harvey Milk. My grades are good, so I think I'll get in. Marcus is helping me apply for scholarships."

"Good," said Nolan. "That's really good. I hope you like the space we designed."

"I'll have to look later. I… I don't want my family to know where I am."

Nolan's heart sank. This poor girl. "I'm sorry to hear that."

She crossed her arms. "I'm trans," she said. "They refuse to acknowledge my chosen name or my real gender. I wasn't safe at home, but I'm worried that if they find me, they'll make me go back. So I came here, and everyone at Rainbow House has been amazing."

"I'm very glad you're safe now," said Nolan. "I hope you become a stellar interior designer."

"Thanks. I wish I could be on TV, but I just don't want…. Well, I'm glad I got to meet you, though. I've admired your work for a long time, Mr. Hamlin."

"Call me Nolan. And thank you."

Grayson had gotten very quiet. Nolan suspected he was thinking about his own traumatic past. Nolan reached over and touched Grayson's shoulder. Grayson nodded slightly, then turned to Marcus. "You do good work here."

Ellen left and the rest of the kids showed up. Grayson shook it off and signaled to the camera to start filming. "Are you kids ready to look at your new common room?"

The kids all cheered.

"All right, let's go take a look," Nolan said for the camera.

The common room had big double doors, so it made quite a dramatic moment for Nolan and Grayson to each take a door and open up the room. The kids then walked into their new space, filling the room with oohs and aahs and little squeals of delight.

Nolan and Grayson took turns walking the kids through each zone. Grayson was a little subdued, and by the time it was his turn to explain the TV area, emotion made his voice crack. He had to pause for a moment before saying, "I'm sorry. Happy tears, I promise! I'm just so thrilled we could make this great space for you. I wish I'd had something like this when I was younger."

Marisol stepped forward and gave Grayson a hug, and then all the kids joined into the group hug and pulled Nolan into it too.

"Aw, you guys don't have to do this," Grayson said.

"We love the new room!" said Marisol. "I don't think we can hug you enough."

Then the kids immediately settled into their spaces. Two of them turned on the TV to play with the game console. Sam found a comfy couch in the reading area and sat down with a book.

As they finished the tour, Marcus carried in a stack of pizzas and put them on the big table in the middle. They brought Travis in too, so the kids could properly thank him for his carpentry work.

"I didn't think it would matter," said Marisol while the cameras were still rolling, "but having an LGBTQ team work the renovation was a really good idea. I think you guys understood what we would need better than anyone else would. I mean, the books you brought in, the DVDs you got, the way you organized the space, all this color! It's so great."

Grayson had been responsible for a lot of the color choices, but Nolan liked it, too. It was a bright, happy space. Grayson wiped at his eyes. "It was our pleasure," he said, sounding watery.

"It really was," said Nolan, getting a little misty himself. "None of you should have to be here—you should all be with loving families—but I hope that you can find a family here. As a gay man, I can speak to the importance of chosen family."

Grayson nodded vigorously. "My chosen family is everything. And family is important."

Nolan was hit with a pang, thinking of family. He had good relationships with most of his genetic family, but the friendships he'd developed over the years, as well as the family he'd tried building for himself, were important to him. He thought again about that baby girl who would soon be part of his life. Would Grayson stay? Would they make a new family? It was overwhelming to think about so much change in such a short amount of time. But it made Nolan happy too. He smiled at the kids.

They stayed for dinner and ate pizza and chatted with the group, promising Marcus they'd come back to check in. Grayson also offered to volunteer if the house ever needed an extra pair of hands. He said he thought it would be healing for him to help out.

Nolan realized Grayson wasn't that much older than these kids. The oldest was twenty-one. Suddenly Nolan felt ancient.

Lord. He'd felt every emotion today, hadn't he?

Grayson came home with him that night because he didn't want to be alone.

"Speaking of chosen family," Grayson said over wine as they sat beside each other on the sofa. "Would it be weird for you to meet my friends?"

"Why would it be weird?"

"I don't know. I have a hard time picturing you all in the same room, but I don't know why. Maybe we could all go out together sometime? I was thinking maybe drinks at this bar I like in the West Village."

"Okay."

"Next week, maybe?"

Nolan wanted to make Grayson happy, which was a strange thing to realize. Drinks were easy. Nolan had once thrived in social situations; he should be able to again. It seemed important to Grayson to have Nolan meet his friends too, so Nolan would do it, even though he was enjoying the bubble he and Grayson currently lived in.

"Sure, we can do drinks with your friends next week."

"Cool. I've told them I'm seeing someone but not that it's you. It'll be an interesting surprise."

"Will it be an issue?"

"I doubt it. I mean, my friend Danny is going to fanboy, fair warning, but everyone else should be cool."

Nolan chuckled. "All right. I can manage that."

Grayson smiled. "What about you? Do you have friends you'd like me to meet?"

"Most of my social circle is still in LA."

"Are you going to tell anyone about the baby? Have a baby shower or anything like that?"

"I don't know. I'm still kind of getting my social bearings back in New York. And I'm worried about jinxing it." Nolan glanced toward the area between his bed and the kitchen that he planned to make the baby's section of the loft. "That's why I haven't bought anything for the baby yet. I guess part of me is worried that if I do, Angela will change her mind and then I will have made all these changes for nothing."

"Isn't her due date soon? What if you get the call tomorrow and have to go to LA?"

"Yeah. I guess I'd better get moving. No party, though. I can't really deal with a party. But I guess I could register. My mother keeps asking me what I need."

"Yeah? Is she excited about being a grandma?"

"Overjoyed." Nolan had to smile at that. He'd called her when he'd gotten home from LA and filled her in. Nolan was an only child, but somehow he hadn't realized his mother's dream of grandchildren had died with Ricky. Being able to tell her it was possible again had brought Nolan a lot of joy too.

Of course, there was also Grayson. Nolan hadn't told his mother about him yet. Maybe it was time to have that conversation.

Grayson leaned over and kissed Nolan's cheek. "It'll be okay."

"Do I look worried it won't be?"

"Yes."

"Oh." Nolan sighed and sagged against the sofa cushions. "Well, yeah, I guess I am. I've just had so much… happen. In the last year, I mean. I guess I'd lost faith that things will work out. I'm sure everything will be okay, but I'm not counting on it until it happens."

"That's fair."

Nolan put his wineglass on the coffee table. "Can you do something for me?"

"Anything," said Grayson.

"I don't want to think about any of this until tomorrow. Make me forget?"

Grayson raised his eyebrow. "With pleasure."

Chapter Eighteen

TWO DAYS later, they drove out to the Cruz house to see how construction was going.

Mike had the full set of plans for the house, so his job was mostly to make Nolan and Grayson's vision a reality. Nolan was happy to see that the house had walls again. Drywall was finished, and currently part of the crew was painting while the other was installing flooring and tile. Mike explained that the kitchen cabinets were expected to be delivered on Monday and the counters the day after, and from there they'd only need another day or two for final touches.

"What about landscaping?" Nolan asked.

Mike opened his mouth to say something, but suddenly someone called him from the other room. "Will you excuse me?"

"Sure. We'll meet you out back."

Nolan didn't have extensive plans for the big backyard, but it was one of the main reasons the Cruzes had bought this house. Nolan wanted to at least lay down some grass seed on a couple of the bald patches and plant a tree or two.

The yard was a hive of activity, though. The production team had set a table with an awning overhead where they were dispensing food and beverages to the construction crew all day. And the crew was also using the back patio as an area to set up a big circular saw that they were currently using to cut tile and floorboards.

While Grayson and Nolan discussed putting a couple of shrubs around the back deck, Mike walked back over to them.

"Everything okay?" asked Nolan.

"Yeah, sorry," said Mike. "The guys here keep asking for my sign-off before they do anything. On one hand, that's good, because they're not making major changes without running them by me. But it's not really necessary. Everyone here knows what they're doing." He paused and smiled. "Okay, what's up?"

They went over the landscape plan before Mike was called away again. Grayson also wandered off because he wanted to see what the construction crew was doing. So Nolan just hung out in the backyard for a few minutes, watching activity buzz around him. The camera crew packed up too, saying they'd gotten enough for the day. Nolan figured he'd wait for Grayson to finish doing whatever he was doing, and then they'd pack it in and head home. In the meantime, he took some photos of the back of the house with his phone so that he could show them to someone at the plant nursery and get some advice about what would look best there. Nolan had opinions about landscaping but would not have called himself an expert.

Mike strolled over again. "Hey, Nolan. I'm glad you're still here. Can I talk to you about something?"

"Sure."

Mike looked around. He gestured for Nolan to follow him, so they walked over to a corner of the lawn far from anyone in earshot. Apparently satisfied now,

Mike nodded. "I'm not very good at this kind of thing, so this will probably not come out the way I intended, but bear with me."

"Is this about the house? Did something bad happen?"

"What? Oh, no. The house is fine. This is more of a personal thing."

That sounded ominous. Nolan braced himself. "Okay."

"My friend Sandy—you know Sandy, he's doing one of your houses—well, his husband suggested I talk to you. He's a big Stacey Lewis fan and saw the show you did a couple of months ago."

"Oh." Nolan didn't like where this was going. He and Sandy had spoken often enough that he was aware Sandy's husband was a fan. And Nolan had only been on Stacey's show once in the past six months.

Mike frowned. "Sandy's husband thought I should talk to you because I know what you're going through."

Nolan doubted that. "I really don't think—"

"I've been married twice." Mike held up his hand to show off his wedding ring. "My first husband was a cop. He was killed in the line of duty. One morning we kissed goodbye and he went off to work and he never came home again."

"Oh." That floored Nolan. It was a lot of information to get from Mike all at once. Nolan hadn't known Mike was gay, for one thing. But he'd also lost a husband. So maybe he did know.

"So I just wanted to say," Mike said, "that I know how hard it is. So if you ever want to talk, I'm here, okay?"

"Yeah, I...." Nolan frowned. He had a million questions. But the only one he could put into words was, "Just tell me, does it get easier?"

"It does. It takes some time, but it does. You'll never forget him—it's impossible to forget those we loved that much—but over time you'll think about him less often. Still, it can sneak up on you. I still have times when, like, I'll hear one of our songs playing from a passing car, and then I'm right back there, missing him all over again. Or I'll find myself wanting to ask him about something happening in the news, because I *know* he'd have feelings about it. And sometimes I look at our daughter and I remember the day we brought her home, or the look on his face the first time he saw her, and I'll think about what a great dad he would have been. She was so little when he died that she barely remembers him. But he really would have been a great father."

Nolan nodded slowly. "I was flipping around channels the other day and I caught part of this cheesy movie Ricky had starred in. I watched it to the end, bawling my eyes out. Worse, it worried me, because it didn't seem like something a sane person would do."

"No, but it's normal." Mike looked off into the distance. "Well, not *normal*. The number of widowers who were married to movie stars is probably pretty small. But you can't kill a cop in New York without it making the news. Worse, there was security camera footage that played on the news constantly in the weeks after he died. I'd watch it, riveted, even though it felt like a bullet to the chest every time."

"Ugh, yeah." At Ricky's insistence, they'd put a hospital bed in the den of their house so that Ricky could die at home, so Nolan had been with him when it happened. He'd been able to tell by the way Ricky's face had gone slack that he'd left. Nolan would never get that image out of his head. But Ricky had been sick for nearly a year, and Nolan had had time to prepare himself, as much as one could be prepared for a loss like that. To have someone taken violently and then have it aired on television repeatedly for weeks, that must have been traumatic.

"But it does get easier," Mike said. "My first husband and I grew up together. He was one of my best friends in the universe. We actually fell in love on a tour in Iraq, if you can believe it. So we went through a lot together, and suddenly he was just… gone. It was the hardest thing I've ever been through. But I distracted myself with work and with raising our daughter, and then despite everything, I fell in love again. So even though I'm married to a great man now, I will never forget my first love. I keep a few photos of my first husband hanging in my apartment. My husband now is comfortable with that. The right man for you will be, too."

"That's… that's good. It's hard not to feel like I had my shot at the One and that's it."

"I don't think we have just one. I think we have people who come to us and who we love when we're at different stages of our lives. And Gio, my current husband, could not be more different from my first husband. My first husband was beer and pizza, and Gio is champagne and caviar, if that makes sense. But I think he's the person I'm supposed to be with at this stage of my life, and God willing, we'll keep each other company well into old age." Mike shrugged. "Or I'm wrong and some calamity will destroy my family tomorrow. I think the lesson is to take each day as it comes and to love the people in your life as much as you can, because you don't know what will happen tomorrow."

Nolan paused to absorb that. He saw Grayson walk across the backyard and take a bottle of water from the cooler at the craft services table.

It often seemed to Nolan that he had no control over who he fell in love with. He'd merely seen Ricky across the room and *known*. He'd had a similar experience with Grayson, though it hadn't been quite as sudden. It had been more of an inkling. Something in him had woken up after lying dormant for a year and whispered *this man*.

"I'm sure you hate talking about this," Mike said. "I just thought, you know, I've been where you are, so if you needed help or just someone to talk to, I'm here. And believe me, I know what it's like to try to make the people in your life understand your pain. Everyone thinks they know, but they never quite understand."

"Yeah. Thanks. This was actually helpful."

"Oh good." Mike smiled.

"So your daughter, you had her with your first husband?"

"Yes, we adopted her as an infant."

"How does your current husband feel about that?"

Mike tilted his head. "Oh, he loves her like she's his own and she thinks he hung the moon. She actually met him before I did. It's a long story." He looked wistfully into the distance. "I won't lie and tell you it has all been fun and easy, but it's good, you know." He smiled. "My daughter is in college now. She still lives at home and commutes to a school in the city. So I'm clinging to her, but I know my days of having her underfoot are numbered."

"I can't even imagine."

"They grow up fast. She was a toddler, then I blinked and she was a teenager."

Grayson walked over to them. "Hi, sorry to interrupt. Mike, Julio asked for you."

"Okay. We're going to wrap for the day in about twenty minutes, so you guys don't need to stick around unless you really want to. But Nolan, you have my phone number, right?"

"I do."

"Call anytime." He smiled and walked into the house.

"What was that about?" Grayson raised an eyebrow.

"Nothing. Well, it seems we're kindred spirits of a sort. But not in a way you need to be jealous of. He's married."

"Yeah, I saw the ring. But that doesn't mean—"

"He seems to love his husband. We just understand each other. Beginning of a beautiful friendship and all that. Come on, let's go."

"His husband?"

Nolan started to walk to the car. "Come on, Gray."

THEY WERE approaching the Holland Tunnel when Grayson decided he had to know what Nolan and Mike had talked about.

Grayson had spotted them having an intense conversation, and Nolan had looked troubled by it. Grayson hadn't wanted to interrupt, so he'd busied himself with grabbing something from the craft services table, but then Mike's assistant Julio had flagged him down and asked him to fetch Mike, providing him with the perfect excuse to find out what was up.

It wasn't any of Grayson's business, which was why he hadn't asked right away, but the more they drove, the more curiosity got the better of him.

"You look like you're about to burst," said Nolan as they slowed down at the toll plaza that led into the tunnel.

"Okay, I do—and I don't—want to know what you and Mike talked about. You can tell me or not, but I am curious. There."

Nolan chuckled. "Well, if you must know, Mike was just offering to be a friendly ear. He told me that his first husband was a cop who was killed in the line of duty, so he understood what I've been going through since Ricky died. He's married again, and he's happy. But he just wanted to offer to listen if I ever needed someone to talk to about Ricky, that was all."

"Oh my God." Grayson pressed a hand over his mouth. Of all the things Nolan could have said, that was the last thing Grayson expected.

"And we did talk for a few minutes, and it did help some."

"You know that I can listen if you—"

"Yes, I know you're willing to hear me, but it's different talking to someone who has been through the same experience you have and come out the other side. He fell in love and got married a second time. I found that reassuring."

"So, we don't have to put you out to pasture just yet," said Grayson, although now he felt a little guilty for being so curious. He felt even more guilty that Nolan had called him on his jealousy back at the house. It wasn't that Grayson was worried about Mike hitting on Nolan—that wasn't even what the conversation looked like—but, *okay*, the thought had entered his mind.

Nolan maneuvered around a car that seemed to be idling in the middle of a lane. The Restoration Channel cars all had EZ Pass installed, so at least they didn't have to go through one of the manned lanes.

Once they were in the tunnel, Nolan said, "Mike said he keeps photos of his first husband around the house, and his new husband is comfortable with it."

"Yeah?" Grayson turned that over. "You don't have photos of Ricky up in your loft. I hope it's not on my account."

"No. I just… I wasn't ready."

"Oh. Because you could put photos up if you wanted to. He was a big part of your life."

"Maybe I will someday. It's still hard. I've got a bunch of photos in a box in the closet."

"Your loft has a closet? I mean, besides that little joke of one in your bedroom area?"

Nolan chuckled. "That door next to the kitchen? It goes to a walk-in closet-slash-storage room."

"Oh! I wondered where that door went, but I didn't want to ask and seem like a creeper."

"I figured, you know, when I felt like I could look at a photo of him and not lose it, I'd put a few out. But I'm not quite there yet."

Now Grayson felt bad again. Maybe his insistence on being in a relationship with Nolan was pushing Nolan for too much, too soon. What was an appropriate amount of time to mourn someone? Maybe one didn't exist. A year seemed like a reasonable amount of time before the one left behind started dating again, but with the baby coming, the situation was weird. If not for the baby and the fact that Nolan and Grayson spent so much time together, maybe this relationship wouldn't feel so important. It would just be two guys casually seeing each other.

But this relationship *was* important. Grayson didn't want to push Nolan into anything he wasn't ready for, but he wasn't going to let Nolan push him away either.

Not that he was doing that now. Nolan actually seemed lighter and happier than he had in a few days. Maybe that talk with Mike *had* helped.

"So how are you feeling now?" Grayson asked.

"About Ricky?"

"About everything."

They emerged from the tunnel and right into a traffic jam. Nolan sighed. "If I haven't said so lately, I really hate Canal Street."

Grayson paused while Nolan focused on getting out of the tangle of streets where the tunnel dumped them, near Chinatown. Once they were headed uptown toward the Restoration Channel offices, he said, "So?"

"How am I feeling? I don't know. The last couple of weeks have been intense. I appreciated Mike talking to me, although of course now I'm thinking about Ricky again. And I'm thinking about you, and how much I like you. And I'm thinking about the baby. And the show. It's a lot, all happening at the same time. It's hard to sort through my feelings about everything sometimes."

"Yeah. I never expected to feel this way either, for what it's worth."

"And what way is that?"

Grayson wasn't completely sure how to voice how he felt. "I want to be with you, and only you, for as long as you'll have me. How's that?"

Nolan smiled. "I feel pretty good about that."

"Good. But, just, I want you to know, you don't have to hide Ricky away. If you find a way to honor him that you're comfortable with, I won't have a problem with it. He was an important part of your life."

"Thank you. I'll think about it."

"Okay." Grayson sighed. "What else is on the agenda for tonight?"

"Ugh, I don't know. I have to talk to Helena about buying plants. Then we have to make the final call on tile for the Dunlop kitchen backsplash. Helena said more samples arrived yesterday and she'd put them in the studio."

"What color were you thinking?" It felt a little strange to shift from an emotional conversation to a work one, but here they were.

"I saw these tiles in a catalog that are kind of long hexagons? I want them in a light minty green."

"Mint? Really?"

"What would you do?"

"I think green is on the right track, but more yellow than mint. Like, uh, pea soup green."

"It's not 1977."

Grayson laughed. He loved arguing about colors with Nolan. "I can picture the exact color in my mind, but I don't know what it's called. Yellower than mint is all I can think of. A very light green, so light that it might look white unless you held it up against something white. Like the pink paint we picked for the bedrooms at the Dunlop house that only looks pink if you look at where it meets the pink ceiling. Subtle color, not gross like you're thinking."

"All right. You may have just invented a color. I don't know if we can order tiles in any color your imagination cooks up, though."

"Shut up. I know the tiles you're talking about and I *know* they come in this color. I saw the same catalog."

"If you say so."

"I do. Just... concentrate on driving, babe. We're almost there."

Chapter Nineteen

THE CRUZES hadn't seen their house since they'd approved the final design plan, back when the house had still been stripped to the studs. Nolan felt that same stomach-churning nervousness he'd felt before they'd revealed the Roberts house. They went through the now familiar routine of making last-minute tweaks to make it look like they'd been designing up to the last possible minute. In truth, they kind of had been; he and Grayson had been in the house finalizing things until 2:00 a.m.

This was their first attempt at designing an entire house. It had been a huge undertaking. Some of the furniture had been the Cruzes' already; they had most of their belongings in storage while they bunked with Lara's parents. Nolan and Grayson had raided the storage unit over the weekend, with the Cruzes' permission, and had taken all the furniture and art they liked. But even if they'd taken everything, the Cruzes now had more house than they had stuff, so Nolan and Grayson still had to supplement what they had. It had meant a lot of shopping for furniture, bedding, and other household supplies. But not having to buy *everything* had been a blessing for the budget, and Nolan had splurged on a beautiful teal sofa that was a bold design statement but fit well into the new space.

So the Cruzes arrived at the door and Nolan and Grayson let them in. Lara immediately screamed, while Jason just stood there, dumbfounded. The first thing that popped out of his mouth was "Hey, there are walls."

"We did a little more than just put up walls," said Nolan.

Nolan led the house tour, explaining the decisions they'd made on the way. The kitchen was where things got really emotional, though.

"It's so beautiful." Lara ran her hands over the counter. "Oh, Jason, can't you just picture our future children sitting at the island for breakfast? I could make waffles, you could make scrambled eggs. We could do the crossword at that little table over there."

Grayson sniffed. "That second bedroom would make a beautiful nursery."

"Oh, you're so right! We didn't want to think about kids until the house was settled, but now that it's ready for us…. Jason, I really think this is going to be our forever home. The place where we raise our kids. Where we grow old together."

"I'm so happy for you," said a watery Grayson.

It wasn't that Nolan didn't feel emotions. He was touched by how happy the Cruzes seemed. And he was glad he could do this for them. The swing in emotion from their distress over their wall-less house to their relief and delight over the finished house was really something.

He and Ricky had redone their house in LA themselves, so Nolan knew firsthand how stressful a renovation could be. He could imagine the relief the Cruzes felt in this finished space.

"You know what I really appreciate?" said Lara. "This tile here. The wallpaper in the living room. All these beautiful, colorful touches that make this different from the same generic house they do on most home renovation shows."

"You guys aren't beige, neutral people," Nolan said.

"No, we aren't! And you understood that. Look at the backsplash in the kitchen. These tiles are so pretty, and they tie in with the rest of the design really well." Lara looked around the room again. "I can't believe I live in a house designed by Nolan Hamlin."

Nolan glanced at Grayson, who didn't look offended. Probably because he was too busy wiping the tears from his eyes.

Mostly, Nolan was thrilled the Cruzes liked the house so much. Jason liked the stainless-steel appliances and the coffee bar in the corner that had been Grayson's idea. Lara loved the tiles and colors they'd chosen for the bathrooms. Jason liked the custom entertainment center they'd built for the living room. Lara loved the teal sofa.

Overall, job well done. That was now three episodes in the bank.

"How do you guys feel?" Helena asked when they got back to the cars.

"Good," said Nolan.

"I'm so glad they liked it," said Grayson, now in better control of his emotions but still sniffling.

Nolan threw an arm around Grayson and gave him a sideways hug. Grayson sniffed again.

"So, like, not to be nosy," said Helena, "but are you guys dating? You don't have to answer if you don't want to. It's none of my business."

Grayson glanced at Nolan, a questioning look in his eyes. So Nolan decided to answer. "Yeah, I guess we are. You're not going to put that on the show, though, are you? I'm not ready to go public with this."

"No, no, I was just curious. But if you change your mind, the Restoration Channel audience loves to really get to know the show hosts. Maybe we could add a couple of talking heads where you discuss what's happening with you personally. Nothing too in-depth, but Nolan, you're adopting a child. That's a big deal. Maybe you could talk about that?"

Nolan's knee-jerk reaction to that was to refuse, but then he thought about those kids at Rainbow House and how he would have reacted to seeing a gay parent when he'd been a teenager. "I'll think about it."

"You should watch a few episodes of *Domestic Do-Over*. That's Travis's show with Brandon Chase. They got together while filming the first episode and wound up moving into that house together. *Very* charming and romantic. But they handled it in a very classy way on the show." Helena smiled. "I mentioned it just so you'd have a model if you want some help figuring out how to do it."

"Does classy mean 'they're gay but don't touch on camera'?" Grayson asked. "Because I've seen a few episodes of the show. When they argue with each other, you can cut the sexual tension with a knife. Like, it's very clear they want to bang each other. But they *never* touch, and aside from those scenes, you'd think they were just colleagues, not romantic partners."

"Just don't make out on camera. But otherwise it can be whatever you want it to be. Restoration used to be a pretty conservative channel, but lately we've been taking it in a twenty-first century direction. Besides, it's not all that different. Even the heterosexual couples don't get too handsy on camera."

"We should talk it over," said Nolan.

Grayson nodded. "We don't have to say anything about us on the show. But if you have to miss filming and I have to do something without you, it might be good to explain why."

Nolan nodded, not sure how much of his life he wanted to make available for public consumption. Talking about Ricky on a talk show back in the olden days was one thing. But now there was a baby involved. "Let's think about it a little."

AS THEY drove out to the Dunlop house a week later, Grayson mulled over the possibility of endings. They were about to film the end of their fourth episode, and whether they did more after they finished the last two would depend on ratings. So there was a possibility these six episodes would be it.

And that would mean he and Nolan would no longer be working together. Between that and Nolan adopting a baby, Grayson wondered if Nolan would need him anymore. Grayson sometimes felt like he was more convenient to Nolan than deeply cared for. He understood that Nolan was not the most demonstrative man when it came to emotions, but he'd gotten even harder to read lately, sometimes distant when they were together. Whether Grayson's perception was accurate was another question, but he couldn't help but worry that without the show, Nolan wouldn't have a reason to see Grayson again. He really hoped that wasn't the case.

But first they had another house to reveal.

The main work they'd done at Maria Dunlop's place was to make her house more functional. They'd taken down some walls, given the main floor as open a plan as Maria could afford—one load-bearing wall had to stay because it was cost-prohibitive to remove—and installed an all-new kitchen. They'd also finished the basement to make a gym for Maria's daughter.

They'd gone a little bonkers with colors in this project, but Maria Dunlop loved mid-century modern design and was open to suggestions. So they'd done light gray cabinets in the kitchen but had found these gorgeous jade green tiles for the backsplash. The living room had an accent wall in a similar green color, and they'd complemented it with jewel tones in the furnishings. Nolan had found a big plush sofa that came in a deep purplish red color that Grayson hadn't believed would work with the green until they got the sofa in the house. Really, designing this house had been a masterclass in color, because in addition to the jade, Nolan had picked a pear-green throw for the sofa and little pops of yellow and pink, and it was bright and lively and all went together. This design was vintage Nolan Hamlin. No beige allowed.

Maria loved it. As soon as she walked in, she was beside herself. The design wasn't for everyone, but it was exactly what Maria wanted. She loved the mid-century touches Nolan had made to the kitchen—he'd picked modern but vintage-looking appliances—and she loved the sight lines on the first floor. Her daughter was beyond thrilled with her new basement gym.

And, of course, when Maria cried about how beautiful it was and how thrilled she was that this house she'd been in for many years finally worked for her, Grayson felt that familiar sting in his throat.

"Oh, here we go," Grayson said, wiping his eyes as they stood in the living room after wrapping up the house tour.

"Oh, Grayson, don't cry!" said Maria.

"Grayson always cries," said Nolan, sounding amused.

"I just have a lot of emotions," said Grayson.

The thing was, though, that these families all deserved functional houses. The Robertses had inherited that old house and needed updates to make it their home. The Cruzes had that travesty of a starter home that they'd fixed to make their forever home. Maria Dunlop now had the perfect home. And, of course, the kids at Rainbow House had a magical common room.

Grayson found himself unable to shake the crying jag on the way home.

"You okay there?" Nolan asked as he drove.

"Just… thinking. Sorry. Ugh, I'm so slobbery and gross."

Nolan reached over and squeezed Grayson's hand. "It's okay."

"It's just that I've never had a *real* home," Grayson said, hating that he was confessing this much. But he figured he should just go for it with Nolan—be honest, explain how he felt, what he desired. Because Grayson was falling in love with the broken parts of Nolan, so Nolan should see the broken parts of himself.

He took a deep breath. "I think I always knew, even as a child, that I was the odd man out. I just wasn't like everyone else in my family. I saw this TV movie once about these two babies who had been switched at birth, and then the kids grew up and realized something was wrong. I always wondered if that was me, if my real family was out there somewhere because I was with the wrong one. But then I'd look in the mirror and realize I definitely shared genes with my parents." He sighed. "I loved New York City when I came here for college and knew I belonged here, but I lived in a dorm, and then I lived on couches or in my car, and now I rent an apartment with two people, but it still feels temporary, somehow. I've never owned property or had a space that truly felt like mine. And something about making these homes for people is getting to me, I guess." He sighed and shook it off. "Sorry."

"Don't apologize. I get where you're coming from."

What Grayson also thought, but did not say, was that Nolan's loft felt like the closest thing to home that Grayson had ever experienced, although it was mostly just because it felt safe and private in a way his own apartment with his chaotic roommates did not. Living with roommates had lost some of its charm lately—fond as he was of getting questions about light bulbs and whether the milk in the fridge was communal while he was miles from home. His apartment felt more like the place he kept his stuff than a real home. It was one of the reasons he spent so many nights at Nolan's. But that was too much to put out there right now.

Grayson grunted and leaned into the seat. What he really wanted to ask was whether Nolan would want to keep him around when he entered the next phase of his life. But he was afraid of the answer.

"Are you okay?" Nolan asked.

"Yeah. I'm good. Just kind of lost in my own thoughts."

"Justin and Peter's house reveal is next week already. You ready for it?"

"Yeah, I think the house will look great. I can't believe we've filmed almost five episodes."

"We'll have to pick a sixth house very soon."

"You know who I want? I want Mrs. Chu."

Nolan nodded. "That's a good choice. I also like that couple with the house near the Jersey Shore. The one with the wife who has purple hair in the audition video."

"Yeah. They're great too, but Mrs. Chu survived cancer."

"You want this show to be a tearjerker."

Grayson smiled at Nolan. "Well… yeah. But happy tears. We'd be doing a good thing for a cancer survivor and a grandma who deserves it. Maybe we can help the Purples next season."

"Ugh, next season. We still have to record all the voiceovers and talking heads."

"Helena suggested we wear soft clothing for our studio interviews. I don't know what that means?"

"Soft clothing? As in soft colors?"

"I don't know. Soft fabric? She says we're supposed to look like we're at home in the studio. But I don't wear soft clothing at home. I dress the same as I always do. Or I wear nothing at all." They were stopped at a traffic light and Nolan turned toward Grayson, so Grayson waggled his eyebrows.

Nolan laughed. "We'll figure it out."

Chapter Twenty

JUSTIN AND Peter were a very cute couple who had been together for six years. The year before, they'd bought a fixer-upper in the Catskills—after years of living in a cramped one-bedroom apartment in Brooklyn, they wanted space—but the challenge of renovating a very old house had soon done them in. So they had a house with a fantastic view of the mountains and that looked beautiful from the outside, but once they'd started digging into the walls, they realized how many problems the house really had.

So as part of the renovation, Nolan and Grayson had overseen asbestos abatement, a lot of plumbing and electrical work, a few feats of engineering to remove some of the walls, and all of that had been so expensive that the design budget was paltry. Nolan had called in every favor possible.

Justin and Peter were a young couple, they loved ultramodern design, and the house had offered Grayson an opportunity to shine. Nolan's aesthetic choices tended to be more traditional and Grayson's were more modern. Nolan was a master at making colors and patterns fit together, but Justin and Peter had taste that was

more minimalist. So Nolan was happy to let Grayson
run with his ideas.

The day before the reveal, Nolan and Grayson
were finishing the design. The modern direction they'd
taken the hardware was sleek and neutral. It wasn't really Nolan's taste, but he liked how things had turned
out aesthetically, and he thought the clients would be
thrilled with it. The color palette was masculine albeit
neutral—mostly white and wood tones—because this
was not a couple who was into florals or patterns or
bright colors.

In some ways, it was nice to decorate for a couple who just wanted a sophisticated living space and
weren't worried about things being cozy or family-friendly. Nolan thought it was good to flex his design
muscles for different kinds of clients so his skills didn't
atrophy. The audience for Restoration Channel shows
was very family-friendly, and they'd designed the Cruz
and Dunlop houses with kids—real or potential—in
mind, but Justin and Peter seemed disinclined to have
children, so why not cater to their tastes?

Grayson helped Nolan place a gray sofa with a bit
of an industrial feel in the living room, then took a step
back. "You don't think it's *too* plain?"

"You're the one who hates accessories," Nolan
pointed out.

"Sure, but, okay, what do you think about blue
and yellow pillows? At least for the staging. This room
feels like a colorless void otherwise."

"Try it and see what happens."

Grayson looked directly at Nolan. "That sounds
like a threat."

Nolan laughed. Grayson rolled his eyes and stalked out of the room, but came back with an armful of throw pillows, which he placed on the sofa artfully.

"That looks okay, right?" Grayson asked.

Nolan had been arranging little trinkets on a built-in bookshelf, but he turned and looked at the sofa. There was a mustard yellow throw tossed over the back of it, and coordinated yellow and blue pillows in each corner.

"It looks fine," Nolan said.

Nolan wasn't completely sure what Grayson was looking for here. Validation? Probably. Nolan had been trying to get Grayson to go with his instincts more, but Grayson didn't always see the stark line between what he thought worked and what the clients wanted.

Nolan had experienced the whole range. He'd decorated the main floor of a house for an actress who had said, "I trust you," before jetting off to Prague to film a movie for six weeks, leaving Nolan entirely to his own devices. She'd been thrilled with the results, so it had worked out, thank God. He'd also been hired to decorate the main living areas of a house owned by a wealthy couple who owned six high-end restaurants in LA, and the wife had been such a control freak that Nolan hadn't been able to so much as look at wallpaper samples or a store that sold tile without her sign-off. He'd learned from years of experience that the client was always right, but also how to judge when he was more right than the client. Grayson didn't quite have that innate understanding yet, but he'd get there.

"I really love this," Grayson said as they wrapped up around midnight. "It's *so* modern. I bet you don't get to do houses like this much."

"No, I don't. People think they want modern without understanding what that means. Usually they just want new finishes. But this couple wanted *modern*."

"I'm really excited to show it to them."

They finished up and looked around for Helena, who had fallen asleep in the super cool black leather chair Nolan had found at a furniture store in SoHo. The chair actually looked really uncomfortable, but at least Nolan could tell Peter and Justin that it was producer approved.

"Hey, Helena, wake up!"

She startled awake. "Oh. What?"

"We're done. You can go back to the city and sleep in your own bed now."

She grinned and let Nolan help her up. "This place is marvelous. I think the viewers will like the departure from the kinds of designs you usually do."

"Yeah?"

"Yeah. Lordy, do you know how many neutral houses I've seen lately, with medium wood tones and white kitchens and farmhouse sinks and the same beige sofa? Not to mention the godforsaken shiplap."

"I kind of hate shiplap," said Nolan.

"That's why I like you."

Nolan laughed and held out his arm to escort her out. Grayson was already standing next to the car when they walked outside, so Nolan hit the remote start and Grayson climbed into the car.

"I hope you know what you're doing there," she said, nodding toward Nolan's car.

"Me too."

"I like him a lot. He's a good foil for you. I guess it makes sense that you'd… agree."

Nolan laughed. "Well, yeah. I didn't expect it. I mean, he's so much younger than I am."

"What are you going to do when the baby comes?"

"That remains to be seen. We've talked and Gray swears he plans to stick around, but I'll believe that if it happens."

"Yeah. Hard to impose fatherhood on a twenty-five-year-old, especially when he had no part in the, er, biological process."

"My thoughts exactly."

"Well, good luck with that. Don't ruin my show. I like the two of you together on screen. I'd hate to have to find you a new costar next season."

"If we even get another season."

"Oh, we will. This show is the kind of thing Restoration viewers love. Two cute gay guys decorating houses for families in need? Yeah, you'll get renewed."

Nolan gave Helena a hug and then walked to the car. Grayson was fiddling with the radio when Nolan got in. "You good?" Nolan asked.

"Yeah, just tired. What did Helena have to say?"

"She thinks we'll get renewed, so she warned me not to fuck things up with you and ruin the second season. But she said it nicer."

Grayson scoffed. "I guess that's as good a reason as any to stay together."

GRAYSON WAS writhing on the bed as Nolan nipped at his neck and was getting ready to reach for the night-stand drawer when Nolan's phone rang.

"Don't stop, Nolan," Grayson growled, shoving his hips against Nolan's.

"I gotta at least see who's calling or it will distract me," said Nolan, pushing away from Grayson and reaching for his phone. "People only call in the middle of the night for emergencies."

Grayson hoped it was a wrong number as he glanced at Nolan's bedside clock, which showed that it was indeed 2:00 a.m.

"Hello?" Nolan said as he flopped onto his back with his phone pressed against his ear.

Grayson started to see through the fog of arousal and began to worry it truly was an emergency. Nolan was right; people generally didn't call at this time of night if it wasn't important. Or a drunk ex. Grayson had an ex who still periodically drunk-dialed him when he got out of the club without a man to go home with.

Shaking all that off, Grayson turned on his side and looked at Nolan beside him.

"Wait, she what? No, I'm sorry, it's two in the morning here. I'm just not…. Oh. Yeah. I mean, it's a six-hour flight, but I could…. Yes, of course. I'll be on the next flight. I'll call you when I land in LA. Okay. Yes. Thank you."

Nolan got off the phone and got out of bed.

"What the hell is going on?" Grayson asked.

"The baby's coming. Angela went into labor early. That was the case worker. Apparently she's on the way to the hospital now. It could still be a while, but I need to get to LA as soon as physically possible."

"Oh." Well, shit. "I thought her due date wasn't for another two weeks."

"Babies don't always adhere to strict schedules."

Grayson sighed and got out of bed. "You want me to come with you?"

Nolan was in the process of pulling a suitcase out of the closet, but he stopped when Grayson said that. "Oh. Um. Well, no. No offense, just, I think this is something I have to do myself. Plus, someone has to be at the reveal tomorrow. Or later today, I guess. I'll call Helena in the morning to let her know, if you want."

It was very hard to process things when it was the middle of the night and Grayson was still trying to shake off sex brain. But he realized that they were supposed to do the reveal for Justin and Peter's house in, yikes, eight hours. "You can't wait until after the reveal?"

"No, I have to get to LA right away. Ugh, I have to book a flight."

Nolan sat back on the bed and started tapping at his phone.

He and Nolan lived in different universes, didn't they? Grayson had been avoiding going back to his shitty apartment in Brooklyn for almost a week, and here Nolan could just book a flight to LA without having a crisis about how to pay for it. Not that Nolan hadn't worked for it, but Grayson wondered if half of why he found comfort in Nolan's world was that it didn't include the same anxieties Grayson dealt with daily. Thanks to Grayson's new salary, he didn't have to worry about making rent this month or for several months to come, but it was a state of being he was still getting used to.

He shook himself off and got up to find something to wear home.

"Don't feel like you have to rush out of here," Nolan said. "I actually had keys made for you a few days ago and forgot to give them to you. If you want to stay here while I'm gone, that's fine."

"Oh."

"I trust you," Nolan said. Then he held up his phone in triumph. "Flight booked. First one out of LaGuardia is at six. I'd better pack."

Grayson sat back on the bed, feeling overwhelmed. Their idyll was over, wasn't it? Nolan would be coming back from LA in a few days with a *baby*. That changed the equation here in ways Grayson probably hadn't even thought of yet.

"You can do the reveal, right?" said Nolan. "I was looking forward to seeing Justin and Peter's faces, but I don't *have* to be there. Nor do I want to postpone until I get back because we shouldn't force the couple to stay out of their house an extra week or two on my account."

"An extra week?"

"Well, yeah. I mean, I'm not set up here yet, and I don't know if it's safe to fly a newborn across the country and I… oh, fuck."

Ah, there it was. Grayson had been wondering when the full force of this would hit Nolan. And something about watching the freakout play across Nolan's face made Grayson snap into problem-solving mode.

"Okay. What still has to get done?" Grayson asked.

"Well, all the furniture is purchased, but I haven't assembled anything. It's just sitting in a pile over there." Nolan pointed at a bunch of boxes stacked up just outside of the sleeping area screen. "And I haven't even started interviewing nannies or babysitters or anything, so I don't know what to do about childcare while we film. I'll have to talk to Helena about postponing the consultation with the Chus. I guess I'll have to do all that when I get back."

"Tell you what," said Grayson. "I can assemble the furniture while you're gone."

"Really?"

"Sure. How hard can it be to put a crib together? The box should have instructions, right?"

"I assume."

"I can't help you with the nanny, but I can get things up. What else do you need?"

"Um. Diapers? Bottles? I bought some stuff, but it's also in boxes and I don't know what else I'd need yet, but—"

"I got it."

"You don't know anything about babies."

"No, but there's this thing called the internet. I can look it up. If you trust me, then trust me to figure this out. I'll get your home all set up for you, okay?"

Nolan took a deep breath and met Grayson's gaze. "I… yeah. Thanks. You don't have to do that."

"I want to."

Nolan got up. Somewhere in his frenzy, he'd put underwear on, so he wasn't completely naked when he walked across the loft and opened a kitchen drawer. He came back with a set of keys. "The square one is the main door downstairs. The round one is my mailbox, but don't feel like you have to check the mail while I'm gone. The hexagonal one is for the loft door. Make sense?"

"Yup. Got it. Seriously, Nolan, I'll figure out what needs to be done here and do it. You can count on me."

Nolan smiled. He leaned over and briefly kissed Grayson on the lips. "I'll probably only be gone a few days, a week at the most. I'm sure there are things to sign and the baby may not be able to leave the hospital right away and… yeah. I'll call or text when I can to let you know when I'll be back."

"Okay."

"You'll be great at the reveal. I know it will go well. Okay?"

Grayson nodded, although he *was* quite nervous about it. Nolan tended to lead the tours through the houses when they did reveals. He had a better way of explaining his design decisions. Grayson would probably only really be only be able to point to things and say, "I like blue." But, whatever. Nolan needed him now. And he'd show Nolan that he could step up and be what Nolan needed.

"Okay," Grayson said. Then he sat on the bed and watched Nolan pack, knowing fun time was over. Things were serious now.

Chapter Twenty-One

THE WI-FI on the plane didn't work longer than about three seconds at a time, so Nolan had no contact with the outside world until he landed at LAX. When he could finally access his voicemail, he had three messages from Clyde, the last of which explained that Angela had given birth, it was definitely a girl, and he'd meet Nolan at the hospital. "She's beautiful," Clyde had added. "The proper number of fingers and toes, great big eyes, and a little nose that will just melt your heart."

Nolan had only brought a carry-on suitcase, so he bypassed baggage claim and got a cab. He decided to go straight to the hospital instead of the hotel Grayson had reminded him to book just before he'd left for the airport.

He called Clyde from the cab, so Clyde was waiting for him right off the elevator on the maternity floor when Nolan arrived. He eyed Nolan's suitcase and said, "So you really came here right from the plane."

"Yeah, sorry. I'm anxious, I guess."

"I don't blame you. There's a private waiting room down the hall where you can stash your luggage. Then I'll take you to meet your daughter. Come with me."

Nolan's heart squeezed. *His* daughter. He still couldn't quite believe any of this was real.

It took another twenty minutes to stash Nolan's suitcase and wrangle a proper visitor's pass to the newborn room, but finally they were walking toward Nolan's daughter, and Nolan's heart pounded.

"Normally, this hospital lets the babies stay with their parents. But Angela didn't want to see her because she thought it would be too upsetting, so they've got the girl in this room down here. So don't be alarmed that there aren't many other babies."

"Okay. That probably wouldn't have occurred to me as something to worry about."

"I know. It's just that you see those cute rooms on TV with all the babies lined up like they're in a display case, and that's not what this is. Sometimes adoptive parents freak out about that."

There was a big window with blue and pink balloons painted around it, but it mostly seemed to show a couple of basinets and nurses bustling around.

But then… there she was.

Before Nolan really understood what was happening—he was somewhat hampered by the fact that he'd been awake for more than twenty-four hours straight—a nurse was placing an infant with a tiny pink hat into his arms.

Something in Nolan changed irrevocably in that moment. He wasn't sure what he'd *expected* to feel, but it wasn't this completely overwhelming love for the tiny human who stared at him with great expectations.

She looked a little bit like Angela. Dark hair peeked out from under the little pink cap on her head. But Clyde was right; she had huge eyes, a cute little nose, and a perfect cupid's bow of a mouth. That was really all of her that he could see because she was wrapped so tightly in a hospital blanket with blue stripes.

"She's… perfect," Nolan said.

Tears stung his eyes as he looked at this baby girl he'd loved instantly. He'd been worried he wouldn't. After all, he'd played no role in her conception. But everything that had happened to Nolan in the past two years hit him all at once, and he started to cry.

"Here, have a seat," the nurse said, perhaps anticipating that Nolan was about to lose it. She led him over to a rocking chair in the corner. So Nolan sat with the baby and started to rock, holding her close to his chest.

Everything that had happened, from the moment he'd said to Ricky, "Yes, let's do it," to the early meetings with the adoption agency and the home visits and then Ricky's diagnosis, played through his head. Nolan held that baby girl close as he remembered Ricky's funeral and the way it had felt like all the dreams they'd had together had suddenly evaporated. He thought about moving to New York, to re-emerging from his hibernation, to meeting Grayson. He pictured Grayson now, awkwardly leading Justin and Peter through the big reveal of their newly renovated house.

Nolan didn't truly know how Grayson felt about children, but he couldn't believe how Grayson had leaped into action after that phone call last night. Or earlier this morning, he supposed. Grayson had insisted he'd set up the baby area of the apartment and buy all the supplies Nolan needed. And he'd made sure Nolan hadn't only packed pants—which is almost what happened—then reminded Nolan to make a hotel reservation. In other words, Grayson had taken care of Nolan, and that was something Nolan just hadn't expected.

"Do you have a name in mind?" Clyde asked.

"I've been thinking about names but hadn't totally settled on one."

He looked at the baby. He wanted to find a way to honor Ricky, but there wasn't a female equivalent of Ricardo that he knew of. He'd been playing around with similar names: Carla, Rita, Ramona… but none of them felt right. Then he remembered that Ricky had been indirectly named after his aunt Raquel, who by all accounts had been a free spirit and someone Ricky had long looked up to. She'd died shortly before Nolan met Ricky, but they'd always been close. It had been Raquel who had helped Ricky come out to his parents, Raquel who had been the first to tell him it was okay to be gay.

That was how Nolan landed on the name Rachel. It was a name he'd always liked. It was different enough from Ricky that the connection probably wasn't obvious, but Nolan would know, and that was what was important. And for reasons he couldn't explain, he thought his little girl even looked like a Rachel.

"Do you want to feed her?" the nurse asked.

"Yes, please."

The nurse helped Nolan unswaddle Rachel so that her arms were free, and then she handed Nolan a bottle. She then proceeded to give Nolan a lecture about formula and nipple sizes for bottles that Nolan only half listened to, because he was too taken by the way Rachel—his *daughter*—stared up at him while she ate.

NOLAN EVENTUALLY went to his hotel. He'd spent most of the day at the hospital. Once the sun set and it became clear that he was almost too tired to stand, the nurse had ordered him out.

The hospital wanted to keep Rachel overnight, just in case. Nolan almost felt empty as he rode in a cab to the hotel. But he checked in, ordered room service, and called his mother to let her know what was going on. He was about to call Grayson when room service arrived, and his stomach growled, so he decided to eat first.

Immediately after he ate, he fell asleep.

He woke up before the sun was up, but it was a reasonable time in the morning on the East Coast. He got up, showered, and realized he still hadn't called Grayson as he got dressed.

So much for keeping Grayson updated.

It was about nine in New York when he finally called. Grayson answered on the third ring.

"Oh, God, I hope everything is okay!" Grayson said quickly.

"Yes, everything is fine. I'm sorry I forgot to call yesterday, but there was just so much going on when I got to the hospital. Once I got to the hotel last night, I kind of just passed out."

"It's okay. How is the baby?"

"Good. Her name is Rachel. Here, I'll text you a photo."

Nolan put Grayson on speaker and then sent him one of the approximately ten thousand photos he'd taken of Rachel the day before.

"Oh, my goodness, she is *precious*," said Grayson.

"How did the reveal go?"

"Oh. Good. It was good. Definitely weird without you, though. Don't make me do the next one alone. But Justin and Peter were thrilled with the design. They really loved all the glass and the wrought iron on the staircase, and they even liked the colorful pillows on the sofa. So I'd call that a success."

"Good, I'm glad that worked out." Nolan rubbed his eyes, trying to focus on the call. "So, I'm going to be out here for two weeks, it looks like. Helena is my next call, because we'll have to reschedule some things if you don't want to do the consultation with the Chus by yourself."

"Yeah, I think that's best. I mean, people aren't tuning in to see *me*. I'm bound to disappoint the Chus if I show up by myself."

"That's not true, but I take your point."

"Still… *two* weeks?"

"Turns out you can't fly with a newborn. And, actually, the doctor is worried about her undeveloped immune system and flying at all when she's this young. So I'm trying to arrange a private flight back to New York."

"A *private* flight. Fancy."

"Expensive. Worth it, though. There's a lot I have to handle here in the meantime. She's going to stay in the hospital another day or two. And I still have a bunch of forms I have to sign. I'm going to relocate to stay with friends of mine in West Hollywood because they have a spare room and a crib I can use. They have two kids of their own, so I plan to pepper them with parenting questions."

"Sounds like a good plan."

Nolan wanted to say something about how he felt about all of this to Grayson, but he couldn't quite formulate words. So he just said, "I really appreciate you helping me the other night."

"It was no problem."

"I know, but... I didn't ask you to do any of it. You just... did it. You're pretty good in a crisis, you know."

"Well, I can think pretty fast on my feet sometimes."

"Thank you."

Grayson was silent for a moment but then said softly, "You're welcome."

WHEN RACHEL was a week old, Nolan rented a car and drove her out to the cemetery where Ricky was buried.

It had been an intense week. Rachel never slept for longer than two hours at a time, and learning to care for her—while everyone around him gave conflicting advice—was thrilling and exhausting and amazing. His mother turned up two days after Rachel was born and got to work explaining to Nolan exactly what to do and cuddling the baby as much as possible. She was overjoyed to have a grandchild, and Nolan valued her help. But now she was threatening to move into the loft, which was too much. "You can visit," he told her, "but I have to figure out how to be a father on my own." That, and he wanted to work out whatever was going on with Grayson before introducing his mother to that whole situation. But he let her have her fill of her granddaughter while she was in California.

Now he put Rachel in the carrier that strapped to his chest. It took a few yoga poses to get himself into it on his own, but he did it and walked with her out to Ricky's grave. He still remembered exactly where it was from all the times he'd come out here when he'd lived in LA. He hadn't been here at all in nearly six months, though, so though the path out to the section where Ricky's grave was located felt well-trod, it felt a little different too. Different flowers were blooming. New headstones populated the landscape.

But there he was: Ricardo Vega. Someone, probably Ricky's sister, had left flowers recently, but they were half-wilted. Nolan replaced them with fresh ones and then sat at the foot of the grave.

"Hi, Ricky," he said. "I want you to meet Rachel. You should be here to meet her in person, but since you aren't, I brought her to you. She's so tiny. She weighs just over six pounds. She eats like a champ, though, so she'll grow in no time. She looks a lot like her mother. I want to give her the best home possible." Nolan sighed. "That home should have been the one I shared with you. I still wake up some mornings angry that you were taken too soon. But it's… it's getting better, I guess."

Grayson popped into his head then. Nolan imagined what he'd tell Ricky about Grayson if he'd been here.

"I've met a man. I don't really know what will happen, but I think he's something special. I never intended to move on so quickly from you, nor did I think it was possible, but I guess sometimes these things just happen. He's young, but I think that might be good for me. He reminds me that I have to live and have fun. I had drinks with him and his friends a couple of weeks ago and then we went to a drag show, and it was the most I've laughed in what feels like two years. I mean, when was the last time you and I just… laughed? Had fun? I think it was that night we went to Megan's house, right before you got really sick."

Megan had been a close friend of Ricky's. She was an editor at a teen magazine; she and Ricky had met during the height of his stardom when she'd interviewed him for a feature article, and they'd hit it off so well, they'd stayed friends. She'd since risen in the ranks to be a senior editor and lived in a gorgeous apartment near the Grove. That night she'd invited a few people over for drinks, and she and Ricky'd had so much fun reminiscing that she'd pulled a plastic bin full of back issues of her magazine out of a closet and they'd howled over old photos of Ricky, his awkward model poses, and the goofy things he'd said in interviews. Nolan hadn't ever laughed so hard… until Grayson had taken him to that drag show. Grayson's friends had been fun and open and game for anything, even the straight guy who had tagged along. The queens were hilarious and talented and had put on a big campy spectacular that Nolan had thoroughly enjoyed. And they'd just… had fun.

"Grayson reminds me to live," Nolan said. "I think I'd forget otherwise. And designing with him has been really rewarding. I didn't think I'd want a partner or that I could handle a relationship with another designer, but it's working well. For now. We'll see what happens when I bring Rachel home. But I just never imagined I'd find someone I connect with again." He took another deep breath and touched Rachel's head. She stirred under his touch but was otherwise pretty deeply asleep.

"I did this for you, Ricky. When they called me to tell me they had a baby for us, I thought only of you. But I realize now that I did it for myself, too, because something was missing from my life. Not just you, but that vision we always had for what a family would look like for us. I wanted a family. I want to make my own family. And I'm almost there. But I will never forget you, okay? You will always be part of me, part of my history and my future. But I'm going back to the East Coast in a week, so I probably won't be visiting you here much anymore." He sighed, caught between loss and life. "I hope you're somewhere blissful and painless. I hope you're so happy it never occurs to you to look in on me. But if you do, I hope you can see that I'm trying to be happy too."

Rachel started to wake up. She squirmed against Nolan's chest and then began to cry. He managed to stand up and rock her a little. "Okay, baby girl. We'll go back to the car in just a second."

Nolan dusted off the seat of his pants and then turned back to the headstone. "I love you, Ricky. I will always love you. But I also know you wouldn't want me to stop living when you left, so I'm trying hard to move on and figure out how to make sense of this life I live now. I wish you were here still, with every fiber of my being. But since you aren't, I'm going to keep living. I'll tell Rachel about you someday when she's old enough to hear it."

Rachel's cries became more demanding. If Nolan had anything else to say, it fell out of his head as his attention focused back on the baby. *His* baby. Then he walked her back to the car.

Chapter Twenty-Two

GRAYSON WOKE up in his bed in his apartment and could hear voices. It sounded like his roommates—Jenny and Kyle—were having an argument.

Grayson pulled the covers over his head, but they were too loud for him to block out. He glanced at his phone. No word from Nolan, who was scheduled to return home tomorrow. With Nolan out of town, Grayson had basically been at loose ends for two weeks, and he'd fallen into some bad habits, like sleeping until lunchtime. Setting up the nursery at Nolan's place had given him a project, at least, but even that was over now.

Grayson made himself get out of bed, and after a quick shower and changing into jeans and a T-shirt—very Nolan of him—he decided to see what Jenny and Kyle were *still* arguing about.

"What's going on?"

"Hello, sleepyhead," said Jenny. "The fridge is broken."

"Oh. That sucks."

Kyle rolled his eyes. "I called the landlord, but the repair guy can't get here until Saturday."

It was currently Thursday. Grayson rubbed his eyes. He'd lived here long enough to know that "the repair guy" was just the landlord's son who, yes, was pretty handy but was likely no expert in appliance repair. So the apartment would likely be without a functioning refrigerator at least until Saturday, but probably longer, since the landlord's son would need some time to figure out that he didn't know how to fix it and call someone else in.

"Okay. That's terrible," said Grayson. Although it was probably inevitable. The refrigerator was hardly state-of-the-art and looked like it had been purchased sometime in the nineties. Working on the show had given Grayson a crash course in refrigerator models, so he knew that they didn't exactly last forever, and this was a cheap one the landlord hadn't bothered to replace through several rotations of tenants.

"I want Kyle to go to the store and buy a cooler and some ice so we can at least keep some of our food from spoiling, but he won't move," said Jenny.

"I have to leave for work in like an hour and I'm not even dressed yet because I've been talking to you about the damned fridge all morning. Why can't you go?"

"I have a paper due tomorrow!"

"I'll go," Grayson volunteered. It wasn't like he had anything else to do until Nolan got home.

Kyle and Jenny both turned to stare at him. "What?" said Jenny.

"I'll go buy a cooler and some ice. They probably sell them at that hardware store on Flatbush, right?"

"Oh. You don't have to do that, man," said Kyle. "You hardly have anything in the fridge, since you're never here anymore."

That was true. The only things of Grayson's in the fridge were takeout leftovers. He'd had to explain to his roommates that he was suddenly home so much because his boyfriend was out of town. Neither of them seemed even remotely put out that he'd been gone a lot lately, since he made sure he got them the rent on time. They were friendly with each other but not close friends, and Grayson figured they were happy to have one less person competing for the bathroom in the morning.

"I really don't mind going," Grayson said. "I don't have anything else going on today."

And that was that. Later that afternoon, after he'd filled a chest-sized cooler with ice and helped Jenny wedge perishables like milk and eggs into it, he went into the living room and figured he'd see if anything interesting was on TV.

He'd designed this space. The couch was "vintage" in that he'd found it at a thrift store, but it was in really good shape. He'd found a purple tweed fabric at a discount store and borrowed Jenny's sewing machine to make a slip cover for it, because the original pattern on the sofa was gray and kind of boring. He'd picked the coffee table up at a stoop sale—Brooklyn's answer to yard sales—and it had seen better days. The blanket he snuggled under now was a throw crocheted by a friend he'd stayed with during his couch-surfing days, the curtains cheap ones he'd bought at a big-box store, the rug was Jenny's, and the TV stand was Kyle's. But he'd been the one to make sure everything in the room worked. He liked this space, mostly because he felt good about the time and energy he'd put into it, but he could see where it was fraying too. One wall had a crack in it that didn't bode particularly well for the building's structural integrity—another thing he knew a lot more about now that he'd renovated four houses. The ancient hardwood floors were scarred and stained. Still, none of that really bothered him because, before Nolan, this space had been *his*.

And yet now the apartment felt foreign. This place had never really been home. It was a temporary stopover on his way to the next thing. He certainly didn't intend to live with Kyle and Jenny for the rest of his life.

But Nolan's apartment was different. Grayson hadn't been staying there while Nolan was out of town, but he'd spent plenty of time in it setting up the nursery. Putting together the crib had ended up being a huge undertaking, and he'd had to call Danny in to help him. He and Danny had spent most of an afternoon assembling the rest of the furniture. There was a dresser that had come already mostly assembled, but it had a removable tray that fit over the top that got a bit tricky. Inside, they'd put a thick pad so that the dresser doubled as a changing table. There was also a little bookcase with the same dark wood finish as the crib and the dresser.

"What else do babies need?" Grayson had asked Danny.

"Beats me. Let me call my mother."

After that, Grayson had gone to a baby store and picked out a rocking chair that matched the other furniture and had it delivered. He also enlisted Danny to help him carry the many bags of stuff Danny's mom had recommended—diapers and bedding and pacifiers and bottles and so many other things, Grayson had started to wonder how such a small person could need so much stuff—and they found places for all of it in

Nolan's apartment. The day after that, Grayson had gone back to the baby store and picked out some little outfits for Rachel. After all, he couldn't have the kid going naked, could he? But somehow he didn't think clothing would be an issue. The photos Nolan had been texting him several times a day indicated that Nolan had also gone a little over-the-top picking up outfits for her in LA, because she was wearing something different in every photo.

But now everything was set up and structurally sound, thanks mostly to Danny, and Grayson had even stretched his design skills a little in picking out linens that complemented each other and finding a stuffed bunny—it was so cute it had made him cry in the store—that he'd put on the dresser.

He flipped channels on the old TV in his living room. When he found an episode of *Domestic Do-Over* on the Restoration Channel, he felt a little giddy at seeing Travis, since he now knew Travis in person. He really enjoyed the dynamic between Travis and Brandon, who always fought like they'd rather be fucking. They were having a seemingly mundane argument about wainscoting in this episode that made Grayson laugh.

Then there was a commercial break, and suddenly Grayson's own face was on screen.

"Coming this summer to the Restoration Channel is an all-new interior design series featuring designer to the stars Nolan Hamlin...." The voiceover paused while several shots of Nolan looking intense while he made various design decisions played in quick succession. "And up-and-coming designer Grayson Woods...." Now there was a pause to show Grayson karate chopping a pillow and then asking Nolan's opinion about something in the Roberts house. "…take on some of the worst houses." Clips of the Robertses and the Cruzes pleading with the camera for someone to help save their houses now played. This was followed by a clip of workers putting up drywall in fast-forward motion, Nolan and Grayson carrying a very heavy sofa into the Cruz house, and a few more rapid-fire clips of Nolan adjusting books and knickknacks on shelves. Then the voiceover said, "Watch *Residential Rehab* Thursday nights this summer on the Restoration Channel or the Restoration Channel app."

Well, that was pretty fucking surreal.

Seeing the promo for the show made it feel real in a way it hadn't to this point. Grayson was starring on a TV show. His name was being splashed all over the Restoration Channel's advertising. And they hadn't even recorded their episode intros or voiceovers yet.

Seeing Nolan on TV made Grayson miss him acutely. And it made Grayson realize that he didn't belong in this crumbling old building in Brooklyn anymore. He belonged in Nolan's loft—with Nolan. This apartment had served him well for the two years he'd lived here, but he wasn't at this point in his life anymore.

And, sure, he was twenty-five, and maybe normal twenty-five-year-olds were totally fine with Grayson's pre-Nolan life of roommates and nights out and random hookups and being drunk on the streets of Manhattan or Brooklyn until the wee hours of the morning—and Grayson had certainly enjoyed that life—but he also longed for the home and family he'd never had. And if he had to choose, home and family would win every time.

But it would be presumptuous of him to move himself into Nolan's apartment. And Nolan's life had just changed dramatically. Grayson hoped beyond anything that he could stay a part of that life, but still, whatever happened, he knew he needed to leave this one behind.

GETTING RACHEL and all of Nolan's stuff into his apartment was a unique challenge. The building had an elevator, so he tipped the cabbie who'd picked him up at the airport to carry the suitcase he'd bought in LA—filled now with all of Rachel's things—while he carried the car seat with the baby in one hand and his carry-on in the other. Once he was in the elevator, he tipped the cabbie again and then rode up to his floor. He picked up Rachel and the carry-on suitcase and then kind of kicked the other suitcase down the hall to his apartment door.

But he was inside now.

"We're home, Rachel," he told the baby.

The first thing Nolan noticed was that no one was home. But Grayson clearly had been there while Nolan was gone—Grayson's leather jacket was draped over one arm of the sofa, and a pair of his sneakers had been left near the door. Nolan found that comforting in a strange way. Perhaps he'd grown to like having Grayson in this space. He'd certainly missed the guy while he'd been out of town.

He put the car seat down and took Rachel out. She made cute little gurgle noises while he carried her over to investigate whether Grayson had set up the crib. The screen he'd bought to section off the baby's "room" was up, so Nolan couldn't see it from the front door.

But then he peeked behind the screen and was genuinely surprised.

The crib was set up and placed against the wall. It was flanked by a dresser on one side and a book-case on the other. Grayson had made up the bed with a sheet with little bunnies on it. He'd put a matching cover on the changing table pad and a plush bunny with a big pink bow on the changing table. The book-case was mostly empty but had a couple of children's books on it. Opposite the crib was a rocking chair that Grayson must have bought, though it matched the rest of the furniture. A pink throw pillow leaned against the back of it.

Rachel started to fuss, and Nolan quickly discov-ered she needed her diaper changed. He put her on the changing table and on a hunch opened the top drawer. Half of it was filled with packages of newborn diapers. The other half had some neatly folded baby clothes.

Once Rachel had a clean diaper, Nolan carried her over to the kitchen. The bottle warmer he'd ordered was set up and sitting on the counter. Nolan opened the cabinet above it and saw that Grayson had moved some glasses around to make room for a half-dozen bottles. There were two pacifiers there too.

Nolan was so touched he nearly cried again, but apparently he was tapped out after the past two weeks. Still, he couldn't believe how much work Grayson had done here. All Nolan had asked him to do was set up the crib. Grayson had done so much more than what Nolan had expected, and Nolan was genuinely touched by the gesture.

This wasn't just a nice thing, though. Grayson had done all this because he truly cared for Nolan.

A half hour later, Rachel was fed and asleep in her new crib, so Nolan called Grayson and told him to come over.

"I'll be there with bells on," said Grayson.

"Well, not bells. The baby's sleeping."

Grayson laughed. "Right, of course."

Grayson arrived an hour later. Rachel still hadn't woken up, but when Nolan heard Grayson's key in the door, he immediately hopped up and ran over to hug Grayson.

"What you did, this is really incredible," Nolan said.

Grayson hugged him back. "I didn't want you to have to worry about anything when you came home."

"Still, you didn't have to go to all the trouble. I mean, the clothes, the rocking chair…."

"I wanted to."

The way Grayson said it made it sound like it was no big deal, but to Nolan, it truly was.

He was in love with Grayson. He couldn't believe he'd let this sweet, caring man under his skin, but he had. It was hard to take his arms away now. He never wanted to let go.

"I missed you so much," Nolan said.

"Oh God, me too."

"I was surprised when you weren't here when I got home."

Grayson sighed and pulled away. "It felt a little weird to sleep here without you. So I was here a lot during the day setting all this up, but I went back to my apartment at night. And believe me, it's been a trial. The fridge broke yesterday, and my roommates have been fighting, and ugh…."

"I'm sorry to hear that."

Rachel woke up then and started to fuss.

"That's her!" Grayson said. "Can I meet her?"

"Of course. Come on."

Nolan led Grayson over to the crib. He scooped up Rachel and showed her to Grayson. She immediately stopped crying and stared at him.

"She's so adorable," Grayson said. "Can I hold her?"

"Okay."

Nolan carefully handed her over to Grayson. Grayson held her and stared at her with awe. It was strange; in the past two weeks, Nolan had almost grown used to Rachel. She'd managed to weave herself into the fabric of his life, although sometimes he'd look at her and be so overwhelmed by her that it felt like his heart stopped. He wondered if it would always be that way. He hoped so.

"What a pretty little girl," Grayson cooed. She continued to stare up at him, her little mouth hanging open, as if he was the most fascinating thing she'd ever seen. Nolan thought it seemed like they were having a moment.

Was there some future where this tableau was something more permanent and less likely to slip through Nolan's fingers? Grayson smiling down at Rachel was fulfilling in a way Nolan hadn't expected. But wouldn't it be great if the two people he loved also loved each other? Nolan had been thinking these two individuals would live in separate bubbles, that Rachel would be his and Grayson would be his, but somehow never at the same time. But here they were.

Nolan wanted that future fiercely. He wanted Grayson to live here and be a part of his life and be a parent to Rachel. He wanted all of it, wanted the life he'd dreamed up with Ricky. But he wanted it in a new way now.

But there was no way he could ask Grayson for all that so soon, so he had to be content to stand back and watch them interact for a bit.

A couple of hours later, when Rachel was back to sleep, Nolan and Grayson cuddled on the sofa and watched TV with the volume on low. Rachel had done an admirable job sleeping through the rambunctious screaming and running of Nolan's friends' elementary school–aged children when they'd still been in LA, and it seemed to be the case today that she slept for two hours at a time no matter what was happening around her.

"You must be exhausted," Grayson said. "Does she keep you up at night?"

"Yes. So fair warning, if you plan to spend the night, I'm going to sleep and she will wake us up every two hours."

"So noted."

"Sleep is more important than sex. That's what the parenting book I bought says."

Grayson laughed. "Really?"

"Yeah. This pattern you're witnessing now, where she sleeps for two hours at a time and then is all cute and awake and then sleeps for two more hours? That's her pattern all the time. It's less cute at three in the morning."

"Okay. Got it."

"You don't have to stay."

Grayson snuggled closer to Nolan. "I want to. I missed the crap out of you while you were in LA."

"Okay. I'm too tired for sex, anyway."

"I don't want you just for your body, silly."

Nolan laughed. No one had called him silly in years. "No?"

"Maybe I like your company."

Nolan hugged Grayson close. "Maybe I like yours too."

"Unless you don't want me to stay."

"No, I do. I definitely do. I missed you when I was gone too. Just, you know. A baby waking you up every two hours isn't exactly what you signed on for the first time you came home with me."

"Sure, but it doesn't scare me as much as you seem to think it should."

Nolan didn't know what to make of that. He kissed the top of Grayson's head and decided to be grateful for their time together now, because he couldn't imagine being twenty-five and taking on a baby he wasn't related to. Grayson was still basking in the glow of their seeing each other again, and Rachel had sucked him in by being adorable and well-behaved. But Nolan suspected that in a few days, Grayson would grow tired of it all and realize this was too much for him.

Maybe that was the troubling thing here. It felt temporary and fragile. Nolan couldn't shake the suspicion that once Grayson saw what he'd *really* signed on for—sleepless nights, messy diapers, and the thrum of anxiety that had vibrated through Nolan's body since the moment Rachel was born—he'd leave. She was so tiny and vulnerable, and it was difficult not to imagine any number of terrible things that could happen to her. And it was Nolan's job now to make sure she was safe and cared for. It completely overwhelmed him sometimes.

He held Grayson close because, for now anyway, Nolan had everything he needed. But he knew it might be fleeting, because if life had taught him nothing else, it was that one never knew what tomorrow held.

Chapter Twenty-Three

"SO, WAIT," Nolan said to Helena. They were in the studio, and they'd just finished filming a segment in which Nolan and Grayson had worked out a design theme for the Chu house. The cameras were gone now, but Helena had asked for a meeting. "The network wants what?"

"Two more episodes," said Helena. "Fan buzz on social media is off the charts for your show. So, look, I've found two more families for you. We can do the house for that couple near the Jersey Shore that you liked, and also this other family that sent a video in. It's a young couple with two toddlers who are stuck living on only one floor of their broken, nonfunctional house. And, uh, strap in, because we're going there tomorrow."

Nolan looked at Grayson, alarmed. Rachel was now a month old, so Nolan had felt okay going back to work. He'd hired a nanny he absolutely adored. She was a perky twenty-two-year-old named Emily who had been taking nanny jobs while she saved up to get her degree in early childhood education. She was great with Rachel and lived close enough that she could get to his place quickly if need be. He'd hoped to postpone going back to work, but the Restoration Channel had a schedule to adhere to, and anyway, he was only really working three days a week. Restoration let him bring Rachel to the studio on days they weren't filming, although he'd also filmed a segment where he explained his absence at the Peter/Justin reveal by saying that he'd adopted a baby. So if he did bring her to filming at the studio, the audience wouldn't be too surprised by a crying baby.

But he'd been looking forward to the hiatus while work was in progress at the Chu house. That promised to be a tearjerker of a project, as it was. Linda Chu was a woman in her sixties who had just gone through a pretty rigorous round of treatment for breast cancer, but her doctor had declared her cancer-free, so she'd decided to seize life by the horns. Her first step was renovating the house she'd been in for thirty years, where she'd lived with her late husband and raised her two now-adult children. Zero work had been done to the house in all the years she'd been there, and it was in pretty rough shape. Linda's kids had no idea how to even start to help, so they'd gotten in touch with the show. So, basically, Nolan and Grayson were now renovating a grandma's house so that it could be the place where everyone went for holidays.

And now Helena was saying she wanted them to do two more.

The next day Nolan drove himself and Grayson out to a house on Long Island, where the Martin family lived.

Grayson read the brief, as had become their routine for in-car footage.

"Kevin Martin works for a social media company, and Debra Martin is a freelancer-slash-stay-at-home mom. Debra has lupus and a few other health problems, which has slowed down renovating this house they bought two years ago. They have two kids, ages two and five." Grayson paused and turned a page. "Okay, so, this house. They bought it two years ago and hired a contractor to fix it, but he was a shady character who left the place a shambles. So they've been saving money for a while to do it right, but in the meantime, half their house is unusable."

They arrived at the house a half hour later. It was a two-story Colonial, just like most of the houses in the neighborhood, and it looked fine from the outside. The front door was ajar, because the film crew was already inside, and Grayson and Nolan were here for the ambush.

Grayson had really started getting into these ambushes. He grinned as they slid through the front door opening, and Nolan found himself getting caught up in it too as they walked down the narrow vestibule.

Here was clearly where the problems began. The floor was sanded but not refinished. The baseboards were missing. The outlets didn't have plates. And this was just the vestibule.

The couple in question were standing in their living room. They both squealed when Grayson and Nolan entered the room.

After hugs were exchanged, Nolan said, "So this is rough."

"No kidding," said Kevin.

"We bought this house two years ago," Debra explained. "When we first walked in, there was something really homey about it. I just had this gut feeling that this was our home, you know? But we wanted to customize it, so we hired this contractor who our friends recommended, but he was… well, what's the contractor equivalent of a quack?"

"Ah," said Nolan.

"He did a lot of things poorly, which makes me think most of his work is not up to code," said Kevin. "We fired him, but then he left our house like this." He gestured around. "But by then we were almost out of money, so we haven't been able to do anything to fix it."

"Upstairs is not usable," added Debra. "The staircase is a hazard, and I won't let the kids on it."

Nolan looked at the staircase and saw right away that that it was missing a railing and that a few of the treads on the steps were not sitting correctly. "Is there anything else wrong with upstairs?"

"Well, we planned to move the laundry upstairs, and the contractor started doing the plumbing work," said Debra, "but who knows if any of it is right?"

So the scope of work here was extensive. The good news was that the Martins had saved money over the past year to fix it. Hopefully the money supplied by the Restoration Channel would be enough to finish the job. Because Nolan's heartstrings were definitely being tugged at.

"We will fix this for you," he said.

Just then, a woman walked into the house with two small children, who immediately ran through the living room and launched themselves at Debra.

Something in Nolan broke then. The previous couples had inspired him and made him want to fix their homes and make them work, but he'd been thinking about each house as a job. This one really hit him right in the heart. This poor couple, with these two adorable little children, were living in this broken, ruined building that had so much potential but didn't work.

Yeah, he and Grayson were going to fix this one.

On the car ride back to the city an hour later, Grayson was uncharacteristically quiet.

"Is anything going on?" Nolan asked. "You're not saying anything."

"I just feel so bad for this family. The house has such a good footprint, and there's a lot of potential to make it a really great place to live, but they got swindled by a bad contractor."

"Yeah. I don't know why, but this one is really hitting me too."

Grayson was silent for another beat before he said, "Well, your life has changed pretty substantially in the last six weeks. You're probably thinking about home and family in a different way."

That was definitely true. "I had a crazy thought the other day about selling the loft. It's fine right now, but in a couple of years, walls are going to be more important."

"Couldn't you just build walls in the loft?"

"I could, I guess. Seems a shame. One of the virtues of the space is how open it is."

"I'm still renting, so I don't even know."

Nolan heard the note of bitterness in Grayson's voice. Grayson seemed pretty annoyed with his roommates recently, so maybe he was tired of that situation. Nolan opted to ignore it in favor of changing the subject.

"Any ideas for the design?"

Grayson did, in fact, have a number of ideas. Nolan couldn't help but notice that he'd gotten more assertive about his opinions in the past few months. Really, ever since the reveal Grayson had done by himself while Nolan had been out of town, Grayson had acted more like a partner and less like a sidekick. It was an interesting change, watching Grayson's confidence bloom.

"I'm excited to sketch it out in the studio," Nolan said when Grayson finished talking. "What do you want for dinner?"

THE LAST straw for Grayson was when he went back to his apartment that weekend to get some clothes and found Kyle making out with some girl in the kitchen.

"You have a bedroom," Grayson said, maneuvering around Kyle to get a soda from the now-working fridge.

"Didn't know you were coming home. It's getting hard to predict. Um. I stored a couple of things in your room. Hope you don't mind."

Grayson went into his room and saw that Kyle had put his guitar case and a box of who knew what on the floor near the doorway. Grayson nudged those things out of the way. He put the soda on his desk and dropped his bag on the bed. Then he went to go use the only bathroom in the apartment and found that Jenny was in the shower.

Grayson had never minded roommates in the past. He'd felt pretty grateful to be able to pay for a roof over his head, in fact. Apprentice designers didn't exactly make big salaries, so a room in a shared apartment had seemed like a gift when he'd first moved in. He and Jenny and Kyle had gotten along well in the beginning. They weren't close friends or anything, but they could spend a few hours together watching TV or eating a meal and have a good time. But he was making pretty good money from the show now—money he wasn't spending because he spent so many nights with Nolan, who seemed to pay for everything out of habit—and he could afford to move out. So if Kyle wanted to use this room and Jenny wanted to tie up the bathroom, well, they could have it.

The catch, though, was that Grayson didn't know where he wanted to move. Should he get his own place? Or should he move in with Nolan?

Nolan had made his intentions pretty clear earlier. If Nolan and Grayson were simply dating, Nolan's family would be an entirely separate entity. Grayson wasn't Rachel's dad, he was just the guy Rachel's father banged sometimes. If that was still the case, there was no way Nolan would let Grayson move into his place. But if Grayson was part of the family, if he and Nolan were in a serious, committed relationship, that changed the equation, didn't it?

Did Nolan want that? Did Grayson?

Well, where did he want to be right now? Not here. Even though Grayson had designed his bedroom, it was his old design aesthetic, before he'd really matured as a designer, and it was so… yellow. And purple. And it felt sterile and no longer like home. And, oh, there was a box of old kitchen stuff in the corner. The popcorn maker an ex-boyfriend had gotten Grayson for Christmas and an old coffee maker that Grayson didn't think worked anymore, and a set of colorful spatulas Grayson had bought when he thought he was going to bake more. Grayson hadn't packed up those things, so Kyle or Jenny must have. It was like they were trying to move him out too.

Grayson went to his closet and assessed what was there. About half of his wardrobe had already been moved over to Nolan's, a few pieces at a time. Nolan had a washer and dryer in his apartment, so Grayson had taken to doing laundry there instead of the laundromat in his neighborhood, mostly so he wouldn't have to hoard quarters anymore. And then he just… left his clothes at Nolan's. He spent more nights at the loft than his own apartment. So of course Jenny and Kyle would think he had one foot out the door.

He had to get out of here.

He'd told Nolan he'd be spending the night at his own apartment tonight, thinking to give Nolan some space with Rachel, but now he regretted that decision. It slowly dawned on Grayson that he belonged in that loft with Nolan and Rachel, not in this apartment. This place had been great once, but he'd outgrown it.

But he didn't want to intrude on them now, so he texted Danny instead.

He met Danny a half hour later at a bar halfway between their apartments. It was kind of a dive, but they made a good burger and had Grayson's favorite beer on tap. It was early in the evening and not even completely dark yet, so the bar was far from crowded. He and Danny got a table in the outside seating area behind the bar, basically just a backyard with some picnic tables and fairy lights. It was a nice evening, though. Warm with clear skies and the beginning of what promised to be a technicolor sunset.

"Okay. Explain all this to me again," said Danny once they were settled with drinks.

"I have three options, I think," said Grayson. "Everything stays the same. I keep living with Jenny and Kyle, I keep seeing Nolan, I keep doing the show. It's all the same."

"I'm guessing that's not really an option, though, if we're having a conversation like this over beer."

"Yeah. I don't think anyone wants that. So I have to decide if I'm *with* Nolan, or if we're just casually dating and I should get my own place."

"What do you mean by *with*?"

Grayson nodded, wondering how out of nowhere this conversation must seem to Danny. Even though Danny obviously knew Nolan meant a lot to Grayson, it hadn't been so long ago that Grayson had found the idea of settling down completely terrifying. Danny had never been in a relationship that lasted longer than a month, and until Nolan, Grayson hadn't really either. "I mean, if I'm with Nolan, I have to commit to being part of this family unit. I'd be in a committed relationship with Nolan, which sounds great. I don't want to be with anyone else. But I'd also basically be a dad to Rachel. And, like, I watched my baby sister when I was fifteen and she was eight, but that's not at all the same thing. And I guess I find that intimidating. But it's not fair to Nolan or Rachel for me to make that kind of commitment unless I'm… committed. Like, I can't decide to go for it and then flake in three months when it gets hard, you know?"

Danny frowned like he still didn't get it. "Okay. What's the other option?"

"We keep seeing each other casually and I get my own place. Probably when the show stops filming and we have no reason to see each other regularly, we'll drift apart."

Danny nodded. "Okay. I'm no expert. But my older sister just got married and I had to go to her husband's bachelor party, where he got drunk and lectured me about love, so I have gleaned a couple of things."

Grayson laughed. "Sure, okay."

"First, do you love Nolan?"

"Do I—?" Well, did he? He'd told Nolan he was falling in love because what he felt went deep, but he'd been expecting some kind of lightning-strike moment that told him yes, this was love. It seemed like the universe was going to make him figure it out for himself, though. Whenever he and Nolan were together, he felt happy. He thought about Nolan all the time and always looked forward to seeing him again. But was that love?

"I think that's the crux of the problem here. He's either a guy you like to fuck after work, or he's a guy you love and want to spend the rest of your life with. And I think you have to decide which of those he is. If he's just a guy you like to fuck, then great. Get your own place, preferably here in Crown Heights so I can walk over and hang out with you all the time, and continue seeing Nolan for as long as it lasts. If you treat it that way, it will probably end, like you said, when you stop doing the TV show together, which *will* happen, because unless you're that born-again couple with eight kids who make everything beige, most Restoration Channel shows usually only do two or three seasons, right?"

"I guess," said Grayson.

"Or, you go for it. If you love this man, if he's who you want to spend the rest of your life with, then you make a commitment. I know this isn't exactly how you saw your life going, but has anything gone the way you've expected in the last five years?"

That was a fair point. "Nope."

"So. Do you love him?"

Grayson closed his eyes and pictured Nolan's face. Earlier that day, they'd spent a few hours in the studio, designing the Martins' house and chatting with Helena about the rest of the season. Nolan had been in a good mood. He'd brought Rachel to the studio, even. He'd filmed a talking head to be inserted into the beginning of the episode about the Martins where he explained that he had adopted a baby. He'd put Rachel in a bouncy chair, and she burbled happily while they debated color stories and kitchen materials.

It had felt nice. Even the studio, which lacked the hominess of a real design studio because it was a set, felt more like a home to Grayson than his own apartment, probably because of the people in it.

"I do," Grayson said. And it was true. He loved Nolan.

"There's your answer," said Danny."

"Okay, but... I don't know if I'm ready to be a father. That's a lot of responsibility."

Danny narrowed his eyes at Grayson for a long moment and then took a sip of his beer.

"What?" said Grayson.

"We've already had a deeper heart-to-heart than I'm really comfortable with, so I'm just going to say this thing and then we're not going to make a big deal about it, okay? Just... I'm your best friend and I love you like a brother. That's where this is coming from."

"Okay. Just say it."

"You're the strongest, most capable person I know, Gray. When your parents kicked you out, you moved back to New York with not much more than a couple hundred dollars and a stick of gum, and somehow you made that work. You got a job and a place to live with zero help from your parents. You know my roommate

Pete? He fills a suitcase with clothes every weekend and goes out to his parents' house on the Island so his mom can do his laundry for him. Aiden's parents pay his rent. And, like, I have nothing against that. This city is a fucking hard place to live. But *you* made it work. You got a job doing what you love, and now you're doing it in front of a huge television audience. You figured out how to succeed in this city all without any help from your family. I'm honestly in awe, because I don't know how I would have gotten by if my dad didn't back me up sometimes. I think you can do anything if you put your mind to it, including taking care of that baby. I mean, look at all the work you did to set up Nolan's loft. Sure, I helped a little, but that was all you."

Tears stung Grayson's eyes. He hadn't realized Danny saw him that way. He didn't see himself that way. The past few years had felt like such a constant struggle that now, when he didn't have to struggle much anymore, he wasn't sure how to handle it.

"Thanks," said Grayson. "I promise I won't embarrass you by saying something schmoopy about how much I love you too."

Danny winked. "Uh-huh. My point is just that if you want to be a dad, you can be a dad. You can do anything."

Grayson didn't think that was true—there were plenty of things he couldn't do—but he appreciated the sentiment. And he was awfully fond of that baby girl. Just last night, she'd woken up in the middle of the night, and Nolan had been sleeping so soundly he barely stirred, so Grayson got up and fed her, and they'd had a nice little moment rocking in the chair.

That had been a pretty fatherly thing to do, hadn't it?

"Okay. Thanks, Danny."

"Anytime. Can we talk about sports or hot guys or Marvel movies now?"

Grayson laughed. "Sure. I mean, if I wasn't in a relationship, the waiter with the dark hair could get it."

Danny turned to look. "Oh, yeah. Oh… look at that. The view is even better from behind."

So they moved on, but Grayson had a better idea of what he needed to do now. The only trick would be convincing Nolan.

Chapter Twenty-Four

GRAYSON HAD struggled with what to say to Nolan so much that they basically just skated by for two weeks.

But most of the season was now in the can. They were finishing up the Chu house this week, the Martins' next week, and a third house the week after. So Helena had set up cameras in the studio in front of a brand-new sofa—it was a real sofa and not the old prop they'd had until then—and planned to film the talking head interviews where Grayson and Nolan explained what was happening in each episode.

"So the idea here," said Helena, "is to make it seem like you're just chatting with the audience from your home studio. I will throw a specific topic at you and then let you riff on it. We'll film it and splice all this in with the episodes."

"Will viewers think it's weird that we're wearing the same thing in every episode?" asked Grayson.

"No. That's why I asked you to dress plainly. I mean, Nolan looks like he always does."

She gestured at Nolan, who wore an oatmeal-colored T-shirt and dark jeans.

"And you look a little more subdued than usual, so I think it'll all blend together. It's not the sort of detail most viewers notice, anyway. We do stuff like this all the time."

Grayson looked down at himself. He realized belatedly that he had on one of Nolan's black T-shirts, which, incidentally, were not just the cheap kind one bought at a big-box store. Instead, it was made of some super soft luxury cotton fabric that had some stretch to it and sat nicely against Grayson's skin. Grayson had paired it with dark tan khakis and a black-and-white scarf with some fringe on it. At some point during filming the show, Grayson had decided scarves were his thing, so he supposed he looked like himself too.

"Roll camera," Helena said.

Eddie, the camera operator, did something, and the red light to show they were filming came on.

"Tell me about the Roberts house as if you haven't done any work on it yet and explain why you are eager to help the Robertses have a fully functional home."

So Nolan and Grayson talked to each other and the camera, mostly about how eager they were to modernize these houses and make these spaces functional, and they argued a little about their design aesthetics, and Grayson tried to crack jokes when Nolan became too serious.

"You *say* modern industrial," Grayson said when they talked about the design they'd come up with for the Martin house, "but your original color scheme idea read a little more 'bruise' to me. I mean, gray and purple look nice together, but if you don't do it right, the house could end up looking like it was in a fight."

Nolan cracked up at that, which was encouraging.

They finished for the day a couple of hours later. While Nolan called the nanny to let her know he'd be home soon, Grayson decided that tonight would be the night. He'd had two whole weeks to sort out his feelings, so all he had to do was lay everything out on the table for Nolan to take or leave. Grayson was tired of living in limbo, and he knew for certain that he was ready to dive into this whole home and family thing. He just hoped Nolan was in that place with him.

"I was thinking," Nolan said a minute later, while Helena was out of earshot, "that I could call in an order somewhere and we can pick up dinner on the way home. I barely slept last night, and after shooting all day, I have no energy for cooking."

"Okay. That's fine with me."

So they walked back to Nolan's place and picked up dinner from a new Japanese-Mexican fusion place—it was mostly tacos with Japanese flavors—and arrived back at the loft in time to let Emily get to the dinner date she had that night on time. Rachel was asleep, so Nolan got right to work laying out take-out containers on the table.

Grayson took a deep breath. "Can I talk to you about something?"

"Of course," said Nolan. "You want a drink? I bought a six-pack of that beer you like."

"Sure, that would be great."

So Grayson waited while Nolan grabbed two beers from the fridge and then settled into his chair.

"What did you want to talk about?" Nolan asked, sounding casual.

He had no idea what was coming. Grayson hoped this would go the way he wanted. "I'm moving out of my apartment."

"Wow, really? That's great. Tired of room-mates, huh?"

"Well, that's part of it, yeah. My roommate Kyle is kind of using my bedroom as a big closet when I'm not there. When I went home the other night, he'd moved a bunch of his winter clothing in. 'Since you're not using it,' is what he said."

"Ugh. I had a roommate in my twenties who—"

"Can I just get this out?" Grayson said. He knew he was prone to tangents when he spoke, but he wanted to try to keep that to a minimum here. At least until he blurted out what he had to say.

"Go ahead," said Nolan.

"So, I decided to move out a couple of weeks ago, and I've been thinking a lot about where I want to go instead. And the thing is… I want to live here."

Nolan immediately balked at that, jerking back in his chair and tilting his head. "Oh, Gray. I don't know if I—"

"Let me explain myself, okay? Because here's the thing. I know that you probably don't want to get married again and I'm not asking for that, but I do know this: I love you and I want to be with you. You keep telling me that I'm too young to want to commit, but my life hasn't exactly been normal by any stretch. And anyway, I should get to decide what I'm ready for. And I'm ready for a home and a family. Working on the show has made me realize that, like I never had before. So what I'm saying is that if you'll have me, I want us. I want you, me, and Rachel, to be a family."

So there it was. But instead of answering, Nolan stared at him.

GRAYSON WANTED to be a family.

Of all the things he could have said, that was about the last thing Nolan expected.

He stared at Grayson probably more than was appropriate, but it felt like his brain had short-circuited. And suddenly he was transported to the moment, years ago, when he'd decided he wanted to marry Ricky.

It had happened in an instant. They'd been out in LA somewhere, shopping for something practical. Nolan couldn't remember exactly what—probably something for Nolan to wear to Ricky's next movie premiere party. The kinds of made-for-TV romance movies Ricky had been making in those days didn't merit splashy red carpets, but usually the studio paid for everyone to watch the movie's premiere in a private event space, and typically everyone dressed up. Ricky had a stylist who picked out event clothes for him, but Nolan had decided that was an unnecessary expense for him, so they'd likely been in some high-end shop trying to find the perfect suit.

They'd been together for long enough by that point that they had a shorthand, and Nolan could tell when he lifted a shirt off the rack that Ricky didn't like, just by the expression on Ricky's face. And something about that had felt so homey and charming. Nolan had never felt connected to another person that way, and he'd decided, in that moment, to propose.

Grayson was right—Nolan was in no hurry to get married again. He wasn't completely against the idea. He wasn't so naive as to think that not getting married would somehow make him immune from facing some other tragedy in his life. But it still felt odd to even think about marrying someone else when part of him still felt married to Ricky.

On the other hand, the man sitting in front of him was someone entirely different. Grayson had walked into Nolan's life and made Nolan feel alive again. These past few months, Nolan had felt whole and human for the first time since Ricky had been diagnosed with cancer. Ricky was gone; he'd want Nolan to move on.

And here was Grayson saying he wanted to be a family… with him.

Wasn't that what Nolan had been after the whole time? He didn't want to replace Ricky, and he knew he never could, but he'd been filling his life with what Ricky would have wanted for him. He had Rachel now. He had a good home and a job he loved. And now he had Grayson.

He'd been waiting for the other shoe to drop since the moment he'd met Grayson, hadn't he? Well, maybe not at first, but definitely since he found out Rachel was on the way. He'd been waiting for Grayson to decide that this whole home-and-family thing was not what he wanted at this point in his life. Except it seemed as if it was. Nolan had listened to everything Grayson had said, and he knew now that all of this was exactly what Grayson wanted. For Nolan, this moment was like letting out a breath he'd been holding for a long time.

So he wasn't sure about marriage… yet. But being with Grayson, he could do that.

"You're not saying anything," said Grayson. "It's been a few minutes."

"I know. I'm sorry. I'm just… thinking."

"I've shocked you. I'm sorry. I just... I needed you to know how I felt."

"I'm glad you told me. I...." Nolan had no idea what to say.

Grayson loved him. And, well, he loved Grayson back, didn't he? It wasn't something that had ever crystallized in his heart or his mind, but the whole reason he hadn't been able to let Grayson go—not that Grayson was willing to be let go—was that part of him had been in love with Grayson from the first moment they'd set eyes on each other. And the truth was, although he'd been holding Grayson at arm's length, he hated nights when Grayson slept in Brooklyn. He hated sleeping in his big bed alone. He wanted Grayson here as much as Grayson wanted to be here, but he'd been afraid to admit that to himself, afraid to want something he didn't know if he could—or should—have.

In a lot of ways, it was still too soon. But it also felt right.

"I love you too," Nolan said. "I don't know that I realized that for certain until just now, but it's true. And I love having you in this space. And if you're really willing to be my partner, to raise Rachel with me and for us to be a family? Then I'm in. I want that for us."

A huge grin broke out across Grayson's face. He shot out of his chair, and Nolan realized he was standing too, before he had a good grasp on what he was doing. Grayson threw his arms around Nolan, so Nolan hugged him back.

"It's going to be hard," Nolan said. "Raising Rachel will be hard, and being together will be hard, and there's so much to work out and sort through, but... it'll be good too."

"Yeah. It'll be good." Grayson kissed Nolan.

Nolan forgot any objections he'd ever had as they kissed. He held Grayson in his arms and wanted to weep with how good this felt. He snuck his fingers into Grayson's hair and said, "I never thought I'd fall in love again so soon."

"And this doesn't mean you love Ricky any less, nor will it tarnish his memory," Grayson said. "It's just a new chapter in your life."

"Yes." He held Grayson close. "Yes, a new chapter. I like that."

"So we're gonna do this?" Grayson said, pulling away. "Because I've already started packing. I could hire a man with a van and get the rest of my stuff over here next weekend."

Nolan laughed. "How much stuff are we talking?"

"Not a lot. It's mostly clothes. I could donate most of my furniture to my roommates, since it's not worth much. I've got a few kitchen gadgets and some linens that are *not* beige or white."

"Uh-huh." Nolan nearly laughed. He couldn't believe he was letting Grayson move in here, but he supposed he did need more color in his life.

"Come on, let's eat," Grayson said. "I'm starving."

Epilogue

THE DAY after they wrapped their first house of season two, Helena decided they should film new opening credits.

Nolan stood in the studio, near the big work table, with the cabinets full of material samples in the cabinets behind them. Grayson stood next to him, fiddling with his shirt. Grayson had actually been the one who came up with what they would say. Nolan thought it was cheesy, but he was willing to roll with it.

The director cleared his throat. "And... action!"

Nolan started, as they'd discussed. "A funny thing happened in the time between wrapping up last season and starting filming this one."

"We got married!" They both shouted in unison as they held up their hands with matching rings.

"Cut!" shouted the director.

Helena laughed once the camera was off. "That was adorably goofy. I loved it."

Nolan smiled despite himself.

"We'll have you do a voiceover for the rest and we'll show clips from the first season while you explain the premise of the show. It should be like the first season credits, but a little longer, since we have more clips to work from."

Rachel squirmed free from the nanny's arms and toddled over. She launched herself at Grayson, who caught her and hoisted her up on his hip.

"Hi, sweetie," said Grayson.

She wrapped her arms around Gray's neck. Nolan's chest felt a little tight. He was thrilled that they'd bonded. And now that her first real word seemed imminent—she spoke in babble almost constantly lately—they'd been talking about what to have her call them each. "Daddy Nolan" and "Daddy Gray" were currently the leading contenders.

Helena plopped onto the sofa and sipped from her water bottle. "Oh, did I tell you? We just signed a new show for the channel. It's this gay couple that buys rough houses and lives in them while they renovate."

"I've heard of people doing that," said Nolan. "I couldn't do it. It's basically camping."

Grayson burst out laughing. "Oh, heaven forbid."

Nolan shot him a look that was meant to be admonishing. He sighed. "Plus, then you're moving every few months."

"I'm sure they have less stuff than you do," said Grayson. "It would be a much easier move than the one we're undertaking now."

It was true. Nolan and Grayson had bought an old Federal style three-story house on Nineteenth Street in Chelsea, just a couple of blocks from the Restoration Channel offices. The house had been well-maintained, but was still nearly two hundred years old. Travis, who specialized in renovating very old houses, had recommended a couple of old coworkers to help with renovations, so now Nolan and Grayson were juggling that while they packed up the loft and tried to decide how best to stage it to put it on the market. Nolan's Realtor thought the loft would sell in the blink of an eye, even though the New York City real estate market had cooled a little recently.

In the meantime, packing up all of Nolan's things had proven to be a larger task than he'd anticipated. Part of that was the sheer volume of Rachel's stuff. How someone so tiny could have so much stuff continued to amaze him.

"You should do more of that on the show," said Helena.

"Do what?" Nolan asked, gathering the toys Rachel had left on the floor.

"Obviously the focus of the show is on the houses you renovate, but I am glad you agreed to do some little segments where we check in on you and your family. What do you think about dropping in on your house before the renovation is done?"

"Sure," said Nolan. He was game. He'd never really opposed making his life public. He often thought that if he'd had someone like himself to look up to when he'd been a kid, he would have found comfort and inspiration in it. Grayson liked to point out that Nolan *had* been that person for him, which mostly only served to make Nolan feel old. Still, he liked the idea of showing their happy family to the world.

It was funny. The misery of his life in the wake of Ricky's death had made him want to hide from the world. And he still had moments when sadness about Ricky would hit him, as if from out of nowhere. Just last week, he'd caught one of Ricky's movies while flipping channels and had nearly lost it. But mostly, he looked back on his life with Ricky with fondness. He'd always miss his first husband. But he was happy in his life now too. And he wanted to shout that from the rooftops. Or put it on TV, at least.

"Cool, let's pick a date for that," said Helena. "I like the dynamic between you two now. And our viewers *love* getting to know the couples. Did you know that people on social media were shipping you two when the first season aired?"

"What does that mean?" asked Nolan.

"It means they wanted us to be in a relationship," said Grayson. "I bet some of them were sitting on their sofas yelling, 'Kiss him, you idiot!'"

"*You* did that at the premiere party, Gray," Nolan pointed out.

"The sexual tension between us was palpable, babe."

Nolan laughed. Yeah, he was happy. This man and their little family had made him happier than he'd ever thought possible after Ricky's death. So, yeah, he was okay sharing that with the world.

"I guess we should give the people what they want," he said, giving Grayson a kiss.

Keep Reading
for an Excerpt

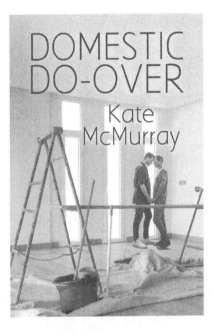

A Restoration Channel Novel

Chapter One

"DREAM" DIVORCE! screamed the tabloid headline. It was the first thing Brandon saw when he got out of the subway. The story was punctuated by a photo of Brandon looking distressed.

He knew he should have taken a cab.

It was a windy, late-winter day in New York, and a recent dusting of snow danced like a cloud across the 14th Street sidewalk as Brandon walked west toward the Restoration Channel offices near Chelsea Market. He tried to focus on those snowflakes instead of his recent, well-publicized divorce, especially since so much of what was being printed in the tabloids was about eight miles from the truth.

And now he'd been summoned to the Restoration Channel offices, probably to negotiate the end of his contract, because his very popular house-flipping show, cohosted with his pretty wife, had been summarily canceled the minute the word divorce was first uttered in public.

Then again, maybe getting off TV would be good for him. He could reopen his old real estate agency and parlay some of his fame into a few clients to get started. He could return to obscurity and not worry about tabloid headlines or television contracts. He could give up trying to make his marriage look like a happy union instead of the fraud it was.

He walked into the reception area and was greeted by a woman who grinned widely when he appeared.

"Oh, Mr. Chase! It's so great to see you. I'm so sorry about the divorce."

He nodded.

"That Kayla was a real bitch, stepping out on you the way she did. I totally understand why you wanted to end things."

"That's not really—" But Brandon cut himself off. It wasn't worth getting into, especially not if the network was about to end his contract.

"Mr. Harwood is expecting you," the receptionist said. "I'll walk you back."

He followed the receptionist to the office of Garrett Harwood, the head of programming for the Restoration Channel, a network that aired mostly the kinds of programming people had on in the background when they stayed in hotels. Home renovation and fashion makeover shows were the network's bread and butter. The channel was incredibly popular, which was the main reason Brandon's divorce was such big news. His show, Dream Home, had been a massive hit for the network… which was probably why everything crashed down on him so hard when the paparazzi caught Kayla out to dinner with her boyfriend.

He steeled himself and walked into the office. "Hello, Mr. Harwood."

"Brandon! So good to see you. Please have a seat."

Brandon debated making small talk first but ultimately decided not to say anything, and instead just sat in the chair across the desk from Harwood.

"Let me cut to the chase," Harwood said.

Brandon's pulse kicked up a notch. Here it came. His time as a minor celebrity with a show on the Restoration Channel was coming to an end.

"I have an opportunity for you."

That was the last thing Brandon expected to hear. "You… what?"

Harwood grinned. "Here's the deal. While I don't regret canceling Dream Home because the show couldn't have continued under the circumstances, you still have a lot of goodwill with this company and remain incredibly popular with our viewership. Even the Dream Home reruns we've been airing on Tuesday nights are getting huge ratings. So we'd like to offer you a new show."

"Are you serious?" Brandon was so sure he was coming here today to get fired that he'd basically already planned out his retirement from television stardom. Part of him had been sad at the prospect of leaving the limelight, but another part was looking forward to it. So much of his life had been given over to maintaining his public image that he was kind of looking forward to just… living.

But no, Harwood wanted him to star in another TV show.

"Here's the premise," Harwood said. "Are you familiar with Victorian Flatbush?"

"That little area in Brooklyn with all the old mansions?"

"The same! Well, my daughter just bought a house there, so I was walking around the neighborhood. Some of those houses are gorgeous, but many are pretty run-down. There are, in fact, six for sale just in a four-block radius, all at bargain prices. Well, bargain for Brooklyn."

Brandon could see where this was going. "Wait, you want to do a show about flipping Victorian mansions in Brooklyn?"

"Exactly."

That would be a hard no from Brandon. Flipping houses in New York City was just too risky, an incredible financial investment that probably wouldn't pay off. Even if one could get the house cheap, the labor and materials cost more than in most other parts of the country. It was why he and Kayla had usually flipped houses in the distant suburbs. Not to mention those old houses often had all kinds of hidden problems and would have to be brought up to code, which could get really expensive. The odds of him turning a profit on a house like that were pretty small.

"I can see you're hesitating," Harwood said. "We could expand out of the neighborhood in the second season and work on brownstones, or make over houses in the outer parts of Brooklyn. But I think the New York angle is key. Show the world that the city is more than just big apartment buildings."

"The financial risk—"

"We'll up your per-episode salary from what you were getting on Dream Home, and the network will go in on every house you buy to help shoulder some of the risk. That's how invested we are in making this work."

That did change the equation. On Dream Home, although they'd received a salary, the financial risk of actually flipping the houses was entirely on Brandon and Kayla, meaning they'd often had to compromise to make a profit. Nothing dangerous; Brandon had always thought an important part of house flipping was to give buyers a place to live that was safe and welcoming. But it meant laminate instead of hardwood in some cases, or not removing load-bearing walls, or buying back-splash tiles on clearance instead of the more expensive ones they liked better—that sort of thing. Kayla had always had a good eye for a bargain and could tweak a design if it was more cost-effective to do so. After they had the requisite fight about the design on camera, of course.

They'd both had roles to play. On the show Brandon was the frugal one who wanted to keep the design practical and attractive to a wide range of buyers. Kayla liked things a little splashier and was willing to spend more on great design even if it meant narrowing the pool of potential homeowners. The reality was that Kayla wanted the profits more than anything and usually introduced something wild and then caved to show that they were willing to compromise.

That they were a loving couple working together on projects they were passionate about. That was the whole story of the show.

"We're calling the new show Domestic Do-over." Harwood held up his hands, miming a marquee. "It's good, right? I love alliteration."

Brandon almost laughed. Harwood was fairly new to the network. His predecessor had only retired about a year before, so Brandon hadn't worked with Harwood much. Brandon supposed Domestic Do-over was a pretty clever name for a show about home renovation.

"Okay," said Brandon. "What about Kayla?"

Harwood shook his head. "What about her? You're not working together anymore."

"No, but… I mean, she still has a contract and…."

"We're buying out the rest of it. This would be a show hosted just by you."

"I know, but—"

"Look, we gave this a lot of thought. We tried to keep Hip Houses on the air after John and Melinda got divorced, and no one wanted to watch it. Our viewers aren't here for our hosts' interpersonal drama. They like happy couples, not bitter exes. But what they do like is a good design challenge. These old houses are bound to have issues. They'll need electrical and plumbing upgrades, probably some structural work, all of that stuff. It adds a plot twist." Harwood lowered his voice a little, mimicking an announcer. "Is Brandon in over his head this time?"

Brandon pursed his lips. He wasn't pleased that Kayla was being left out. They'd been partners for a long time, and he wasn't sure he was interesting enough to carry a show by himself. Although, of course, a divorced couple wasn't good for the Restoration Channel brand.

"If it helps," said Harwood, "we've been talking with a local contractor who specializes in restoring old homes, and he's interested in coming on board. Great guy. Lots of sex appeal, but a little rough around the edges. I think the viewers will love him. We're committed to this project. We just need a host."

"In other words, you're doing the show with or without me."

"Well, yes. But we want you. You'd be a fantastic host. You know this market well, you know how to flip houses, and the audience loves you."

"I don't know. It's still a huge financial risk."

"Tell you what. We've got our eye on a house right now. It's been on the market for almost four months now, so the asking price is negotiable. Go take a look at it. I think you'll fall in love with it. If you don't, then that's fine. We can find another project for you."

"Or buy out the rest of my contract."

"Or that, but let's keep an open mind here. We've got you through the end of the year, right?"

"July."

"A few more months, then. Still, you know we love you. We want to keep you as part of the Restoration Channel family. We'll find something for you to do. But I think you'll see this house and love it on sight. Here, let me give you the information."

Harwood turned around and rifled through a folder on the credenza behind his desk. Turning back, he handed Brandon a piece of paper. It looked like the printout from a real estate website.

The photo of the house made it look haunted. Several windows were boarded up, the paint was clearly peeling badly, and the front door looked like it had been knocked off one of its hinges. According to the data on the paper, the house had been built in 1917. Five bedrooms, three bathrooms, about 3,000 square feet. The asking price really was a bargain, less than a million dollars in a neighborhood of $3 million homes, and if it had been on the market for four months, it was likely overpriced, even at that.

"All right, I'll go look at it."

"I knew I could intrigue you. We really want you for this project, but no pressure. If you're really done, we can negotiate the end of your contract the same way we did with Kayla."

"Then let me look at the house and sleep on it."

"Great!" Harwood stood, signaling that the meeting was over. "I look forward to hearing from you, Brandon."

THE HOUSE was on Argyle Road, a few blocks south of Prospect Park in Brooklyn. Brandon had known this neighborhood of old houses was here but had never been to it before. He walked down Church Avenue from the subway station until he got to the road he was looking for. Six-foot-tall brick pillars with stone flower boxes on top signaled the start of Argyle Road, so Brandon turned.

And was suddenly transported.

Church Avenue was a bustling thoroughfare clogged with buses and cars, with crowded sidewalks, people rushing between the shops or running toward the subway station. It wasn't pretty, as such. Although the neighborhood had historical significance, the section of Church Avenue between the subway station and Argyle Road was mostly big discount stores and bodegas, crumbling brick architecture, and the occasional empty storefront. Brandon had walked by a shop proclaiming "fresh fish" on a big neon sign, but it smelled like some of those fish had been sitting out in the sun for a few days.

Then he turned onto Argyle Road, and it was like he was in an entirely different universe. It was quieter, for one thing. There were fewer people, and trees everywhere. Before him was an entire street of large detached houses, well-maintained lawns, and vintage streetlights. It looked more like a wealthy suburb than Brooklyn.

The houses were amazing.

They were a mishmash of styles. A tall Tudor house sat across from a Queen Anne, which was down the block from a Greek Revival home with columns across the front, and there was even a Japanese-style place that looked like a pagoda. Some of the houses were breathtaking in their size and beauty, painted a variety of colors—navy blue, white, yellow, mint green—and some looked like they should have been condemned years ago. Albemarle Road, which intersected Argyle, had a row of landscaped islands through the middle, green space in a borough where space was a premium.

Brandon cursed. How dare this neighborhood try to charm him! He'd wanted to resist this so much. The brown street signs indicated he was now in a historic district—which meant getting permits for renovations from the city would be a unique challenge, yet another reason not to do this—but man, he'd love to live here.

Then he arrived at the house, and it did indeed look like something out of a horror movie. But he had the code to the lockbox, so he punched it in, took out the key, and let himself in.

The inside of the house was… pretty bleak, actually. The front door opened into a narrow hallway and a staircase. There was an archway to his right, which led to an empty living room. The brick around the fireplace looked like someone had already taken a sledgehammer to it, and the ancient wallpaper was peeling. The rest of the house was more of the same. The layout inside was boxy and compartmentalized, the hardwood floors on the first floor were stained and scarred, there were mouse droppings in the kitchen, and the beige carpeting that covered the entire second floor smelled like dog.

And yet.

Brandon could see what this house had once been. The metal grate over the fireplace was an ornate piece of ironwork. The swirls in the wood used for the bannister on the stairs to the second floor were unique—Brandon hadn't seen anything like it in a long time. The wallpaper was actually kind of neat in the places where it wasn't a peeling, discolored nightmare, and Brandon could imagine what the main living areas had once looked like. The crown moldings, the wainscoting on the second floor, the archways.... No one made houses like this anymore. The kitchen had clearly been renovated sometime in the late seventies, but even that had a certain kind of charm, from the orange tile someone had chosen to the boxy design of the cabinets.

Before he knew it, Brandon was mentally making over the space, deciding which walls he'd remove, trying to determine if the floors were salvageable, imagining what a modern kitchen could look like with a few touches—light fixtures, tiles—that would nod back at what this house had once looked like.

Shit.

Brandon wanted this project. He knew all the hazards. He'd have to pay for an exterminator to fumigate the bejesus out of the place first. The walls likely held asbestos, outdated electrical systems that would have to be brought up to code, and pipes that needed to be replaced. But the structure seemed sound. The floors creaked in a few places, but Brandon knew how to fix that. He could make this house into something spectacular and sell it for twice the current asking price.

He pulled out his phone and called Garrett Harwood. "I'm at the house," he said when Harwood answered the phone.

"And?"

"I love it. I'm in."

KATE MCMURRAY writes smart romantic fiction. She likes creating stories that are brainy, funny, and, of course, sexy, with regular-guy characters and urban sensibilities. She advocates for romance stories by and for everyone. When she's not writing, she edits textbooks, watches baseball, plays violin, crafts things out of yarn, and wears a lot of cute dresses. She lives in Brooklyn, NY, with two cats and too many books.

Website: www.katemcmurray.com
Twitter: @katemcmwriter
Facebook: www.facebook.com/katemcmurraywriter
Instagram: @katemcmurraygram

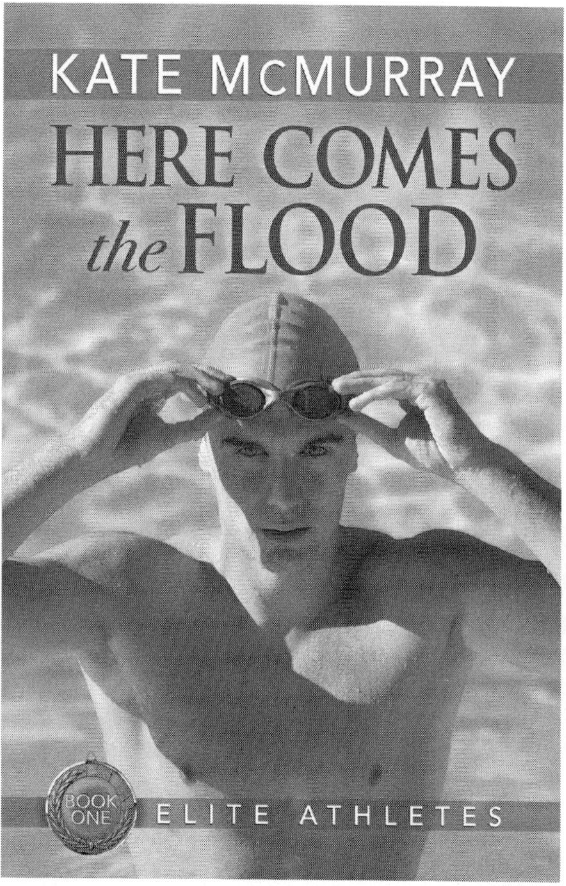
KATE McMURRAY
HERE COMES the FLOOD
BOOK ONE
ELITE ATHLETES

An Elite Athletes Novel

Two years ago, swimmer Isaac Flood hit rock bottom. His alcoholism caught up with him, landing him in jail with a DUI. After facing his demons in rehab, he's ready to get back in the pool. He stuns everyone at the US Olympic Trials, and now he's back at his fourth Olympics with something to prove.

Diver Tim Swan made headlines for snatching a surprise gold medal four years ago, and then making a viral coming-out video with his actor boyfriend, the subject of splashy tabloid headlines. Now his relationship is over and Tim just wants to focus on winning gold again, but reporters in Madrid threaten to overshadow Tim's skill on the platform.

When Isaac and Tim meet, they recognize each other as kindred spirits—they are both dodging media pressure while devoting their lives to the sports they love. As they get to know each other—and try to one-up each other with their respective medal counts—they realize they're becoming more than friends. But will the relationship burn bright for just sixteen days, or can it last past the Closing Ceremony?

www.dreamspinnerpress.com

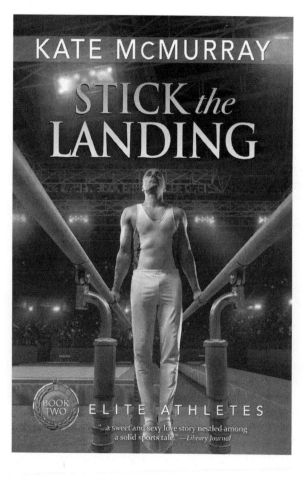

KATE McMURRAY

STICK *the* LANDING

BOOK TWO ELITE ATHLETES

An Elite Athletes Novel

Jake Mirakovitch might be the best gymnast in the world, but there's one big problem: he chokes in international competition. The least successful of a family of world-class gymnasts, he has struggled to shake off nerves in the past. This time he's determined to bring home the gold no matter what.

Retired figure skater Topher Caldwell wants a job as a commentator for the American network that covers the Olympics, and at the Summer Olympics in Madrid, he has a chance to prove himself with a few live features. He can't afford to stumble.

Olympic victories eluded Topher, so he knows about tripping when it really counts. When he interviews Jake, the two bond over the weight of all that pressure. The flamboyant reporter attracts the kind of attention Jake—stuck in a glass closet—doesn't want, but Jake can't stay away. Topher doesn't want to jeopardize his potential new job, and fooling around with a high-profile athlete seems like a surefire way to do just that. Yet Topher can't stay away either....

www.dreamspinnerpress.com

An Elite Athletes Novel

Sprinter Jason Jones Jr., known around the world as JJ, is America's hope to take the title of Fastest Man in the World, the champion of the Olympic 100-meter sprint. Two years before, a doping scandal brought his winning streak to a crashing end, and even though he's been cleared of wrongdoing, he's finding it hard to escape the damage to his reputation. At the Games in Madrid, no one believes he's innocent, and officials from the doping agency follow him everywhere.

It just fuels JJ's determination to show them he's clean and still the fastest man on earth.

If only he wasn't tempted by foxy hurdler Brandon Stanton, an engineering student and math prodigy who views each race like a complicated equation. His analytical approach helps him win races, and he wants to help JJ do the same. But JJ's been burned too many times before and doesn't trust anyone who has all the answers. No matter how sexy and charming JJ finds Brandon, the Olympics is no place for romance. Or is it?

www.dreamspinnerpress.com

THERE HAS TO BE A REASON

KATE McMURRAY

WMU: Book One

Dave is enjoying his junior year at a big New England university, even if none of his relationships have been especially satisfying. He plans to hang around with his best friend Joe and focus on his studies until he graduates, and then he'll figure out the rest.

Meeting Noel changes his plans.

Noel is strikingly beautiful and unlike anyone Dave knows. Something about Noel draws Dave to him—an attraction Dave doesn't feel ready to label. And even if he was, why would Noel be interested in Dave? And what about Joe? He hates Noel and everything he represents, and he might hate Dave if he finds out about Dave's secret desires. So Dave will have to keep those feelings hidden—along with his relationship with Noel.

But Noel has fought too hard for his identity to be Dave's dirty secret. Will Dave tell the truth and risk the life he's always known… or live a lie and risk losing the love of his life?

www.dreamspinnerpress.com

WHAT'S THE USE OF WONDERING?

KATE McMURRAY

WMU: Book Two

Violinist Logan has spent most of his life train-
ing for a career in music. But as the pressure mounts
during his junior year, he questions whether playing
in an orchestra is the future he wants, or one chosen
by his parents. His new roommate—that annoying jerk
Peter from last year's production of Guys and Dolls—
complicates matters. Crammed into a dorm room with
the overconfident but undeniably hot accounting major,
Logan can't stop snarling.

Then Peter sprains his ankle building sets, and Logan grudgingly agrees to play chauffeur. But instead
of putting further strain on their relationship, spending
time together reveals some common ground—and mu-
tual frustration. Logan discovers he isn't the only one
who doesn't know what he wants from life, and the ani-
mosity between him and Peter changes keys. But just as
the possibility of a happier future appears, Logan gets
a dream offer that will take him away from Western
Massachusetts University—and Peter. Now he has to
decide: will he live the solitary life laid out for him, or
hold on to Peter and forge his own path?

www.dreamspinnerpress.com

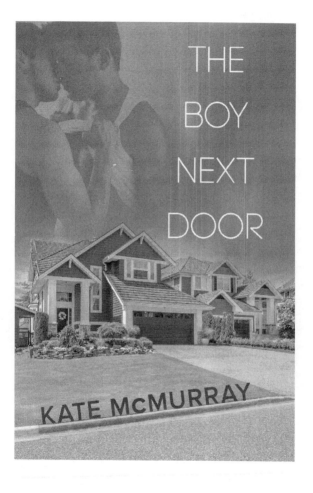

THE
BOY
NEXT
DOOR

KATE McMURRAY

Life is full of surprises and, with luck, second chances.

After his father's death, Lowell leaves the big city to help his sick mother in the conservative small town where he grew up. He's shocked to find himself living next to none other than his childhood friend Jase. Lowell always had a crush on Jase, and the man has only gotten more attractive with age. Unfortunately Jase is straight, now divorced, and raising his six-year-old daughter. It's nice to reconnect, but Lowell doesn't see a chance for anything beyond friendship.

Until a night out together changes everything.

Jase can't fight his growing feelings for Lowell, and he doesn't want to give up the happy future they could have. But his ex-wife issues an ultimatum: he must keep his homosexuality secret or she'll revoke his custody of their daughter, Layla. Now Jase faces an impossible choice: Lowell and the love he's always wanted, or his daughter.

www.dreamspinnerpress.com

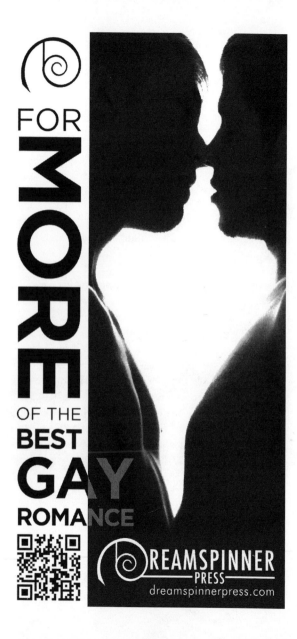